THE ANCIENT ONES

c.b.strul

Odom's Library

ISBNs:
(Paperback) 979-8-9889275-0-1
(EBook) 979-8-9889275-1-8

Front cover image by Aurelia Lozano
Book design by c.b.strul

First printing edition 2023 in United States

www.odomslibrary.com

The Ancient Ones

TABLE OF CONTENTS

THE ANCIENT ONES

PART I - TETSET

One

In the shadow of a great mesa on the western edge of a continent that might one day be known as an America, the rushing wind of an encroaching monsoon season blew to welcome the mantra of a ceremonial song of joy. The Ground Sloths heard it in the teosintl fields but payed it little mind. The Elder Armadillos listened near a stream on the outcrop of a small wood, though it did not bother them either. And even the Great Crows sat crouched in the trees above, giving only the slightest inkling of acknowledgement to the growing rhythm coming from the town beyond.

A large pyre was lit in accordance with the old rites. Piles of teosintl, squash, and coney hide filled the surrounding tables. And the women of that splendid Tetset tribe harried more such crops to the site in a luscious, linear dance of communal pleasing, maternal loving, and compassionate familial rearing. As soon as one dancer placed her burden she would turn and disappear into the orange and red monsoon sky of twilight leaving the next in line to take her place; a signal that the rains should come again and take their old crops away in order that they may receive new growth in the days to come.

From behind a full and heavy cloud, the moon broke free in that same sky the sun still occupied. This sight led the men of Tetset into a calamitous uproar of joy for the moon was the bringer of water. The women completed their tasks abruptly and opened their ranks to these men who took control of the ceremonial space with pride and violent whimsy. They spun from table to table; knees branching out into brazen kicks, arms extending and contracting to their bodies in perfect balance. With their arrival came cacophonous new chants patting the old rhythm down into submission. The words of their great song of birth:

The Mother the Father that make me
The Sun and the Moon that will bake me
The Raft on the Rivers that take me

One girl then stood out from the others, a girl of about fifteen years wearing a beautiful ceremonial dress of lapis blue chiseled throughout with dynamic lines of white. Feathers branched out from her arms, legs, and headdress giving her the look of a great forgotten bird from lore. She alone in the company did not dance. She stood perfectly still. Stoic as a sleeping volcano. And all the others moved and danced fluidly around her presenting her with gestures of love and awe.

Her name was Blue Flower. And this was the day the gods would see fit to end her people.

Two

From amidst the male dancers, a single restless youth quit what he was doing so he may approach Blue Flower to steal some words with her before the conclusion of the ceremony. He was not unhandsome, though his behavior always came with a sort of awkwardness like he never could quite understand how to be in the world as it was. His name was Silent Wolf and he asked flirtatiously, "Hey Blue Flower! Why don't you smile, hmmm?" His hands shook a little as Blue Flower's eyes met his own.

She did not know how to settle him, how to make or allow his energy to feel anything but alien in her presence. But she was not unwilling to try and play his game. She continued to hold her smile back with some effort and spoke. "Does the Oak Seed smile at the wayward Coyote, Silent Wolf?"

These words were meant as an invitation of sorts, and Silent Wolf leapt on them too greedily, "It would if it knew that Coyote could carry it to its favored patch of soil." He was baiting her with a heavy coat of blood sheen weighing down his words, but she did not bite so he blurted out with frustration and discontent, "Still, I am no Coyote coming in the middle of the night to steal you away, Blue Flower. I am a man who stands before you on a happy evening just before the bloom of this land." His desperation noticeably thickened the air, "Would you not share a smile with me even in such fine times? Long ago, when we were younger, I recall the feeling that I could not get you to stop smiling my way. I still struggle to understand why this behavior had to change so irreversibly."

Blue Flower looked markedly into Silent Wolf's eyes with intense contemplation. She did not know how to make this one happy. He was an honest boy, yes. And perhaps in some other life another girl very much like her could have fallen in love with his unfortunate wit and unrefined boldness. But she was not and could not be that girl. She was meant for another purpose. Her teacher had prepared her well and boys such as Silent Wolf were merely a distraction that she could not allow herself. He watched her hungrily as she made up her mind. Finally, she forced a very fake, very wide, toothy smile.

Silent Wolf, sensing his failure, rolled his eyes and nearly spat out his words, "One day you will come around." Dejection and remorse filled and emptied him.

In defeat, the boy turned and rejoined the dance. Blue Flower did not mean to, but her lips parted anyway, and a chuckle broke free from the back of her throat. She did not mean to be cruel, but what was a girl to do when she was not allowed to feel as she knew this boy felt? Still, from deep within her, Blue Flower sensed a gnawing ideal that even Silent Wolf deserved to find love and for some reason she could not put into words, Blue Flower felt guilty for not being able to give it to him.

Three

Lingering just outside the town of Tetset, there existed a hilly meadow that in the springtime would sprout the most fascinating breed of Poppy Flower. The elders of the tribe at that time of year would send youths out to extract these flowers and some of their seedlings to craft medicines and inks and jewelry with them. Had the current season been Growth, and had those rituals been in progress at that time, perhaps the tribe could have escaped and survived the night. But as things were, this being a cruel time and the Season of Low, the hills remained unexplored and left forgotten. None of the one hundred from Tetset could see the fifteen or so warriors of the Hen'Bon'On clan waiting there for the dark order to be given.

War paints marked their faces like insects climbing in various patterns of circles and lines up to their mouths and onto their eyelids, through the long piercings extending from their nostrils. Down their necks onto their chests the paints crawled, splotched, muddled - making the Hen'Bon'On appear anything but human.

Quietly, the men began to scuttle out from their hiding place. Slowly at first. Then the anticipation of the moment to come swept into their feet and they began to run toward the fire beyond the walls, pikes and arrows clenched firmly between their fingers.

Four

Back amidst the town, the music came to an abrupt conclusion. An elder woman had finally stepped forward to transition the reaping ceremonies — the tribe's prayers to the skies for rain and regrowth at the ends of the Low harvest season — toward their natural finale. Mother Tree was her name and she hollered a joyous bellow, raising her arms to the heavens, her sleeves drooping all the way to the ground. She spoke loudly with confidence so the whole tribe could hear her, "In death we become one with the land the sea and sky. In life we are entrusted with the keeping of this cycle: Birthing, Binding, Sewing, Reaping." She paused a moment to look down toward Blue Flower, standing alone in her place of honor away from the crowd. Mother Tree smiled and Blue Flower returned the expression genuinely this time. "Young seedling of our people! On this eve, you will bud and blossom as your namesake would in the beauty of the moonlight. And the harvest will see you and know it is time to ripen in kind. The crops will journey toward us from the reaches you will travel, your footprints will produce a trail back to us and Tetset will be fruitful once more." Mother Tree extended her hand out to the youth. Blue Flower approached and took it in her own and Mother Tree whispered, "Come child."

Together, the two women walked into the darkness north of the town toward an old grove near the teosintl leaving the rest of the tribe to enjoy the spoils of the ceremony.

Silent Wolf wanted to follow them. He was curious as to what that last piece of the ceremony entailed. That and he still felt he and Blue Flower had more to discuss in the darkness. But an elder man, seeing the error the boy wished to commit, stepped in his path. He was the leader of their tribe and so named for it Chief Tetset, strong and hardy. And he laughed off Silent Wolf's insolent attempt to evade him, clasping his shoulders in a gentle but firm embrace. He said, "Silent Wolf, leave the women in peace."

And the boy obeyed.

Five

Mother Tree led Blue Flower with purpose toward the old Magnolia near the stream known as Antan on the outskirts of the teosintl fields. Before this night, in the Season of Growth, the Magnolia would have been leafy and vibrant with its namesake flowers in a brilliant white. In later years, were someone to approach the once life affirming tree, they would find sharp, gory, red petals. Though none who would have known the difference ever did pass that way.

Completely unaware of the fabrics of time that would tear and untangle in this night, Mother Tree lowered herself to her knees on a patch of patted soil before the old Magnolia gesturing to Blue Flower and saying, "Sit child. We have much to discuss."

Blue Flower did as she asked kneeling before Mother Tree and allowing her mind to wander to the strange whispering hum that emanated from the breeze-blown teosintl beyond. A flash of lightning lit the sky in the distance but no thunder accompanied it and Blue Flower returned her mind to the task at hand. "What great insights can you offer me teacher?" she asked it with sincerity.

"Though I may seem wise to you, young one," Mother Tree sniffed the air and felt a shift in things, "I can offer very little comfort at this time. You will soon pass into the realm of myth. Like the great glyptodons of old, you will venture out into the unknown. And like with those once glorious creatures, I doubt you and I will ever cross paths again." The woman stopped a moment to clear her throat. She was heartbroken to know this day was upon them. Blue Flower could see a strange sort of pain overtake the older woman's mind and wondered at this, but in little time Mother Tree continued, "You have already begun your journey I can assume." She looked down at Blue Flower's knees contemplating, "How long has it been since your first bleeding?"

The girl fiddled with the hem of her ceremonial skirt now, attempting to overcome her discomfort with the topic. "Many moons now," she whispered, "and I have bled many times since." She let the hem of her skirt go at last having finished saying what she felt she was supposed to say.

"Yes. Then your connection to the moon is well founded." Mother Tree smiled and tapped above her own heart twice. "Do you bleed this evening against the full moon?" She asked without any sense of discomfort at the question.

Blue Flower raised her eyes to look at the reaping moon, now the only deity remaining in the sky. "I do." She said it a little louder hoping to sound proud for her own body, though in truth she felt ashamed. She was not meant to have the womb of a mother or the fleeting joys the other girls would know of their outer organ. She was intended for this one greatness, this one task asked of her and others like her once every fifteen years, to leave her tribe and find nature, to show it the path to Tetset — a task of which she must not expect to return.

"This is good child." Mother Tree reached and rummaged through her satchel in search of something small and difficult to grip. She pulled a rag from within, just a plain white rag sewn together with apparent haste by one of the women of the tribe. Natural holes riddled the thing all over. But for its limited purpose, it would suit fine enough. As she held the fabric toward Blue Flower, Mother Tree continued, "Soak this rag with your blood and place it in the hole of that tree. Then you will be ready for the next phase of your journey."

The younger woman accepted the rag without hesitation. With purpose, she tucked the threads between her thighs and moving her shield aside, applied as much pressure as she thought necessary. A moment passed. She removed the thing, replaced her shield, and raised the now vibrantly bloody fabric up to the level of her eye. She rose to her feet then and in the stutter step choreography Mother Tree had been teaching her these last several months, Blue Flower danced like a small bird toward the white Magnolia tree.

Arriving at the trunk, she caressed the barky exterior with the back of her hand as if the tree were some long lost familiar and she the consoling one. Her knuckles found a crevasse large enough for the crimson cloth. Gently, she tucked the rag within.

Having done this, Blue Flower turned to smile back at Mother Tree. But something was wrong. As Blue Flower looked in the direction of Tetset, she was surprised to see raw heat... A Fire! And far too much of it. Somehow the fire pit must have wriggled free of its containment and now those flames were heading toward the two of them and the Magnolia; toward the Antan; toward the highly flammable teosintl. An accident. Surely this was an accident.

That's when she heard the howl, like a beast in pain. But this was not the voice of some beast. This was a voice she had known: an older man from her tribe who often shared his water with her. He was screaming out from beyond. Blue Flower felt her feet take action without the command of her mind. She would run back into town as quickly as she could saving as many of her people as she could find before this terrible fire had a chance to consume them totally.

Yet, she never made it back to the path. A lighted arrow hit the ground in front of her with a presumptive thump before she ever left the grove. So she turned her attention to finding the source of this aggression somewhere in the dark. All she could see was Mother Tree's face beside her. The old woman had moved quickly to Blue Flower's aide, an all too knowing look on her face.

Mother Tree forced her satchel into Blue Flower's hands hissing, "Into the teosintl quickly child!"

"But—" Blue Flower tried to argue, both because she wished to help her people — to fight this faceless horror — and because she feared the crop might catch and burn around her.

Mother Tree would not listen, "Do as I say!" She screamed this time. Her eyes were too wide. Her hands too shaky. Her jaw quivered with fear. Blue Flower took in all of these unappealing attributes knowing that this was uncharacteristic of her former teacher. The cold of it settled over her and she understood that this was a truly dire moment for her. Her journey must begin here and now. Not in the morning or with any of the additionally planned ceremonies and fanfare. Her life as she had once known it was gone. So Blue Flower took in one hard breath. She wanted to embrace Mother Tree. She wanted to cry in her lap and listen to one more story about the great Water Birds of myth. She wanted to laugh of warm meals at large tables and sing to her ancestors. But that time was already a distant past. And Blue Flower ran.

Six

The Hen'Bon'On clan surged through the town of Tetset wielding fire and pain. Painted men destroyed structures of clay and grass with clubs and pikes and arrows. The Tetset tribe was not prepared. Chief Tetset bared his teeth and fought valiantly against the initial assault, but he could not himself reach the armory. Fire breeched his path and he had to settle for a small ceremonial blade with half the reach of the Hen'Bon'On weapons. He strafed without his artillery, bounced and weaved against the attackers, took at least three of their ranks along with him to their deaths.

Silent Wolf saw the man fighting in his bravery and found a similarly small ceremonial blade on his person. He would emulate the death of his chief. He would go out as a hero would. He hoped to commit himself now to that warrior's fate, but in his first attempt to lash out and swing at one of the painted men, Silent Wolf was struck in the back by an unseen foe running through the town at a sprint without resistance. The boy was beaten and beaten by two such men until he could not move. Until he could only watch with muzzled vision.

He had witnessed his chief run through five times with pike and arrow. He had witnessed his village crippled with clubs and searing fire. And Silent Wolf knew that he had failed. In an instant, Tetset was lost.

Seven

Blue Flower sprinted through the teosintl. Large stalks came up to meet her, swatting and bruising at her arms and head. She thought of her people, of Mother Tree, of the terrible fire and the arrow that landed at her feet. *Who are these attackers?* Her people were a peace loving tribe. Only choosing war when there was no other choice. She was not aware of anyone who would take up arms against them. What would even be the point? They had little wealth but what Antan provided — and that only amidst the rainy seasons. They had little power in the region and kept out of those petty squabbles between the Koff and the Denato peoples. *Who would do this? Why?*

A stalk of teosintl smacked Blue Flower in the face and she stumbled backward and fell to her knees. She rubbed the pain on her face away and refound her footing, peering backward to ensure that she still was heading away from the flames.

But as she looked behind her, she noticed a figure in the ominous, wispy silence of the field. *A shadow*, she thought. A shadow. Yes. But a living breathing shadow. Imposing as it approached, Blue Flower quickly took it for what the paint on its skin hoped to conceal. This was clearly the shape of a man. Strong, glistening muscles shown like lapping waves reflected against the distant fire light. She did not recognize the symbols upon his body, though she thought them terrifying in the moonlight. Where could he have come from? She was so far out now. Had he been following her all this way? Why her? Surely one fifteen-year-old girl could not be worth such a pursuit. Blue Flower did not know what to do. This beast man clearly meant her harm, but she did not wish to give him the satisfaction of catching her in a race knowing she fled in fear. She was not weak and she and her people did not deserve to be treated this way. No. If she were to be defeated, let her be defeated facing her enemy.

She spoke out of the silence, surprising the man, "Who are you? Why do you soil this celebration for us?"

The man's eyes became visible then as he tracked her down amidst the stalks. They looked strange, almost too focused in Blue Flower's opinion as they stared toward her own silhouette. Yet, the man did not move toward her. He lingered, his right hand brushing at something up against his chest. Finally he spoke, a voice rough from the smoke, but somehow gentle and clear all the same, "Why do you run when you do not know?"

His words were a perverse kind of thought game to Blue Flower. She did not wish to give him the pleasure of making her seem a fool. Yet she did not have an answer for him. She tried to find the words as she stared at his form in the darkness. And she saw something glimmer for a brief moment in his left hand. Was it a blade? Had he been holding it all along? Or had he just now pulled it from some hiding place with evil intentions? *Well two can play at that game,* she thought. After all, she had Mother Tree's satchel in her hand. She knew the contents from her ceremonial training and if she was very careful, she could reach within without being discovered in this odd light.

But she had left the man waiting for an answer and he did not want to wait any longer. He took a first careful step toward her. She felt wildly around in the bag as he took that second step. Then her fingers felt the shape of a small vial beneath the water sac. He took a third step and she tugged upward unsheathing the vial from the satchel. And with that motion, the man threw his caution away and leapt to stop her. But Blue Flower was quick.

The vial sprayed open releasing the pungent peppery liquid directly into the man's face, Blue Flower shouting, "Be gone with you demon!" as she turned and sprinted away toward the desert mountains beyond. She had rid herself of that threat with ease. It only occurred to her much later and after a great deal of recollection that the feared blade of her assailant had not been a blade at all. Rather, he had been holding an odd little sort of circular mirror — liquid in texture, with an otherworldly craftsmanship to the tool, but a mirror all the same.

Eight

As for the man, he writhed on the ground in pain. In his suffering, he could only hope the others had been captured safely. That this would not all be a total loss. After a time, he did not know how long, the pain began to dissipate to the point that he could open his eyes once again. The clouds had parted enough that the moon shown through, its color now a deep, dark red. He got to his feet and walked slowly back toward the fires of Tetset.

His name was Qotle and he felt as though he had just awoken from a dreadful nightmare, one in which his hands and words were not his own. Still, he stood now in the ruins of Tetset, sun rising at last in the distance to reveal the damage that had been brought upon this place. Not by him directly of course. That task had been carried out by the other members of his clan. Qotle had remained on the perimeter of the teosintl fields waiting to capture the stragglers. He had seen none. Or had he? He recalled a woman's face, fearful but resilient. Had that happened to him? His eyes still itched with redness. But they were his eyes. And he was not a "demon" as the woman had shouted. No. He was Qotle. And he had not seen a soul out there in the fields he decided at last.

The burning houses of the night were now a series of small rubble fires allowing Qotle a clear view of the surrounding landscape and the heaps of bodies. He knew some amount of death would be required to fulfill the Spider Woman's wishes, but he had not expected this. At least thirty Tetset lay dead or dying in the wreckage. And five of his own clansmen had perished as well. For the first time, Qotle began to wonder about their mission. He saw Ginjiyo giving out orders to Hen'Bon'On men across the way. He watched those men gather up their captives, some twenty or so Tetset women and children firmly tied hand and foot, but with enough give in their bonds that they could walk themselves the several days journey to the canyon where they all must go.

And then Qotle noticed the man, the only Tetset man remaining. He was being ushered along with the rest of his tribe looking... well Qotle imagined he himself must look as bad as that Tetset man given his lack of sleep and that lingering pain in his eyes. Qotle decided what was done was done. Now it was time to return to the Spider Woman.

Nine

Silent Wolf was crying. His blurred vision had finally normalized as the sun rose and he could at last make out the extent of the destruction. His house was gone, his village, half of his tribe. He wondered if Blue Flower had escaped to her death journey, but decided it was more likely she had been stopped and killed prematurely in the night.

Two men approached him in diminished war paints, streaked with sweat. They spoke to each other in a language he could not understand. One of them grabbed him by his armpits and forced him to stand, then to walk, though his bindings made that difficult. Silent Wolf did not fight back. He had nothing left to fight for.

He was forced to join a small assembly of women and children. Those who had not had the strength to defend themselves, those who were easily captured. It occurred to Silent Wolf for the first time in his life that, contrary to all of his greatest wishes, he was one of these — easily captured — helpless. The tears came again, this time for the loss of his own sense of self-worth.

Out of the corner of his weary eye, he saw the body of the man he did not deserve to look at. He tried not to, but now he knew just how weak he was, so he gave up and stared as long as he dared at the run through corpse of Chief Tetset. His hand extended outward. It had been run through as he had attempted to defend himself and looked a bloody stump. Dried, paste-like blood smears had soaked and hardened against the former chief's clothing and his face was frozen in a state of shock, pain, and mortal anguish.

In an attempt to blind himself, Silent Wolf raised his eyes and looked directly into the sun.

Ten

She made it, at last, to the edge of the teosintl. The stalks had acted as an elaborate maze to Blue Flower in the darkness, but now that the sun had risen, she could more easily navigate her way to the end of the crop all the way to the unwelcome beginnings of the harsh and vast desert beyond. Blue Flower was so very tired. Already she felt her memories of the ceremony she had spent so many months preparing for were of some distant event. It felt as though a hundred years had passed her by in the span of a single night. As she peered off toward the rock and dust ahead and the mountains beyond even that, great epochs of past (the birthing of the world) and future (the killing and death of it) came up to meet her. She wondered tediously if all of this had been preordained; her tragedy, fear, and strength against this adversity... or the final moments she had spent in her town of Tetset, a home that had loved her so well. She was already meant to die. So why had she been allowed to survive to complete some foolish task when it seemed apparent that others who were meant to live had most likely perished? Her sacrifice would be for nothing.

Like some fiendish nightmare, a huge beast rose up from the stalks beside her. Blue Flower felt her survival instincts kick in once again, then falter, then disappear altogether. She no longer had the energy to fight back. It had been sapped from her by the long night. So it was fortunate that this creature did not seem to care about her presence here. Raising her eyes to meet the beast, Blue Flower realized she was at this moment standing beside a megatherium: a giant ground sloth. These animals, while bear-like in stature and dominant presence, were not carnivorous and usually only attacked when spooked or threatened. Blue

Flower felt relief flow through her veins as the ground sloth bit off the dense, craggy end of a teosintl stalk and lowered itself back onto all four of its legs. She lost sight of it beneath the tall plants.

That creature could have just as easily been hungry for flesh today — she had heard such stories before — but luck would have it that the sloth had filled itself already. Apparently, the universe wanted her to live a bit longer. Though earlier she felt certain her journey had ended before it could even begin, now something inside of Blue Flower told her to try and be strong. So she was strong — for her people, her pain, her heart. She picked herself up and walked on toward the mountain pass beyond.

Continuing her ceremonial journey, she climbed and stumbled over large stones and dips in the earth, squeezing herself between the tight enclosures that sometimes packed the inner walls of the mountain pass. She felt herself channeling a goat sometimes as she leapt against one surface and then another. Her legs were so weak. Her back was on fire. Sweat trickled down her brow for a time and then she had no sweat left to give. And her eyes kept asking her to close them, to let them sleep.

Yet Blue Flower persisted through that narrow path. She had to make her way out to the lands beyond before the storms could catch her here and sweep her away into the undying lands. She became acutely aware of the banded snake playing sand percussion in spats with its tail somewhere behind her. These external motivators and others like them helped her to continue pushing on through that last stretch of mountain where she approached a sort of natural threshold out to the greater world.

Her eyes saw only deserted lands. Vast plots of nothing for days. Directionless, Blue Flower decided the sun would guide her forward. In the evening, she would walk against it. In the mornings, she would approach it. And at midday... at that time she would rest so the sun could make up its mind. Out amongst the great earth stones of her desert, she was but a girl enshrined like one in a chrysalis in the vastness of the universe.

Stopping a moment, Blue Flower reached into her satchel to retrieve the life giving water sack for perhaps the fifth or sixth time since her journey had begun. It felt noticeably lighter, but she was woefully thirsty and began to drink. Then the water stopped pouring... stopped dripping. Blue Flower's dry lips told her she was in danger of transforming back into the soil.

Even so, she continued her long walk, the sun baking her almost constantly. At this point, she had forgotten how long she had travelled. This was and would be her life, she felt, for as long as she dared to continue living it.

Once she had been caught fully exposed in the edge rains of a monsoon. She attempted to catch rain water to replenish her supply, but she did not have the right tools for this and the hole in her water sack was too small a target for too many raindrops.

Once a coney leapt out of hiding a ways ahead of her, but while her mind dreamed of hot meat, her fingers would not move quickly and the hare bolted before she could act on her fancy imaginings.

Blue Flower had lost her strength. Her will had almost left her.

Eventually, she approached a region of strange, tall, and slender stone pinnacles. Knowing of this place from stories, she was aware that no water could flow here or nearby. She also knew that she was finally and thoroughly spent. So Blue Flower found a good sitting rock. She reached into Mother Tree's satchel one more time and pulled from it an unused reeded instrument known in her language as a kopa. Placing her fingers on the small holes that riddled the shaft of the instrument, she began to play a soft, sad song.

Her eyes were so blotched with sun sickles that she could hardly even see. Not realizing how close she had come, she finally gave up, dropped her kopa to the dust beneath her, closed her dying eyes, and hunched her shoulders down to her knees. Her last breath left her body. Her final thought was of emptiness and the unforgiving nature of a world she had once imagined prized and cared for her like one would prize the beautiful evanescent flora that was her namesake only to leave it to compost after it had begun to wither and lose its beauty.

Blue Flower did not know that she was at that very moment being watched, studied, heard by something intelligent — something from another distant place in the universe that just then happened to be skillfully clinging to the upper wall of one of the taller pinnacles. It held itself up there with its sixteen powerful and dexterous fingers and toes. Blue Flower could not know that her feet had intuitively led her to salvation. She could not sense the presence of another.

It was a bizarre creature, taller and thinner than a human and hidden behind an ovular mask of turquoise with quarters of red and yellow above where the brow would be. It hung from the pinnacles above with its sixteen powerful and dexterous fingers and toes. The place where the mouth might have existed instead contained a flat, round, and black apparatus that appeared to serve no immediate purpose. And there were small, triangular markings beneath the upside-down mountain-shaped eye lenses. Above that, two thick rectangles pretended to be eyebrows. Between the red and yellow forehead, more black and white triangles pushed up to the apex of the mask where the hard material then met with many dark grey, shining plumes; lapping waves of feathers.

Shrouded in a dark sort of cloak, the body of the Being could not yet be seen, but a glance at its neck and any occasionally protruding appendage would imply that this thing was far too slender to have derived from any tribe of man known.

The Being leaned out of its position resting on one wall of stone. It straddled its long legs between that surface and another and it scuttled down the large rocks with ease. The feathers on the back of its head expanded and contracted as it went. Once it was close enough, the Being leapt down to the desert floor. It landed quietly beside the dead girl, but did not go to her immediately. The kopa, it seemed, was of more interest to the thing at first. It lifted the woodwind up with some confusion, placing its eight fingers along the holes where Blue Flower would have placed ten. Only then did the Being come to remember the girl hunched down in a heap on the stone below. It lifted Blue Flower up and bounded across the arid landscape with the majesty of a gazelle.

Eleven

Silent Wolf had failed to blind himself. He had failed to save his people or keep himself from being captured. He had failed to do anything. He sat in a clump of prisoners — women and children of his tribe — and wallowed in his own self-pity.

From the front of the group, he could hear the proud words of the old woman, Mother Tree. Apparently she had not yet surrendered, though she was as much a captive as all the rest of them. She invoked the words of the angry sun saying, "I will bake the transgressors into the pit. Hear me, I will make it be that those who spite me shall become as the salt fields. Never again shall the rain waters pass their way. Their children will birth without breath and their lips will run dry without the moon to provide them..." Well, she was angry, that much was clear. Though their captors did not seem to care about her words, Silent Wolf and those of Tetset who listened found themselves wondering if their faith could bring them through this struggle.

For his part, Silent Wolf was doubtful. If he were to be their only warrior, then Tetset had no warriors. He was nothing. He was less than nothing.

A nearby child named Dusty Boy asked in a whisper, "Why do you not fight older brother? Why do you not use Mother Tree's words to give you strength and smite these men?"

Silent Wolf rolled his eyes at the young one. The stakes were impossible and he had already given his mind up to the circumstances of prison. As he looked up and watched the guards prepping for their journey, he replied, "Tetset gave itself up in the night. Blue Flower was its hope. Not me. And Tetset abandoned her to the wild... to the fires of the desert, she would have gone... to death." He had not before allowed himself to consider how he felt about Blue Flower's purpose within the tribe. Now that he had too much time to think, that was all he could think about. Tetset had sacrificed that beautiful girl on the day of her birth. She had never been a walking breathing one of them. Silent Wolf had loved her and she did not have the power to meet him halfway because she was already dead.

"You are a fool Silent Wolf," Dusty Boy whispered back to him. Well Silent Wolf had already figured that much out for himself. What did he care if the others knew it too?

Twelve

Blue Flower had only died for a moment, perhaps a couple of hours... could a day have passed? When she finally opened her eyes, she did not know where she was, or why it was so much cooler in this place, or what that odd dripping appendage was hanging just over her face and mouth. The walls of the cave were all mossy stone and grey and red. Some mineral deposits colored the stones with starkly beautiful layers of crushed sediment. Droplets of water had been falling onto her face from the appendage and she realized it bore an off resemblance to some of the water pots of Tetset at the end, though there was an extension of metallic tubing coming out the back end of the thing that did not look familiar to Blue Flower in the slightest.

She shook off the small puddles of liquid that had been forming around her eyes and chin where the drip had missed its mark. She sat up slowly, feeling the ache in her muscles from the long journey she had just taken. She followed the metal tubing with her eyes to see it extend from wall to stalactite-covered ceiling. Her sidelong glance brought her attention to a cluster of humming bricks formed from that same metal. The boxes were new with no signs of rustication. If Blue Flower had known much about metal, she would have recognized that none of those components could have been there for very long. But all of it was beyond Blue Flower's comprehension. Her people had not been metallurgists. Tetset had never imagined the need for stronger, more durable materials like these. Still, she marveled at the shine of the stuff.

More metallic objects lingered beyond those boxes, with soft, velvety surfaces inlaid atop them. What this substance was, she had even less of a clue about. And why were there so many shiny finger-sized circles and sticks jutting up from just below the velvet? Had all these things been built by someone? They did not appear natural — not like anything Blue Flower had ever experienced.

Eventually, she decided she should stand in order to see the rest of the room. Her aches seemed to dissipate as her sense of disoriented curiosity overtook everything. Now on her feet, she realized the room was much smaller than she had initially thought. She would have been able to walk from one end to the other in perhaps six long steps if she hadn't suddenly become distracted by the other creature with its back turned to her behind the place where she had been sleeping.

The Being was lanky and peculiar. Of course, her eyes went first to that bizarre mask. But then she noticed its four-fingered hands as it tinkered with a device that projected a blue light into the air. *How odd,* she thought. Within that blue light, Blue Flower saw her kopa raised — floating — without strings to hold it — hovering by the power of that light. Symbols surrounded the kopa, shapes resembling scratch marks left on trees by predators marking their territory. These marks were ethereal, lacking the necessary substance to make them appear real to Blue Flower's uninitiated eyes and at first she began to feel pangs of panic and anxiety. But her curiosity quashed those other emotions. She decided to speak to the Being, "What are you doing?"

Then it was the Being's turn to be startled. It turned too quickly around accidentally knocking over its experiment — the blue light flickering out — the symbols dissipating — the kopa falling helplessly to the ground. The Being leapt up into the air with its powerful legs, latched onto the ceiling, crawled upside down to the farthest, highest corner of the room it could find and held there like a spider.

After its fall, the kopa rolled across the floor until it came to rest at Blue Flower's feet. In her own surprise at the Being's reaction, she barely noticed the tap of the reed there. "Why are you frightened?" she asked. The Being did not respond, staring at her through its mask. "Can you understand me?" she pressed again. The Being hung in stillness a moment longer before finally lowering its hand and pointing a long finger down toward the kopa at Blue Flower's feet.

Blue Flower knelt down to collect her instrument. She held the kopa up and asked with some confusion, "This?"

The Being made the same pointing motion once again, so Blue Flower raised the instrument to her mouth and awkwardly blew a note through the reed.

More intrigued than frightened, the Being finally released its fingers and toes from the cavern ceiling and elegantly jumped back down to the floor. It approached Blue Flower, walking on all fours, and began sniffing at her like a dog might. Blue Flower rushed through too many emotions all at the same time, but ultimately settled herself. She knew it was quite odd to be in the presence of a creature such as this and she began to giggle. So the Being stopped circling, rose to her eye level, raised its own fingers, and began to pantomime the playing of the reed itself. It then pointed to Blue Flower as before.

"Alright, I get it." Blue Flower said with some delight. She was not in her right mind, she was acutely aware. But this creature, she assumed, had saved her life. She was already beginning to feel some semblance of a friendship forming here and she wanted to keep the darkness of the recent days from her mind. So she lifted the kopa again to her mouth as the Being clearly wished. She sighed as she settled on what she would play, and decided it would only be right to replay her lament from the desert pinnacles, the last song she felt she had any reason left to play.

She let the notes linger this time, playing the tune with her full heart. She allowed her mind to think of Mother Tree and that brave look she had seen on her face just before she ran into the teosintl. She recalled the spreading fire of Tetset and all of the excitement and fear that had rushed into and through her that night. She thought of the man in the field and the long walk through the mountains of loneliness — of how it felt at last to die. How sad she was to not have been able to continue, to summon more of the earth to find her tribe. How she knew that they would no longer be there to receive the gifts she was sent to retrieve for them. And she knew with certainty at this that she had in fact died. How was it that she was alive then?

As Blue Flower scrolled through those thoughts, the Being stared across at her, enthralled. And as Blue Flower approached that final question, the Being lifted its arms exposing each forearm and the components of metallic suit it wore there. A small collection of piano-like keys existed on the inner wrists. The Being then rose to its full height allowing the feather-like appendages on the back of its head to expand like those of a peacock in heat. It tapped key after key — and the feathers danced — and a new melody erupted outward from the Being — a strange and elaborate new song.

Blue Flower had to stop her own playing, she was so startled. But the Being pointed to her kopa once more, and she realized that the two melodies were meant to mingle and harmonize. So she began to play again.

It was extraordinary, this girl from a primitive tribe was jamming with an alien born of a world thousands of lightyears away. And somehow they were both speaking the same language. Blue Flower's mind raced. She began to forget, truly forget, about everything else in the whole damn world. The Being's motions were hypnotizing as it danced. Then, suddenly, everything fell into blackness.

Blue Flower's senses took a veritable gut punch. The rug had been pulled out from under her conscious state. She had no body. No self. All she had was the darkness. And a tiny dot off in the distance that seemed to be approaching very slowly at first. Then the dot picked up speed until all of the hollow space she could perceive was completely filled with it. She took a moment to recognize the shape of it; the Being's mask floating before her in that dark place. She felt the presence behind the vizor. Sentience? Breath? Eyes?

Then the field of teosintl was real before her, not just a memory, but physically there, touchable, true. Blue Flower struggled to breathe as the emotions of that night took her over completely. The fire in Tetset. The screams. Had she heard them before? She recognized every voice. A plague of violence tearing through.

She collapsed into the Being's waiting arms. Back in the cave. Back in the present.Thoroughly winded and on the verge of unconsciousness, Blue Flower asked, "Did you... see it too?"

The Being did not respond to her question. It held her in its arms like a mother holds her baby. It walked her back to the drip system and laid her gently beneath the water. It ran its long, four-pronged hand over her eyes. Blue Flower fell into a deep, dreamless sleep.

Thirteen

As she opened her eyes, Blue Flower knew instinctively that she was no longer in the cave. The Being's mask rested, staring at her from a counter beyond. But the mask's owner was nowhere to be seen. So Blue Flower decided to explore her new surroundings. The moment she attempted to move however, her body smacked against something. She tried again and a third time to sit up before the realization overtook her that something for some reason was holding her down. Straps of glossy material elasticated across her shoulders and legs. Blue Flower had never seen a safety harness before, so her first thought was of imprisonment. She struggled against the barricade and her hand accidentally brushed against the exposed contraption at her waist. The harness came undone with a click.

Blue Flower sat up abruptly to survey the interior of the new space. It occurred to her that something else was wrong. The room was very compact, the walls fully metallic with myriad unknown devices directly installed across each surface. In fact, not one bit of surface space seemed devoid of practical use and purpose. Still, Blue Flower wracked her brain for something else entirely was the matter. She had not, according to her senses, been lying down as if on the ground or a bed; she had been lying upright as if standing in midair. Once the safety harness was removed, Blue Flower unwittingly had floated several inches away from the table that had been holding her. And as she attempted to "sit up", her entire body went with her in a very slow, very surprising summersault.

She came down face first toward a nearby surface and pressed gently with her fingers propelling her backward again. She carried on like this for longer than was necessary, feeling both bewildered and playful all at once. After a while, Blue Flower remembered herself. This was not the time for playing around. She should be frightened by her present circumstances. So why did she feel such a sense of enjoyment out of this floating sensation?

She turned her head and noticed another area beyond and through a body sized porthole. "Hello?" she called ahead. Pushing off from a wall behind her, Blue Flower swam through the air. She spiraled into a diving position as she fell through the opening into a slightly larger area. This time, she did not change her trajectory to explore the inner workings of the zone having gotten used to the visuals of the place. The walls looked so similar to the others as she allowed her peripherals to do their work, so she instead made directly for the closed, silvery surface ahead of her.

Placing her fingers on that slab of metal, a spark clicked against her skin. She pulled her hand back to kiss away the brief pain. And the door shot open.

Beyond was the night sky as Blue Flower had never seen it before; the stars too radiant and bright, the void overwhelmingly black. She was so enthralled in what lay before her that she took no notice of the maskless Being at the other end of the room. "Where am I?" Blue Flower asked herself not expecting an answer.

The Being guessed what she wanted to see. It stood at a small podium laid out with flat controls on velvety monitors, and it tapped here and turned there and the whole structure around them began to lurch and turn. Blue Flower watched the sky shift before her eyes, stars flurried by and away from her until she was instead looking down upon a massive and beautiful orb covered in shades of blues, greens, and yellows. White patterns swirled and shifted below. And Blue Flower was again confused and surprised for she had never seen her world from that perspective and could not know what it was she was looking at. "I don't think I understand." she said after a moment, turning back to look into the eyes of her alien friend.

This led to a different emotion from Blue Flower. One of love. The Being was elegant and beautiful once removed from its strange costume. It had wide, trusting eyes inset within a glossy, shield-like face with fronds sloping backward into that plumage that Blue Flower realized was not a part of the mask at all, but an extension of the creature within. The Being had no mammalian mouth, rather it wore a sharp and delicate beak of sorts that did not differentiate in color or texture from the rest of its smooth, azure and violet skin.

The Being's eyes were smiling at Blue Flower and it tapped playfully at its controls once again. The structure, or more accurately, the shuttle churned into gear with each motion of the alien's fingers. And the colorful orb came closer and closer. Blue Flower felt the speed in her body and she struggled to catch her breath. Excitement overtaking her, she fought against the g-forces to speak out again, "We were..." a deep difficult breath, "above?"

While the Being may have understood the intention behind Blue Flower's question, it could not translate those words. Actually, the Being was starting to get rather annoyed that Blue Flower had taken so long to figure out what was so obvious to it. Without looking up at her, the Being mimicked the playing of Blue Flower's kopa.

At first Blue Flower appeared stupefied, but then lightning struck and the alien's request sunk in. "Oh!" she must have said to herself for she couldn't have been speaking to the Being, "I will get it." And Blue Flower turned back around and swam through the door.

Arriving back at her harness bed, Blue Flower searched and searched until she noticed the reed tucked away in a pocket next to where she had slept. She collected the instrument hungrily and shot herself impatiently off to the starry room her companion had occupied. The shuttle shuddered and reclaimed its calm as Blue Flower reentered through the door. Kopa in hand, she was already speaking. "You need me to play this thought," she said, "though I do not know the way." She raised the reed up as if offering it to the alien, but when the Being only stared back at her, she felt an uncomfortable resolve and said contentiously, "Okay. I will try."

Raising the kopa with reticence to her mouth, Blue Flower closed her eyes and cleared her mind of all thoughts but the one question she had intended to ask. Then she contemplated a moment. *Must the notes of my song make the words somehow? Or is it my intention that has played the biggest role in our communication to this point?* She settled on a bit of both and, targeting her thought about the world from which she had come and the stars and sky where she was increasingly beginning to believe they then were, she blew just one ridiculous note and held it slowly forcing it to raise higher into the next octave. She stopped once she reached the top of her range and opened her eyes to look again upon the Being.

It cocked its head to one side contemplating Blue Flower's actions and then came round to a firm decision. The Being began tapping at the buttons of its podium in a sort of rhythm and quite abruptly shoved one of the longer controls on the panel all the way forward. With this action, the atmosphere of the orb in their viewport shoved aside and the shuttle burst through the cloud tops into an ocean of oxygen.

Blue Flower screamed. She could not help herself. The ground of the vast desert near Tetset rose up to meet them.

However, as she turned back to try and holler at the Being to stop, she felt a pang of shame. The alien looked so happy; eyes scrunched and filled with excitement. And just as Blue Flower was about to lose her nerve again, the Being flicked another control and the shuttle shot sideways instead, the sands of the desert moving along beneath them like a roaring river.

Still not getting the hint, Blue Flower asked another question, "What are you doing?!" And the Being instantly made her pay for saying words rather than playing thoughts. It pulled up on a control and the shuttle swung a full ninety degrees back up toward the sky.

Of course, Blue Flower was none too pleased at having her stomach wrenched into so many knots from these rapid and unusual movements. But a trickle of sense came back into her and she raised the kopa again playing something, anything to make the Being stop what it was doing. It heard her, but it no longer cared. The alien was having too much fun and it decided it would be even more enjoyable to change the shuttle's trajectory on the girl a few more times before it was done.

Fourteen

Now Silent Wolf walked the vast desert in bondage, one inconsequential component of a line of unnecessaries; he and the women and children of former Tetset. The invading Hen'Bon'On men would occasionally shove a Tetset who moved too slowly, though to be fair, they all moved too slowly these last two days. They had been given little nutrition or water, and their legs were all bound so movement and the desire to move came both with trepidation and dissociation.

For his part, Qotle watched the lone man from Tetset with a keen eye. He behaved as one defeated, but the Spider Woman had warned Qotle of the pride and wildness of these men. So Qotle kept his focus trained on the man and little else. The others could deal with the loud elder woman at the front of the line, apparently the only Tetset who had not yet surrendered. She was not Qotle's mission.

Ahead of him, Silent Wolf noticed one of the Hen'Bon'On soldiers had stopped moving, a look of stupidity on his face. Silent Wolf watched the man raise his arm into the air and point off toward the horizon. So Silent Wolf followed the finger's trajectory with his migraine-heavy vision. The sun was low in the sky and getting lower. The stars would be out to play soon. But from within the soft glow of the sun, a small object of false light shot out across the horizon. The object changed direction once, then again, then a third time. Even Silent Wolf in his depressed state could understand that something was off. Had he at last gone completely mad? The object dissipated back into the sun as if it had never really been there at all.

No. He was sober enough. He watched the object reappear once more. It was heading right for him.

Qotle did not notice the others had stopped. He only watched the one man. And he found himself growing irritated, for the man had chosen now to begin daydreaming. He nudged the man between his shoulder blades with a stick and spoke out with words he knew the Tetset could not understand. "Hurry up child of death." he said, "Do not hold up the line."

That's when things became muddled. A voice, one of Qotle's own men, began to shout and, for the first time in their long march, Qotle was forced to take his eyes off of his mission. Against the background of the setting sun, Qotle peered off to the spot where all of the other Hen'Bon'On men were looking. An object; he knew it to be a shuttle. It was headed their way, moving far too quickly for them to escape on foot.

As the shuttle rapidly grew in his vision, it occurred to Qotle that the line of prisoners had broken. His men were scattering among the hills. The man of Tetset was gone.

Fifteen

In the cockpit of the Being's shuttle, a rapid change had come upon Blue Flower. From absolute, uncontrollable terror, her thoughts had eased into a euphoric sort of pleasure. The lands they traversed at this absurd speed were becoming increasingly recognizable to her until, at long last, the line of humans — the line of Tetset — appeared in the distance. She watched them become larger, more human in size, as they came closer and closer. Unthinking, Blue Flower hollered with elation, "My people! You have found them!"

And even though the girl had spoken with her human words, the Being knew her sense of joy from that look in her eyes. It felt pride knowing it had done well by her and began to bob and bounce its shoulders to a happy rhythm — though its fingers never left their station, and its focus never lost validity. The girl's people were down there. The Being wanted to collect them for her — wanted to prove to her that they could be friends — could help one another. It thought about this even as the line of prisoners began to break apart.

The Being's task was becoming more and more difficult by the moment. These were not simple controls it was handling and the friendly humans running around in every direction would be frustratingly hard to parse apart from the ones that had done the capturing. At the same time, the Being had to worry about keeping the shuttle on course and in the sky. That would have been enough of a challenge all on its own.

Sixteen

A strange assortment of chimes and high pitched buzzing frequencies emanated from the approaching shuttle. They flowed down toward the scattering crowd, here raising a Tetset woman, there swirling a dust pile around a young boy, until eventually one of those frequencies came to enshroud Silent Wolf. He stopped his awkward, chained sprint and stood now in shock balancing precipitously on the edge of a low rock cliff. He felt his body being lifted into the air like it had no weight to it and a sense of fear and revulsion began to build within him. The sound held him and his ears could not figure out where to sort it — music, howl, the hum of teosintl. He was lost in the vibration.

Qotle spotted the man in the crowd at last. He sprinted on toward him even as others in his peripherals seemed to unhinge from gravity. One of those sounds was taking his mark. The Tetset man tremored lightly with that unearthly buzz. Qotle felt concern for this one. He needed the man with him, needed him alive and relatively unharmed. The Spider Woman demanded it... He lunged forward toward the man smacking his upper body against the other's and in a heap their two forms tumbled down the side of a rocky hillock Qotle had failed to distinguish from the rest of the landscape.

The ache and pain simmered through Silent Wolf's muscles and he noticed himself choking hoarsely for air. But he was no longer vibrating. Perhaps that was a victory of sorts. He felt the other man beside him shudder as he attempted to sit up. *Was he alright?* For the first time since their meeting, Silent Wolf felt it necessary to address the Hen'Bon'On that had captured him, "Have you saved me?"

Qotle took a moment to respond, the pain of their fall reverberating through his head, and the language of Tetset, not being his first tongue, took a moment for him to process. But he found the words and spoke as simply as he knew how, "In a way." Then he remembered himself; his mission, his own people. Qotle stood up tall, ignoring the agony in his shaking bones. He must call to the others in the canyon. He must reach them before the shuttle succeeded in taking their prize away from them. Digging through his satchel, Qotle sliced his fingers on the glass he realized must have shattered in the tumble. But he was not one to give up, and working through the added pain of these fresh cuts, he managed to grip a large enough shard for his purpose.

The glass was black like jet or obsidian with a sheen to it that, when raised to the sun, could reflect rays of light an incredible distance. Silent Wolf watched the man aim that reflection off in the direction toward which they had been heading. He contemplated the man's resolve and — perhaps — his kindness in saving him from the alien beam. He asked, "Why would you do this?"

Without taking time to really consider the question, Qotle chose to shoot off a series of phrases the Spider Woman had taught him. "The shuttle up there belongs to a very troubling form of insect. You belong to something greater. And your purpose has yet to be satisfied."

Silent Wolf peered up toward the small cliff edge from where they had fallen. The sounds of fear and dismay echoed beyond and he could see the people of his tribe buzzing as their bodies climbed into the sky. Dusty Boy lay limp in the air like one who has just succumbed to a seizure and a terrible sense of foreboding struck Silent Wolf. That shuttle meant to do Tetset more harm than these other men had. Again, he felt helpless. He did not see any way he could be of use against a force such as this.

Seventeen

Ripples of sound cascaded across the desert floor before Blue Flower's eyes. Her pupils reflected that strange warping air around her tribe's bodies and she honestly began to believe in the concept of hope again. That warmth within was filling her up. Her smile was growing. She watched the members of her tribe float towards her like bundles of leaves and flower petals in a slow and peaceful cyclone. They were not yet near enough for Blue Flower to make out the expressions on their faces but she had begun to recognize some individuals from their dusty clothes and body shapes. There was Bird Cries; a young energetic girl she had looked after from time to time in her own youth, for they were perhaps five years apart in age. And Boy Who Plays With Fire; a child who had truly earned his name one night when he had nearly burned down their entire village... one of the few males she had noticed in the bunch. And there was Mother Tree whom Blue Flower so greatly wished to speak with again.

She wondered, however, what had become of all of the adult men. Chief Tetset would not have abandoned his people and Blue Flower felt a sickly pessimism about the man. But surely some of the others would have escaped. *Silent Wolf would not have given up so easily*, she thought to herself wishing she had a better point of reference than this chaotic display. This could not be all that was left. Still she had to remind herself that nothing was certain in this life. She should have been dead, yet she lived. Likewise, others were meant to live, yet she believed so many of them now dead. And she wanted to mourn for the men, for Silent Wolf though she knew this was not the time to do so. She cleared her mind and spoke to the alien in the corner, "You are saving them. Thank you my friend." This time she remembered herself and tried to play that sentiment into her kopa.

The Being was very busy controlling the anomaly of hovering frequencies with geometric precision. But in hearing the girl's bittersweet thank you tune, it felt akin to her somehow. For the briefest of moments it looked her in the eye. It knew Blue Flower then and it hoped that in time she would learn to know it. But in that same moment, all of the shuttle's sensors shot on and the Being realized something had gone very, very wrong.

Eighteen

Silent Wolf could not understand what he was looking at. First the shuttle, then the sounds, and now the sky itself was alight with a new burst of energy. From off in the distance an arch, like the tail of a comet, blazed forth penetrating what was quickly becoming a very crowded horizon line. This new, shipless energy curved and hurtled until it burst directly into the side of the shuttle above.

Tetset fell from the sky. The entire tribe smacking in terrible clumps of meaty flesh to the hard stone of the earth. The sound of it was sickening. The alien shuttle came down next. Metal scraping violently against the stoney desert floor. The harsh noise of too much air bursting out of a ruptured organ magnified by a thousand. And then, there was no sound at all. Silent Wolf fell to his knees, unable to move, watching the place in the sky where it had happened. He did not understand. He did not want to. He felt like vomiting, like laying down in that spot and never getting up again. Even his vision was beginning to blur. His chest was so near to bursting.

His mind dissociated then. Like the snap of a finger — the snap of a neck — a broken bone — or two — or all of them, every bone in a body... and his anxiety subsided; was gone, leaving an abominable emptiness like a well that could never again be filled. Silent Wolf's home was gone, his people all dead, and he had not lifted a finger to help them. He swallowed deeply and spoke with a new voice — despondent, "What was that?"

Behind him, the Hen'Bon'On man seemed a cruel, muffled reinterpretation of a world that otherwise no longer existed. He was another man of how many other men that occupied this continent and world. But at least he was another living thing.

Those suddenly seemed in rather short supply to Silent Wolf. Only he, himself and this other man — the brief glimpses of shocked members of the capturing tribe as their heads barely cusped the ledge above — these were the only true examples Silent Wolf had left to him of what a living human looked like. The Hen'Bon'On man's words came through with clarity, "Come. I will show you."

The man from the other tribe extended his arm to Silent Wolf and Silent Wolf reached up and took it.

Nineteen

Blue Flower coughed herself awake. She was huddled and partially buried amidst the rubble and wreckage which had heaped up against one wall of the cockpit. Within the Being's shuttle, the world was in shambles. Lights flickered on and off in staccato with electrical currents still leaping out from one broken connection or another into the aether. Once smooth walls had become covered and pocked with bulbous abrasions as if some massive hand had reached out and squeezed the hull of the shuttle into a crumpled half-form of its previous self. The one time perfectly clear viewing port of the room now opened up into the elements, its glassy material having shattered in the crash.

Wincing, Blue Flower pulled her legs out from beneath the fallen technology. A vibrant pain coursed from her right hip across to her left shoulder. But in her state of shock, she could not tell if any of her person had been irreparably damaged. Her legs were still able to walk anyhow. Blue Flower coughed again and asked a question to whoever might be listening, "How are we still living?"

She got no response from the Being. It did not seem to be moving over there in the corner. It dawned on Blue Flower that she was likely the only one who had made it. She hoped desperately that she was wrong. Still, she did not know if she could trust the Being after what had happened. Had it in fact meant to cause her more pain? Why would it keep her alive just to force her to witness this new massacre?

Regardless of the discrepancy, Blue Flower found herself more immediately worrying after her fallen Tetset. So she began wading through the rubble toward the missing viewport. The alien atmosphere of the shuttle visibly leaking out into the desert beyond like miscible bubbles one might see floating under water. These bubbles fizzled and twisted in a hazy sort of fountain up through the air. Presumably, an element so light would have eventually made its way straight up and out of the atmosphere, an impossible to contain (for humans anyway) aerosol cloud of plasma. But right then, Blue Flower could see that plasma trickling away with her naked eyes there was so much of it. She stepped past that strange cloud out into the desert beyond.

Tripping, Blue Flower crossed the threshold between technology and that barren wasteland she had hoped only a day ago she would never have to see again. She felt a thin certainty that the desert would be her inescapable forever home, a terrible trap for a creature who had become vaguely aware of a hidden vastness the universe had forgotten to tell her about just over her head. A harsh pain shot through her shoulder as she tried to use her arms to regain her footing. Yes, she was definitely bleeding from the place on that shoulder where she had only been aching a moment before.

As she raised her eyes, however, all of that pain went away. Overwhelmed by a new and horrible sensation called dread, Blue Flower looked out across the far too shallow graveyard — the final resting place of her bloodied and dying tribe. Nothing she could do to help them. Nowhere for her to hide from the harsh sight of them. Small fires shined an eerie light across the landscape and Blue Flower could not look away.

Between the wound and the smoke she began gagging. Had her lungs been damaged? She hardly cared one way or the other at that point. But as her wheezing fit subsided, Blue Flower realized she could hear a faint whisper... a human voice coming from somewhere out there amidst all of that gore.

She pulled herself out of her anguish and forced herself back to her feet, shouting, "Hello! Is someone there?"

The whisper came again. So Blue Flower began to walk carefully through the field of corpses and fire, hoping... hoping for what? A survivor? Could anyone survive this... this terrible thing that had happened?

A voice she wanted so badly to hear came to her then, but not in the way she had wished — not with strength and pride. No. The voice clawed up to her, a broken whisper, too weak. "Blue Flower," said the whisper. The woman, her teacher, her mentor, Mother Tree lay crumpled against a boulder; bloody, frail, broken, and forgotten.

"Mother Tree," Blue Flower spoke uneasily as she rushed to the old woman's side. She kneeled down to be with her, this unthinkable version of the woman she had spent so many years looking up to. The tears instantly sprouted from her eyes as she understood the dismal extent of Mother Tree's wounds. "What has happened to you? Are you okay? Can you move?" But Blue Flower already knew the answers to those questions and many others she might have spoken in her sorrow.

Still, Mother Tree answered her with care and clarity, "Blue Flower. I will die soon." She did not move anything but her mouth and eyes, raw with obvious agony. But she forced herself to speak clearly, quietly, "My bones are already ashes and I cannot move them. But the earth has given me one final bit of joy." Her eyes tried to smile but the pain quickly sucked the forced joy from them. "I did not think I would ever see you again. If this is to be my last vision in this life, then it is a good one."

"Mother Tree." Blue Flower could not stop saying her name, knowing this was the last time she would have reason to say it.

"Do not fear for me now child." Mother Tree carried on in her feeble way, "I have lived. I have seen the great procession of life. And I have known my joy. Will you do the same for me?"

"I—" Blue Flower wanted to respond. But she noticed a change come suddenly into the dying woman and somehow it seemed she was not talking any longer to the flesh and blood form of her mentor. Rather the strength and spirit of the woman had forced itself free in one final, desperate act of will power.

"My time is coming rapidly," the spirit of Mother Tree said with that new strength, "I believe you have a friend who needs you now far more than I do."

"A friend?" Blue Flower asked the ghost.

Then Mother Tree managed to raise her thrashed and broken arm. She pointed a now skinless finger bone off toward the battered shuttle behind them. And her voice sounded like that of a young woman, "The two of you have many things to accomplish. More to see than the tribe could ever have shown you. But *she* needs you now, or this future will never come to pass."

Wide-eyed and fighting to process what she was experiencing from the half-dead woman, Blue Flower questioned again, "How do you know this?"

"I am with them now." Said the younger voice, the spirit voice, "I speak with them as I speak with you."

"Who Mother?" Blue Flower was stunned as she watched the breath of the woman change back to the true dying breath of a broken thing. Her skeleton hand collapsed to the ground with no muscle to power it and her eyes began to roll away until only the veiny whites showed.

But somehow the lips still managed to speak one last time even as the life-force had clearly gone from the woman. "The gods that breathe."

And then, even that mouth was dead. Blue Flower sat with the body. *The only living thing left in this desert,* she thought. She breathed in her sorrows and frustrations, and forced herself to stand. She was not the only living thing left in this patch of desert, for there was another she now had reason to believe she could trust who needed her help.

She spoke aloud to the corpses of Tetset as she made her way back to the shuttle and she said, “You may all be gone. But I am still here. I will stand for you. I will become your justice... somehow.”

Twenty

It did not take Qotle long to gather up the other fifteen members of the Hen'Bon'On tribe. They were the only ones left. The smoking wreckage of the alien shuttle lay ruined and ugly a ways off and Qotle had to work to keep the men's teeth from chattering as they stepped over the bloody mess splattered across the surrounding stones. The group demeanor was becoming tried as a result. No one had come into this expecting the result they now faced.

But, in short order, the men were able to refortify their soldierly demeanors and resume their march back to their canyon home. They traveled at a much faster pace now that they only had one captive to look after and, given their superior numbers, they no longer felt any need in restraining the lone Tetset man's legs to keep him from running away.

They walked the desert path a great many miles, crossing rough and craggy terrain, taking shortcuts where they could find them over sharp hills they would have had to circumvent had the women and children survived. They ate only small rations, some few crops they had salvaged from the Tetset celebration they had sacked. And they continued on in this way, not stopping or even speaking to one another until they arrived in the very early morning at Kyun'Bon'On — The Fingers of All and the most sacred river of the Hen'Bon'On peoples. It was a miraculous sight to Silent Wolf whose own people had never taken pilgrimage this far to the East.

Every man of the group paused in soldierly rank and file. Silent Wolf took them in, the Hen'Bon'On. He watched with confused reverence, recognized the cultural similarities those men seemed to share with the hunter groups of Tetset. The

Hen'Bon'On men kneeled in ceremony as if praying to the water itself for forgiveness. Silent Wolf's own people had done this during the Low festivals at their Creek Antan only a few days ago. The men reached down in unison with cupped hands and raised the imprisoned water high into the air as if first offering it to the Monsoon which had somehow still not touched this land. Those hands then lowered below the men's waists as if making the same offering to the dry patches of soil along the banks, still untouched by the currents of the great river. When neither the sky nor the land asked the men for a share of the water they had claimed, the soldiers lifted their palms to their mouths and drank. One of the men began to hum then — a low, elongated note that Silent Wolf imagined would never end. Others joined in with the humming. With more water, they began to wash themselves. Their war paint melted away. And Silent Wolf felt a jarring loneliness come over him. He saw the faces of the men of his own tribe upon the faces of these men who had killed them. It was so shocking that Silent Wolf had to shut his eyes to try and find his senses again. When he opened them, he saw that the men's faces were of the others and not of Tetset at all. He knew then he had begun the long, winding process of going insane.

Qotle approached the captive noticing the man had not come to the river with the soldiers in order to drink. He offered him water from his own hands, but the man did not seem to want it. So Qotle sipped at what remained in his palms and walked a short distance away to take a seat on a large piece of driftwood nearby. He felt disconnected from his men. Out of sync. Ever since that night in the teosintl fields he had not felt himself. Or, if he was being completely honest, he felt more himself than he had in many years. He listened for the Spider Woman in his mind. But she would not come to him. She had not properly communed with him since that girl had burned his eyes and choked him. Or was that a different man who had endured that humiliation? Qotle did not feel humiliated. Far from it; Qotle felt a renewed sense of himself. His bloodied hand, now washed clean from the river Kyun'Bon'On, felt strong as it had when he was a child, before...

Qotle decided not to revisit that memory. He stood up from his driftwood seat and whistled out to his men. It was time for them to go home.

Twenty One

Coming to a sheer cliff, Silent Wolf stopped to examine his captors once more. They seemed relieved, in high spirits even as they approached the edge. And without looking, the first two of them turned backwards and leapt, disappearing into the abyss of the canyon beyond. Silent Wolf felt a shudder work down his spine as, slowly, he approached that ledge as well. His eyes might as well have popped out of his head as he glimpsed the bottom of the hole in the ground a great distance down. A fall from this height to the bottom would kill a man a hundred times over and Silent Wolf audibly gulped. But, of course, the first two men who had jumped had not fallen to their deaths. They gripped the wall with firm, crooked fingers — feet sliding along a ledge projecting out from the rock a mere three inches wide. Perhaps these men had done this climb so many times they simply no longer feared it, but somehow Silent Wolf doubted a man could ever really forget that kind of fear. Still more of his captors were hopping down onto that ledge with the same sense of abandon.

Qotle approached the Tetset man. He could see the fear in his eyes and recalled the first time he himself had ever done this climb. A boy of seven, he had not yet earned his name. The Hen'Bon'On elders, all gone now, had been so proud of him for he had never flinched, though the sweat slipping down his brow forced his eyes closed and the wetness of his palms made him slick. But he had made it to the wider path and down to the true home as all other proper Hen'Bon'On had done. As, Qotle knew, this Tetset man would do. And he remembered the elder's words to him all of those years ago, *"There are three ways into the canyon, though one of those is death. When the monsoon swirls there is only one way, and only in between the rains. You will take this way today so you may know it in the water."* Qotle was pulled all at once from the memory for the Tetset man was speaking.

"Why do we travel this way?" Silent Wolf whined the words, "Down this path of all places?"

"All human life emanates from deep within the heart of this canyon." Qotle spoke as the elder had spoken to him, though he wondered at the words. "I wish to show you our past so that you may begin to understand our future."

The Tetset man hesitated, obviously unconvinced. And Qotle had to force back a childish laugh.

"Come." Qotle continued, "It is not so dangerous if you know how to use your feet."

Silent Wolf contemplated the captor's words. He thought briefly about the possibility of falling, about his own death. And he remembered how the others had fallen. Should he die here, his death would not be so different from theirs. So he steeled himself and walked past the man who had been speaking to him. Silent Wolf fell through the air, the wind brushing against his skin, but only for a brief moment. Then his legs jolted to a stop, his knees taking the majority of the hit, his knuckles cusping into the crevasse just overhead. His leap had not been so aggressive as those of the others, but he accomplished the task and now he began to feel a sense of pride returning to him — seeping back into his bones. He had chosen to follow these men, to dangle here on the cusp of life and death. Something within him was trying to pretend that he was not, in fact, a prisoner any longer, for he, himself, had made the choice. He thought it might be his inner survivor trying to stave off the inevitable. He would learn in due time that this assumption was wrong.

The sun moved rapidly through the sky on that day as the work of footing and fingering the different levels of the wall required consummate concentration. Occasionally, Silent Wolf would turn his head and catch a brief glimpse of the other wall behind him. The sun's rays lit the stone so magnificently, reds and oranges streaked across his vision, and Silent Wolf completely forgot himself and where he was. On one of these occasions, he nearly lost his footing sending a crumbling barrage of rocks tumbling down the incline to a place where his body might have broken. But he held on somehow and for some reason he could not completely understand, he continued to survive.

His eyes brushed over the canyon bed below. Any vegetation appeared abnormally small; a mere illusion of distance. And there was a river that twisted, surged, and slowed amidst the curves of the boulders down there. Silent Wolf wondered if this was the same river they had visited the night before.

Kyun'Bon'On, that canyon was the sacred place where the great river went to die. Though Qotle and his fellow tribesmen knew, in fact, that the river's resources did not completely deplete themselves there, rather the waters lived a sort of second life as they bled down into underground pools, subterranean chambers beneath the Lady's Temple toward the canyon's end. And still those waters found a way beyond even that place reforming another smaller body of water some many miles to the East. In that way, the river never truly died. Even greater than that strange immortality, in some years the river would unexpectedly enlarge, overtaking even the highest walls of the canyon. Yes. Sometimes "The Fingers of All" were angry fingers that would take life without hesitation. If not for the Spider Woman, all of Hen'Bon'On would have drowned the last time Kyun'Bon'On had shown such fury.

But Silent Wolf knew none of these things at that moment. He only knew the beauty of the tamed river beneath him. And he marveled at the thing recalling some small bit of childish joy.

One of the Hen'Bon'On men nudged him and Silent Wolf realized he was holding up the line again. He turned to face his grip holds and discovered the path had grown beneath his feet. While he daydreamed, they had reached the wider and much safer portion of the path to the bottom. He tested his footing and, seeing that the men ahead of him were no longer clinging to the rock face with their hands, Silent Wolf let go. He sighed with deep relief, for surely what came next would be easier than the last several days and nights.

Twenty Two

It was a long, meandering walk to the base of the canyon. A sort of fever dream of lolling calm scorched through Silent Wolf's blood all the way down. And he began to feel the guilt of all his living days flow into that empty place in his stomach where Tetset had once existed. Calm collapsed into tedium, aches into genuine pain. Silent Wolf was fading, floundering as he wrestled with his survivorship. His false assertion that he was now free only made him feel worse as the long walk plodded on. *Blue Flower would have made a better last than me*, thought Silent Wolf. *She was always accepting of the true nature of our people. I am not Tetset as she was. I should have taken her place among the dead, and she mine among the living.* He was not looking forward, not looking up. His head hung low and all he saw was rock and dirt... and water.

Slowly, the Hen'Bon'On had led him back to water. Large puddles rose up to his shins. One of the men stopped before him, leaned over and collected the liquid in his hands. That man sipped a little, turned, and offered the stuff to the dehydrated Silent Wolf. This time Silent Wolf did not refuse. As he sipped the water, he felt one last pride-filled piece of himself chip away. He felt naked. His hate, his pride, his anguish and passion all removed. Should he have refused the offering, he might have died and thus retained some small aspect of the Tetset person he had been: the proud warrior that protects his home at all costs... the dutiful one that would sacrifice himself if it meant there was even a possibility that it could preserve the tribe's lasting impression on the world at large. Blue Flower had been this way. Ultimately, Silent Wolf had not. Instead of further committing to the ideal of this sacrifice, he drank of the ending pools of Kyun'Bon'On and lived... and lived and lived... something no warrior was meant to do.

He lifted his head up and finally noticed something far off in the direction in which they were heading. Something large and utterly overwhelming glinted against the reflection of... of what? The moon? Silent Wolf had lost all sense of time, but he knew there was no sun in the darkened sky. Still, lights flickered from... windows? This was not firelight. Silent Wolf had never witnessed anything like it or the structure it occupied.

Spires of mica rose higher and higher up the far distant canyon walls, seemingly cut directly from the stone, until they reached the top. Silent Wolf thought that if he had come from the flat land on the outside of the canyon, he would never have known any of this was even here. But from where he stood, a great tower loomed before him tucked neatly into the bosom of the canyon earth which held the structure in a firm embrace.

"What is that?" Silent Wolf spoke more to himself than to anyone around him.

But Qotle accepted the question as genuine and he lurched into the response he had been planning for this very moment, "That is the place I have promised you." he said, "The Temple of the Spider Woman."

Silent Wolf took a deep breath. The morning sun broke the line of the top of the canyon. How many days had it been? How many hours? The sun was up again. All of the lights from within the mega-structure, the temple, all at once flickered out.

The man formerly of Tetset stood there, silent, mouth agape as the daylight bounded off the huge building, so spectacular, so foreboding in full view. Silent Wolf felt himself forgetting everything else he had ever known. Indeed, this was the day he would be reborn.

Twenty Three

Carefully, Blue Flower approached the gaping entrance to her companion's shuttle. She stepped across that thin veil between past and future recalling the place where she had tripped only moments ago. Regret filled her as she realized what the bump in the ground had really been — a severed human leg — a Tetset leg. Too late, she looked away. Instantly, she found herself distracted from the image's attempt at searing itself into her mind, for in plain view, across the way, lay the Being, maskless and struggling as it had been pinned down by rubble on the cockpit floor. Its eyes were wild, rolling to and fro in search of some way to free itself.

Blue Flower climbed across the rubble, blood trickling down her abdomen as she leaned in to try and lift the heavy tech that bound her friend to the ground. Though she was slow with her injury and perhaps not strong enough regardless, she still knew she had to make the attempt. She was actually managing to budge the largest component; a velvety screen with a great deal of piping and silky thin rope coming out the back which it had torn away from its mounting behind.

The Being saw the futility of the girl's attempts. It needed to clear her mind as well as its own. So it flared out what feathery appendages it could get loose from the rubble and shrieked out a pain soaked, harsh and violent song through the timorous husk of its body.

Darkness. Blue Flower was once again blinded by the music. No. Not blinded by it... shrouded in it. Her mind floated in the vacuum of the Being's strange language. A truly terrible chord strung against her and the Being's colorful mask filled her perspective. The mask. Why?

She felt as though she had been struck in the chest as she looked down into her friend's maskless and worrying eyes. She shook her head with uncertainty and tried again to remove the velvety screen.

But the Being had to insist she listen or this would all have been for nothing and it would die there and then. It forced out another agonizing spray of music.

Again, darkness for Blue Flower. The void filled around her more urgently this time, not with the mask, but something else, more awkward, more obscure... A small bag. Slowly, the bag inflated and retracted to the methodical pattern of lungs breathing air.

"I do not understand." Blue Flower spoke to the vision.

More music. The bag disappeared. In its place and all around her Blue Flower stood with her own body in a desaturated world. She understood she must have been looking at a memory because the shuttle sat in perfect shape before her against an unbloodied desert landscape. The Being, completely unharmed, stepped out of the ship with curiosity in its eyes. It did not wear its mask in the memory either.

Blue Flower was swept away then into a realm of macro abstractions. Tiny particles of dust wizzed around her. So tiny. She comprehended their size — even as she stood amidst them — even as the myriad molecules grew to the size of her own body. She was moving with them, as if one of them. And they were all heading toward a great mountain. No. Not a mountain. It was the Being's face, naked, enormous, filling the space where desert landscape should have been. Blue Flower and the dust particles flowed forth and were unceremoniously sucked up into the Being's massive nostrils.

Falling back into the desert, Blue Flower returned to her own scale. She watched the desaturated memory again. Now the

Being leaned down to close a sample of stone into a small casing. But something affected the Being adversely and it collapsed to the dust struggling to catch its breath. It crawled weakly back into the open shuttle bay.

Time leapt forward. The Being stepped out of its shuttle once again. This time, it wore its turquoise and triangle rich mask. Blue Flower tried to study each detail worrying that the whole interaction was taking too long. Then she spotted it — the small, inflating, deflating bag. It clung to the back of the Being's mask. It was a breathing apparatus.

"Oh yes I see." Blue Flower gasped in amazement. She was suddenly back in the shuttle wreckage, real time upon her again. She knew how the Being wanted her to help. Quickly, she turned and ran toward the door at the rear of the cockpit. It was malfunctioning and would not open on its own, so she had to grasp at a small gap between the metal and force it open herself. She could see little trails of her own blood forming beneath her, but she decided that was inconsequential at the moment because — she had managed to open up a large enough crack in the door to fit her body through. She stuffed herself in and found the inner chambers had sustained far less damage than the cockpit (though much clutter had fallen from the walls throughout). *We must have smashed into the earth face first,* she thought, *broken all our teeth in the process.* Then she spotted the thing she was looking for and b-lined toward it. The mask. It was laying sideways on the floor. It had not taken damage. She reached out and grabbed it, tucked it beneath her good arm, and rushed back through the crack in the doorway leading to the cockpit. She climbed across the rubble as before and kneeled down at the side of the Being.

Gently, Blue Flower placed the mask over the Being's head. It clicked down smoothly and Blue Flower looked to the breathing apparatus on the back. The bag expanded. The Being's body relaxed. Blue Flower felt herself breathe a huge sigh of relief as the alien began to push with renewed strength against the rubble. She leaned back in to help with the smaller items which lay across her friend's legs saying to herself as much as to the alien, "I have you. You will be new again. I promise."

PART II - THE GODS THAT BREATHE

One

Standing in her private chamber, in her mica tower built from the very walls of its canyon home, the Spider Woman reached her mind across the void to try and commune with the members of her raid party; the Hen'Bon'On men gone off to seek out and capture her missing "ingredients." Some five laborious days had passed since she had last heard from Qotle, and for reasons she did not understand she still could not raise him. Fortunately, she was able to attune herself with the other members of the group — Ginjiyo was particularly susceptible to her mind speech. So the Spider Woman reached out to Ginjiyo instead.

He showed her that they were close. Very close. He showed her that the men of the raid party were all safe, including Qotle. So she stopped worrying for his life and instead began worrying for his mind. Ginjiyo also showed her the reason the alarm had sounded, why the turrets had been armed; that the extraneous members of the Tetset tribe had all perished. The Spider Woman marveled at the miscomprehension Ginjiyo showed. He lacked a clarified vision of the craft they had shot out of the sky. And the Spider Woman thought about the tremendous waste that had come out of the sloppiness of their attack. She had not wished to use humans in this assault in the first place, they were so inconsistent. But she had had her reasons in the end.

Probing Ginjiyo's mind further, she could see one of those reasons now. All was not in vain, for the boy, at least, had made it through the desert with them, quite alive. She knew instantly that she had Qotle to thank for this. Yet the girl was not there... not with them and nonexistent in and across their collected memories. She: that vision in the Spider Woman's mind that had spanned across the epochs of space and time to haunt her. Based on what Ginjiyo showed her, she knew the girl had not perished with the others. She had not been present for any of it. So where the damn was she?

The Spider Woman tried to raise Qotle one more time for something within her told her that he would know more, but this attempt too was unsuccessful. And as she thought and pondered on these uncharacteristic failings of her psychic powers, she remembered her physical self. She realized she was about to have a guest. As any good host would do, she should march downstairs to meet this progeny of the forebears of man.

Two

That tower grew larger in Silent Wolf's eyes with each step. It was now to the point that he could at last make out the speckling details of the upper windows with more than just a passing assumption of what he was looking at. And as he and the other men crossed through a particularly narrow corridor of the lower canyon, and out the other end, the base of the temple became clear as well. Silent Wolf did not expect to see this base camp. Why should it exist when the tower (still under some form of construction) could house, in his estimation, ten or twenty tribes within its walls? Silent Wolf then noticed something else that, for reasons he did not understand, made him quiver; his subconscious fought to raise a question that he did not wish to consider openly. So he put it off. The two large orbs seemingly buried halfway up in the base racks at the forefront of the camp. He would have easily identified them as turrets if he had ever seen such things before.

Shielding himself from the queasy thought bouncing around his head, Silent Wolf decided for the first time to indulge himself and his captor in some small talk. "Do your people claim this land?" Silent Wolf asked the question lamely.

Qotle was happy to hear the man speak again. The silence of their hike had not been kind to him these last few hours. The thought of coming home — something that only a few days ago had been all that occupied his mind — now seemed shrouded in perilous uncertainties. He hungrily took up this new conversation, "We fight for the right to it." He said those words and considered them a moment knowing this response was an inadequate one. But for the life of him, Qotle couldn't remember so many things that had been rote memory to him before, a frustrating side effect of his disconnect from the Spider Woman. He searched his existing memories and grasped for a slightly more satisfying explanation. "This canyon is sacred to us. And the Spider Woman asks that we keep it." As the words left his mouth, it occurred to Qotle that even they did not feel accurate anymore.

Fortunately for the Hen'Bon'On man, that was the moment the first of the fentiums decided to burrow out of a hole in the southern turret. The creature pressed out into the open air of the arcade of Bo'No'To, the Hen'Bon'On name for this sacred city. The fentium was tall, lanky, and scarlet red. To the untrained eye it may have looked like a massive, red stick bug, perhaps two heads taller than the tallest living man. Qotle was used to seeing creatures such as this on a daily basis. Since the day the Spider Woman had rescued him and his people, hundreds and possibly thousands of fentium had found their way up from — Qotle didn't know where within the earth's depths — to aide the lady in her various missions, most prominently the building of her great temple.

If Qotle was used to seeing things like these, it was plain immediately that Silent Wolf was not. The boy of Tetset had gone pail and sweaty all over. His fear returned to him like it had never left at the sight of this new monstrosity, a scar across his perceptive faculties. "What is that??" He choked out the question.

"Do not be afraid." Qotle stepped out in front of the boy. "Ho there!" As he greeted the fentium a sense of normality entered back into Qotle's mind. He really was back home after all that had happened. He said to the creature, "We return with the Spider Woman's first request!" Qotle gestured toward Silent Wolf adding, "This young man, destined for greatness." But Silent Wolf did not look destined for greatness at that moment. The boy was crying again, quaking in his boots. The fentium just cocked its head sideways like a confused puppy.

"Qotle!" A young, female voice shouted from across the yard.

"Shi'Yun!" Qotle's eyes brightened and he smiled with all the teeth he could make visible at the sight of his little sister. Shi'Yun rushed down the steps of the great temple, raced across the long divide of land, passed the fentium, and sprung forward, nearly tackling Qotle to the ground. Qotle caught her in his arms and saved them both from tumbling with a happy spin.

"You have returned from your long journey." Shi'Yun did not try to catch her breath, "I am so glad."

She was a cute little girl of six or seven years and Silent Wolf, watching the reunion scene, felt himself clambering through too many conflicting emotions. Longing. Jealousy. Empathy. He could hardly process a single one.

Qotle placed Shi'Yun back down and chuckled, "Yes little sister." He then turned his eyes to Silent Wolf again and spoke with a heavier voice, "Though my mission is far from over."

"Oh please don't leave me again!" Shi'Yun prattled on, "I hate it when you are gone. I fear for you so on your hunts."

"You do not need to fear for me, Shi'Yun." Qotle placed his hand on his sister's head and jokingly messed her hair, "I am strong like the spirit of the warrior from the elder's tales."

So this man's name is Qotle, Silent Wolf thought to himself, *He has a sister who cares for him and he lives in a town at the base of this canyon with...* Silent Wolf eyed the fentium once more, but the creature was already going about its own business. So Silent Wolf, not feeling threatened at the moment, put away his cowardice and began to look around past the two orbs at the front of the city.

Bo'No'To was not a city as modern man may recognize one, at least not on the surface. There were doors and windows bored into the canyon walls beneath the large temple, and within each of these openings one would find chambers extending straight beneath the earth for perhaps two miles all around. These chambers would serve as apartments and communal areas during the stormy seasons, though to be completely honest, many of them remained quite empty all the year round. The Hen'Bon'On peoples were not so numerous as to need all of this space. And, in fact, it had only been on the insistence of the Spider Woman that the humans had even allowed so much quarrying and construction by the fentiums in the first place. It was becoming a vast and intricate cave system that seemed to be getting a little bit bigger with each passing day.

More fentiums were making their way out into the arcade accompanied by some few humans; women, children, elders — all the likes of those whom Silent Wolf had so recently lost. He didn't mean to, but something within Silent Wolf switched on... new wheels were turning in his head. He projected his love for his lost Tetset tribe onto these people and, being far too weakened from his recent journey, being all too completely compromised by those terrible emotions that had been resisting and working their way through him, Silent Wolf could not recognize the manipulation being played upon his mind by the strange presence that was then slowly approaching the entry steps of the temple.

Silent Wolf, that strange presence seemed to speak to him from that place, though words had not been spoken.

He jumped at the utterance of his name there in that place that could not possibly have known him from any other creature in all the universe. Silent Wolf, not under his own power, and not understanding why, turned and looked up toward the top of those enormous steps. And at last he saw her.

The Spider Woman was not necessarily terrible to look upon. In fact, she shared many latent human traits — a pair of arms with hands, elbows, shoulders — a mouth with puckered lips — a nose — but her skin was red, her legs hidden behind a sort of gown that implied a number greater than two, and when Silent Wolf reached her eyes, he realized that while the bottom two beneath her brow were distinctly similar in shape to his own, the other eleven were rather obviously not. Those extra obsidian irises formed patterns of fives on left and right getting smaller the farther they existed from the center. But at the center of that sharply elongated forehead, there existed that one big eye that seemed as though it could reflect the whole of the universe within its deep blackness. Silent Wolf then noticed that each eye, including the two more human ones, housed multiple pupils. Yet somehow Silent Wolf did not feel himself balk at the sight of her as he had with the fentium. Rather, he realized that he found her features strangely beautiful, that he felt his mind begin to clear when he looked at her, that even though nothing at all made sense anymore in the whole world, somehow her presence there did.

"How do you know my name?" Silent Wolf asked, not considering that the words had in fact been mind beamed to him.

So the Spider Woman spoke aloud in kind, "I know many things, young one." Her voice was gentle and soothing, though contradictory in its robust deepness, "I know of the end of your tribe. I do apologize for the terrors that have been inflicted upon you these days past." She watched him and saw no change in his demeanor, which was good. "I know of your love unrequited." At that, she saw Silent Wolf bristle. That was also good. "And I can show you the pathway back to that love." The Spider Woman then extended her hand forward as if the boy were meant to take it. Though the distance was too substantial between the ground where he stood and the top of the steps. She said, "Come."

Only then did Silent Wolf really seem to waver. He was not entirely hers yet after all. But that was alright. She would have him in time.

"My people no longer live on this earth." Silent Wolf spoke, "I know this fact. I know that evil was done to them." He looked sideways at the orbs... the turrets... behind him. "Though I do not understand the reason. You speak to me of love. Why should I listen?"

Pulling her outstretched hand back to her core, the Spider Woman began to thread her fingers fluidly through the air. An odd sort of dance; at once beautiful and flowing; at once forced and tugging. She manipulated a small pocket of space before her, pulled some unidentifiable element from the opened air like crystalline string — like a spider's webbing. She held the element forth and Silent Wolf, gobsmacked by this new sorcery, had to get a better look. He climbed the stairs like a little boy, filled with awe and wonder.

As Silent Wolf approached, the Spider Woman began to play with the string, wrapping it like a game of cat's cradle. "Young child," she spoke methodically, "the pathways do not know malice. Though malice may be done. Take my hands and I will make it clear to you that I am not your enemy." She wove the string back in on itself and shoved it, in plain sight, back into the aether from whence it came. She then held out both of her hands again to Silent Wolf. This time the boy was close enough. He took them and with a great strength, the Spider Woman lifted him up into the air and placed him delicately down on his feet on the top of the stairs beside her. Silent Wolf was hopeful and unshaken by the action... more boyish than ever before. The Spider Woman smiled. "Yes. You will follow as I have foreseen.

This way." She turned — stopping only for a moment to look off in the direction of Qotle and Shi'Yun still distracted by the joys of their reunion — and walked back through the entrance of the temple. And for his part, Silent Wolf did follow.

Three

As large as the structure appeared from without, the Temple of the Spider Woman was even larger within. Cavernous, alien rooms led to other equally massive spaces beyond to the point that Silent Wolf found himself really contemplating just how small a thing he was. He was a teardrop in an ocean amidst these newly discovered zones of the world. In the main hall alone he could look all the way up to a ceiling that touched the very height of the canyon walls. As if from a dream, or perhaps it was a nightmare, Silent Wolf gazed upon several tremendous sloping pathways — as of the moment unfinished, but already so much larger than his Antan in width and scope. These were fragmented, glittering pathways or bridges that rose and fell from one level of the space to another and they were made out of many strands of that ethereal web-like material the Spider Woman had shown him outside. Hoards of fentium crawled along those bridges unharmed, pulling additional cords of the material. That webbing had an odd presence once stretched out between levels. It seemed to charge with glowing energies the likes of which Silent Wolf could not begin to fathom. A sizzling sound would often accompany balls of light thrusting belligerently through the inner workings of the cords — like the plasmic origins of lightning born of a primeval universe.

Then Silent Wolf became aware of just how many of those fentiums infested the space. Hundreds of them in direct view of his current location — like ants in a hill — popping in and out through unseen tunnels within the framework of the tower. At first he had taken the shells of their bodies to be the inner walls of the structure. But slowly, awfully he realized that those walls were moving, shuffling — fentiums going about constructing, adjusting, cleaning — whatever it might be that a fentium or an ant might get up to in its busy day-to-day life.

Silent Wolf spoke to relieve himself of the creeping feeling all over his skin. He asked, "What is this place?"

And the Spider Woman was right there beside him answering, "Young boy, there are many things I would like to show you... in time." She lingered, studying him a moment. She had an emotion within her eyes that Silent Wolf could not contextualize. Still she kept them moving, walking toward a surprisingly small opening against a back wall of the otherwise massive main hall.

The door was perhaps four feet in height. Silent Wolf would have to duck to make his way through. He wondered awkwardly how the Spider Woman, who was taller than him, would herself manage the task. He looked up noticing that a few of those charged pathways seemed to converge on that space, seemed to stab through the wall above the opening, bleeding energy into it. *For what?* He wondered.

"Go ahead," the Spider Woman smiled as she spoke, "step inside. You will see something that will forever change your life. It will make you stronger. This I promise."

Silent Wolf didn't know if he liked the sound of that. But he didn't see much of a choice in the matter. And given the myriad ways in which his life had already been changed of late, he decided it probably couldn't get much worse. So he bent his head down, hunched his back as low as he could get it, and pushed open a stone-slab door pressed against the hole.

Four

It had been several days since the incident in the desert. The shuttle had taken long to repair if not because both Blue Flower and the alien were more heavily injured than either wished to admit, then certainly because they simply did not have the correct components to make the necessary adjustments to the engine and hull. Life support was another matter altogether. And whenever the Being needed Blue Flower's aide in some task she had to arduously reach out to her primitive mind in complicated musical overtones. She could understand perhaps only half of the information presented to her in each of those visions, but she was resilient nonetheless and the Being found itself growing very fond of her iron will.

That being said, the limited repairs they could make were slap-dash at best and the Being knew they would have to travel a great distance to get what they needed. So they agreed to give up on the hull adjustments for now and focus all of their efforts on the engine mechanics, at times even tearing the hull back further to harvest the precious metal it could supply.

The end result of all of this work would have been comical to the two of them if it didn't make the long flight so miserable. The broken and mangled husk of the shuttle would have to fly some five thousand miles at suboptimal speeds over potentially fierce, storm-prone waters. The two travelers would have to take turns operating the shuttle's mechanics in a cockpit that remained cracked wide open to the elements. Worse still, Blue Flower's shoulder was not healing well. Yet she would not allow her friend to take longer turns than her as it had seemed to be suggesting in its latest song.

Presently, Blue Flower's turn was ending for the day and the Being approached her at the command station and relieved her for what would be a handful of hours. She stepped away from the panel and peered out at the water beyond. Having wrapped herself in some of the additional fabrics from the exterior of the pouch Mother Tree had gifted her, the wind could smack at her through the gaping hole in the hull all it wished. She had hardened herself and grown used to it, though her skin was always dry, her lips always chapped, and her fingers could never seem to shake the terrible cold from themselves... especially not in the injured side where the skin around the wound was festering with shades of yellows and greens. Blue Flower did not completely understand where her friend was taking her. All she had had to do on her shifts was monitor the engine's gages to make certain no irregularities cropped up. She marveled that the Being had been able to program their course so the shuttle was automatically going in the right direction — West across the ocean to a place where repairs could be implemented. She felt the Being's pain as it felt hers... and she trusted it.

From the sea below, a luminous and massive creature breeched the surface. It had huge fins each the size of the shuttle and its obsidian skin wore a beautiful, glossy sheen. Blue Flower looked on at the thing with incredulity, for she had never known such a beast could exist in the world outside of camp fire stories.

Five

Within the new space, Silent Wolf found himself surrounded by flat, watery surfaces on all sides; walls, ceiling, floor — all appearing to reflect off of one another in an endless cuboid dance. Light energy would occasionally pulse along just beneath the surface of those mirror ponds.

After a moment's hesitation, Silent Wolf tested the water with his left foot. To his surprise, it was somehow solid. Even though ripples would occasionally break across the surface, they were nothing so large as to be able to trip the boy. He took a full step onto the moving mirror floor. Then he took another. Before he had a chance to look up, he was already pressing against the back wall. He touched it with his left index finger and though the wall felt as solid as the floor had, new rings of ripples formed from the place his finger had disturbed.

Silent Wolf tried to step back and nearly lost his footing as a wave of the mirror stuff nearly six feet tall cusped up against his body from behind and forced him back toward the rippling wall. As he approached against his own will, Silent Wolf feared he might be crushed. He shut his eyes tight and he felt his face press up against something cold. His hands splayed to either side, helpless. But the wave and the wall did not hurt him.

Eventually, realizing he was still alive, Silent Wolf reopened his eyes. He was shocked when he recognized that he was somehow inside the wall. It was peculiar; gelatinous. Yet he could still breathe and see... *See what?* He struggled, as he so often did, to comprehend what he was looking at or what he was feeling. He even struggled to recognize his own thoughts, for they had begun to sound like someone else's. The gelatinous wall continued and Silent Wolf knew that the wave was still propelling him through it. He watched and waited in exasperation until the wall ended, breaking into drippy liquid on the other side. He dropped out the back end of the goop onto cold rock. His hands and knees bruising easily against the hard surface.

Silent Wolf was free of the wave and he felt himself laugh, for he was not dead. But where was he? A small cubby of a room, built in stone and nestled gently behind a wall of soft-hard squishy stuff. He scratched his head and rubbed his elbows with his aching palms. And he studied the stone walls through a thin veil — a waterfall. Something had been crafted on those stone walls beyond; cave drawings, freshly formed.

The boy put his head through the waterfall to see the images close up, though perhaps he had come too close. His eyes struggled to make out the bigger picture and all he could see were details. But at least he wasn't trying to see it through the spray of water.

What 'It' was, was an incredibly elaborate series of images that seemed to be telling a story. The first thing Silent Wolf's eyes went to was a perfectly recreated image of the alien shuttle which had attacked his people on the walk in the desert. *But how is this here?* He wondered. There was an image of a tree on fire next to this. And then what appeared to be a huge stampede of ground sloths and other creatures he could not quite make out. The next image seemed to imply that these forces were converging on some huge obelisk. Just past that, Silent Wolf swore he was looking at an image of Blue Flower in the arms of... a faceless man. The two seemed to be lovers. *Why show this to me?* He was becoming perturbed. *Blue Flower should be long dead by now and none of this other stuff makes any sense at all.*

Frustrated, Silent Wolf pulled his head out from beneath the gloss of the waterfall. He pondered on, looking at that image of Blue Flower and the man. Then he noticed his own reflection staring back at him from the water's surface. It rested perfectly over the blank face of that man and it was smiling, though Silent Wolf did not feel that smile's presence on his actual face.

Six

The Spider Woman remained by the small opening waiting with anticipation. She had an idea what he might see within the mirror room. Yet she worried over how it would make the boy react. She had seen this moment on one of her mind journeys along the pathways, but this had been one of those unfortunate pivot moments when two possible futures had diverged from the same spot. The Spider Woman hated those kinds of moments, specifically when other individuals held the keys to them. Silent Wolf's imagination was the key to this one and it made the lady feel impractically helpless. So she stood there waiting for the boy to come out of his hole and tell her in which version of the future they would now be living.

Finally, after what felt agonizingly like three hours to the Spider Woman, Silent Wolf emerged, dampened by plasma and wearing one of those awkward human expressions she had had so much trouble reading. She asked as calmly as she knew how, "What did you see?" She did not require him to answer. The moment the boy had stepped back out from the mirror room she had instantly been able to regain access to his mind. Yes. She felt it; his lack of understanding; his evolving attempts at comprehension. It felt right. He was turning rapidly into the version of himself she had hoped he would become. The future pathway she most desired was opening to her. So she smiled and pretended not to care and said with the kind of dignity required of a host, "No matter, I will explain what I can in time. You are weary, I know. Let us get you to rest."

The Spider Woman then summoned a nearby fentium and the underling led Silent Wolf through the main hall toward one of the pathways that wound through the room like a grand staircase, though there were no steps on it, only the slow and peaceful incline passing from story to story and continuing on almost to the very top of the structure.

Silent Wolf followed the insect obligingly. He was, after all, very tired. As he walked he contemplated. He did not know what it was, why the Spider Woman was so eager to help. After the loss of his tribe — of Blue Flower — he had been left in tatters. Now these people, these Hen'Bon'On who had intended to take him prisoner, did not treat him as such. They claimed to desire friendship when Silent Wolf could only see darkness.

Seven

That day Silent Wolf slept very badly. He tossed and he turned in his hollowed out pocket in a burrowed wall of one of the temple's cave-like rooms; a sort of bed that might well have been comfortable to any member of Tetset who had been so used to sleeping directly on the ground, though in those times they would have had their relative's bodies around them to help soften the night. Having been through such a terrible journey, Silent Wolf would not find comfort any time soon. He slept with terrible visions all that day and two more nights beyond that. In his dreams he saw Blue Flower rising from the ashes of the wreckage of the alien shuttle. He saw her in shadows growing larger than he could ever have imagined. Now a shrewd giant, she held a kopa to her lips and commanded a massive army of shadow creatures Silent Wolf could not contextualize. What he could make out — what he could readily see and comprehend — was her intense rage... Her desire for vengeance. He knew this deep down in his bones to be true. Blue Flower was angry. Blue Flower was alive.

Silent Wolf's eyes opened with a shot. He suffered from cold sweats and quivered with the fearful realization that he was nothing and she was everything. If he could only find out what had happened to her on that night — where she had gone — how she had survived. If he could only see her and talk to her, maybe they would have a chance to be that thing she had never allowed them to be. The pain within him roiled over and then, from afar, some nameless and faceless thing quashed that thought process altogether. He felt neither pain nor worry. He was numb not of his own resolve or emotional intelligence, for he had so little of either of those things...

It was the Spider Woman's will. She crawled ever through the chambers of his mind, fixing the human to her liking, seeking to find the core of the man that she must pull from within the boy. She would need that man when the ultimate moment came at last.

Eight

On perhaps the seventh day of flight, a massive tree line mercifully came into view across the horizon, though Blue Flower's onsetting illness kept her from seeing the sight firsthand. The previous day she had begun to sweat and burn up to the touch. The Being unwrapped her shroud and found the severity of her injury had spread to her neck and chest. Infected veins of black ran as far across the girl's body as there was body to look upon. So the Being had taken her back to the inner room, washed her, and reconnected her to the drip system for her own good. The alien returned to the misery of the cockpit and did not leave her post until they arrived at their destination within that distant wood.

The Being lowered her shuttle into a small gully that would have been impossible to spot amidst the trees if she didn't know precisely where to look for it. As the craft descended the daylight all but disappeared beneath the bamboo canopy.

She — for the Being was in fact a she named for the melodies meaning "Crow" and "Mother" — felt a need to hurry. Her human friend had been too greatly battered and had not been willing to take care of her body, and Crow Mother felt genuinely responsible for her now. She had not brought the girl back from one nether, her earlier wounds of exhaustion, only to let her die again from another otherwise curable sickness. So she had resolved to collect Blue Flower first thing before looking after her own lesser wounds. The Jomony would help. They had taken good care of the others when Crow Mother's people had first arrived. Surely they would be just as genial toward a native of this world.

Crow Mother finally left her post, the shuttle well settled on firm soil. She hurried back to the room where the sickly Blue Flower suffered, collected the human, and rushed her out the breeched hull of the shuttle. Gently, she lay Blue Flower down on spongy green moss and sprinted on all fours to the tree stump she knew as the place of summoning. Rhythmically, Crow Mother tapped the broken foliage. Percussion! She belted out a howling song of emergency hoping she was not already too late.

Blue Flower, trapped in her feverish slumber, briefly managed to peel her eyes open to see the alien hurriedly tapping away at its drum. *How odd,* she thought. Odder still, she thought she could see the trees and bushes around them begin to rustle and sway to the rhythm. She assumed that, in her illness, she had begun to hallucinate. But she was wrong. The flora really had begun to move to Crow Mother's song. Had Blue Flower been more sober, she might even have seen the funny little clay people waddling out from their hiding places behind those bushes to see what assistance the refugees needed of them. But Blue Flower's vision began to split as the fever took her again, her mind circling the drain.

The Jomony were silly little things to Crow Mother. They resembled dolls in shape and she knew them to be fabrications of some lost culture whether of this world or another. Not truly alive by modern scientific standards, the Jomony none-the-less had the surprising ability to think for themselves and problem solve in real time. This had made them exceptionally good companions to The People; the name of Crow Mother's species — for on their home planet they were the only "people" capable of contemplative thought and understanding... something that had rapidly changed over the last handful of decades. By the time that change had occurred, however, The People did not know any other song to define themselves by, so the title remained.

As the Jomony emerged from their bushes and trees, Crow Mother changed her song to emphasize Blue Flower's location over on the moss. The little clay robots sped off in that direction to "administer repairs."

Nine

Blue Flower would never really know just how close she had come to dying for the second time. She opened her eyes assuming she had been dreaming but quickly discovered that she was in exactly the same spot as her fantasy had left her. A mossy patch — in a glade — in an unknown forest. The difference was, Blue Flower could not see things swaying in her vision to the Being's frantic music, yet the music persisted. She noted that while in her dream state she had had no control over the functions of her arms or legs, now she was fully capable of movement once again. As she sat up, she realized that she was surrounded by little clay dolls who tinkered about still touching her in places she had imagined pain existing only a moment before.

No pain remained, so Blue Flower stood up, a little anxious of the close proximity to the clay dolls. She regained function in each of her limbs and stepped and even walked. The little guys dispersed with not a word. And Blue Flower, being a curious girl, watched them as they trotted off toward her friend's shuttle. They swarmed the hulk of metal and began twisting components back into shape and Blue Flower lit up with understanding. "They are fixing it!" she said with instinctive pleasure at the realization. She turned toward the sounds of drumming in the center of the glade and saw her friend there batting away at the tree stump. The Being met her eyes through its mask and she assumed it was smiling at her. It shrugged and kept on playing.

Then Blue Flower felt a tightness in her hand. She raised it to eye level and saw the blackness of her veins there. For a moment, she was frightened, but one particularly interested clay doll stopped its work on the shuttle, turned its head one hundred and eighty degrees and approached her without having to turn the rest of its body — for the back and front of a clay doll was interchangeable. It gently raised an arm to Blue Flower's still darkened hand.

"Can I help you?" Blue Flower asked with confusion.

The clay doll took a moment to process the language and then in a robotic sort of drawl, responded, "I will help you." The robot touched Blue Flower's index finger and she felt a pinch there. She would not have believed it if she had not been seeing it with her own eyes, but the blackness within her veins seeped forth from that finger and vanished into the outstretched arm of the robot helper.

Blue Flower gasped, "You have healed me."

"Yes." The clay doll responded.

Blue Flower raised her hand in the air toward her drumming friend to try and show it what had happened when she noticed another of the little dolls was repairing the Being's wounds as it played. Her alien had brought them to this place knowing they would receive excellent care from these little toys and Blue Flower smiled and said to the doll who had aided her, "You are our friends."

"Yes." The Jomony said again after a brief pause.

Blue Flower accepted the one word answer. She was just happy to be able to communicate with something in a language she actually understood, though at this point she still could not contemplate just how advanced the technological workings of the Jomony had to be in order to make such communications possible. Rather, Blue Flower had to assume it a strange sort of magic or sorcery such as her elders had once told stories about. Whatever the case, she accepted what she was seeing and decided to approach her friend to see what it wanted to do next.

The Being nodded to Blue Flower as she closed the gap between them and she took this to mean she should be seated. So she sat crosslegged on another mossy patch a few feet away from the drum stump. When she was settled into her position, the Being stopped its drumming. At the same exact moment, the clay dolls stopped working — not just repairing the ship or the Being — they sagged in place, no longer operating at all.

"Why have they stopped?" Blue Flower asked craning her head back to scrutinize the still and silent forms within the glade.

Crow Mother was happy that they had survived their journey, but she was growing tired of the human's obtuseness. For the moment, she figured it would be quicker to return to that obvious pantomime of playing the reeded instrument. It had worked before.

The girl looked a little embarrassed and Crow Mother felt badly, but enough was getting to be enough and still the human rattled off words she could not understand...

"I suppose I should be getting used to this by now." Blue Flower said the words out of sheer habit as she dug through the thin remains of her satchel and raised the kopa to her lips. The tune Blue Flower presented was quick, sad at first, but ending in a flurry of excitement, then repeating on coda. She thought about skin stitching itself together over time and the blackness seeping from the pinprick in her finger. She hoped that the flurry would help imply a sense of healing; of getting better. Blue Flower smugly wondered at the prospect that she might really be getting the hang of this form of communication after all.

Listening attentively, Crow Mother found herself admiring the human's denseness. Truly, Blue Flower was not very good at getting her point across in the language of The People, but she kept on trying — hoping — Crow Mother could always sense that feeling of hope and wonder even in the girl's darker moments.

Still, this new tune of Blue Flower's hardly made a lick of sense, so Crow Mother decided to help the girl out. She returned her hands to the drum matching Blue Flower's melody by half. This resulted in the Jomony all tilting their heads and reawakening from their brief slumber at the same time — something Crow Mother had known would happen, for the Jomony could only remain active during extended periods of percussive melody, a side effect of the constant thrumming of the core of the planet from whence they had come. One of the little creatures had relayed this information to Crow Mother when they first met. Though due to this phenomenon, the Jomony had many long gaps in their collective memories. *A strange sort of food,* Crow Mother mused, *almost as if these robots had been specifically created to work alongside the musically inclined People of her race.* Yet they were foreign to her, and she was foreign to Blue Flower and the natives of this world. *Perhaps,* Crow Mother thought, *perhaps it is time I show this girl the truth behind the bonds we now share.*

Crow Mother raised her plumes and began to sing a new harmony both of sadness and raw power. It rolled beneath Blue Flower's melody like a dirge until it found its turn to break free and force the other melody to evolve. And to Blue Flower's credit, she was able to play this game. A very fast learner of some things, to be fair. For a brief moment the sound was everything to the two women from opposite ends of the galaxy. They were as if two leaves in the wind circling one another, rising up and down as the air saw fit to move them. A great wind came through the gully then and swept them both away.

Ten

Blue Flower stood amidst that velvety blackness once again. It was becoming a familiar place to her. She knew that their harmony had brought her here like before. But where was here? The last time this happened, here had become a silhouetted version of her own world and the alien shuttle therein. This time, that was not yet clear. What was clear — or rather becoming clear — was the vision of the Being's mask again, beckoning Blue Flower forth into a world she had never seen before. The darkness parted. The mask faded away.

What was this new place now expanding before her? It was hilly and jade green with all sorts of unknown vegetation. It did not appear to be Blue Flower's Earth, the shapes were all wrong. Something was coming; stumbling, frolicking. No. Many somethings. They became clearer in Blue Flower's vision. Was it really — could it be —? It was the Being, naked as a lark with long, pluming feathers extending out from her spinal column and elbows. Her skin was violet and azure as Blue Flower had seen before, but it glowed so beautifully against this strange atmosphere. She was surrounded by other members of her race, hundreds of others just as bare skinned as her, and just as happy. Blue Flower could see the happy on them. She felt the happy permeating the air of the memory. She felt warmth. She heard them sing. They all sang together; a happy song. It came in waves, washing over her like a welcome breeze.

Yet something was not quite right. The sky was changing color. It had been a surprisingly beautiful shade of pink — then green like the plants — then sickly green like... like something Blue Flower did not want to think about. Too much sharp, vomitous, green light pierced the atmosphere harshly illuminating all the surface of this once pleasant world.

The herd of naked aliens stopped tumbling and playing all at once to gaze upon a new and unwelcome apparition in that sky. A massive, mica shuttle... not a shuttle... a ship, made for war; acts of atrocity. Blue Flower understood this immediately. The feeling in her gut hammered hard against her memories of Tetset. For the first time, she was seeing the face of the one responsible for the deaths of all her people.

Almost the face of a human, Blue Flower knew it for what it was; a Spider. Those eyes. All those eyes. What hidden depths could this terrible creature see? Why did it come? Why did it appear to smile too widely as it watched out its viewport on that warship? It gave the order to strike. The energy built up within the ship's canons and burst forth spraying cascading light illicitly — crushing down like hail across the planet's surface. It was so similar in appearance, that light, to the beam which had struck their shuttle. It was the same. The same source. The same technology.

Soil erupted from the hills below with new volcanic activity sending the herd into fumbling panic. They tried to run, to escape that terror, but the ground began to shatter around them.

Time leapt and leapt within the visions. Crow Mother had made this happen intentionally. She knew her audience would understand the broad strokes, but perhaps the details would be a bit too confusing until such a time when they could communicate more directly. Crow Mother wondered how she could make that happen. She realized she had reached a critical moment in her song. Now it was time to change the rhythm.

From Blue Flower's perspective, this change of pace was rapid and disorienting. She felt her mind spinning across the great expanses of time eventually pausing to watch her friend — now clothed for safety from the elements — rushing through an impeccably clean laboratory. The Being vaulted through an open doorway as a great explosion erupted upward in the distance outside, visible through a velveteen window — a monitor. The alien then stood on a hard surface that must have been fabricated by her species... Blue Flower had never imagined something like asphalt before. As Crow Mother witnessed the puffing cloud growing in strength — closing in on her position — she rushed toward a vessel waiting for her on the tarmac. Other Beings awaited her aboard that vessel and welcomed her with strenuous excitement as she approached its circular threshold. Blue Flower watched and knew then that her friend's planet had been compromised, her herd depleted.

Suddenly, Blue Flower's mind was inside that vessel. She could tell at a glance that it was meant to hold a great many more of the species than had made it aboard. She felt it propel itself and all within it high into the sky and she braced herself (though of course she was in no danger). Then Blue Flower focused her attention toward a window and somehow she was outside of the vessel, floating bodiless in the dark of space. She watched her friend's world — the jade greens turned to crumbling blackness — the hills turned to soot. She lay witness as the alien's world evaporated into a trillion little pieces before her very eyes. She watched her friend's vessel barely escape as the wreckage propelled toward them.

The alien vessel was alone then, barely moving against the void. Blue Flower knew she was still playing her kopa back in the gully. She played her thought well enough that Crow Mother could understand it. She played, "This Being is just like me." The music slowed. The dreamworld dissipated. The song, at last, had ended.

Crow Mother felt she could make sense of that thought. Her attempts at communicating her message had been received. She was exhausted, but this elaborate use of the stump had been worth the outcome.

Eleven

A tear traced Blue Flower's cheek as she came back to herself. Reality settled in. She blew two final notes in the sequence of the Sad Gully Song. She stopped. The Being completed her own notations and dropped her hands away from the tree stump. The clay dolls were still; frozen. The breeze had passed and not even the trees were swaying. Together they sat in empty silence contemplating each other — hating the nature of the universe they both had been forced to occupy.

Blue Flower thought mostly of pain, death, and destruction. She choked on anger and hate. She could not find the light within herself.

Crow Mother watched her with keen understanding. She had, after all, felt the same emotions as the human. Grief had been Crow Mother's consummate companion these last several years. So Crow Mother knew from experience that such an emotion could not be circumvented. One must work through the pain, not around it. This would take some time.

Breaking their silence, Blue Flower said, "I... I am sorry." She could think of nothing else worth saying and the tension of the still robots, the trees, the emotion of hate nearly overtook her again.

Fortunately, Crow Mother understood that inaction was not the right medicine for her human friend. She raised her hoofish hands and began the pitter pat of a beat on the tree stump once more. The Jomony resumed their procedures and Blue Flower was forced away from her morbid machinations. The world was, somehow, alive again.

Blue Flower rose to her feet and approached the alien. She worked her way through the crowd of robots, some still stopping to touch her body here and there where a wound may still have lingered. She no longer cared that the Being could not understand her words, she felt she had to say them, "How do you do that? How do you let it go so quickly? I cannot. It is so fresh in my mind. This terror. This hate. This desire for vengeance."

The alien's mask raised up with an edgy stare. Blue Flower felt the lamenting quality behind that vizor. Though she could not see it through the reflective surface, she knew she was wrong. The alien had not let go. Blue Flower would have continued her little speech though her heart was no longer in it. The Being had been landing drum blows at each emphasis point of Blue Flower's statement and somehow this helped the girl to believe she had actually been heard this time, even if the words did not directly connect.

It occurred to Crow Mother then that they were each only communicating broad strokes of emotion in their current state. Something should be done to address their language barrier. She quickly changed her drum beat to a rhythm of summoning. The wind returned to the gully and Blue Flower was nearly thrown backward from the sheer force of the breeze. Yes. The call had been heard. The others would be arriving soon.

Twelve

Silent Wolf did not wish to leave his room. That would require facing the impossible truth that he did not any longer control his faculties. But if that was the case then it could not have been Silent Wolf at all that wished to stay away from the Hen'Bon'On. No. There was a small piece of Silent Wolf still within him. It was draining out but it was there.

Contemplating his terrible string of dreams, Silent Wolf's mind wandered deeper into the abyss of his rebirth. He could not go back the way he had come, yet how could he keep going forward? The world was becoming such an awful place to have to live and yet — he was thinking about Blue Flower. His thoughts always went to her when they had nowhere else to travel. Especially amidst those crazy dreams. She was mounting something. Coming for him. He could see the moment when she would find him and he would come out to meet her in this canyon. He wondered how such a meeting would go. Could he bring himself to tell her what was happening to him — that he was changing? He couldn't understand it himself so how was he supposed to express to another how lost he was becoming?

The Spider Woman's web entrapped him across the epochs and he was slowly numbing beyond recognition, losing all sense of what was real and what was not. Still, Silent Wolf did manage to cling to the strange idea that Blue Flower was out there doing something — always searching — always trying to come for him. Was she alone at this moment right now? Did she know that he was the one she was meant to come for? Would they recognize one another in that seemingly distant future? Or would they be as strangers meeting for the very first time? Silent Wolf felt the Spider Woman press deeper into his mind. He did not try to fight it. How could he? The boy had been so very weak. The Spider Woman would make him strong.

Thirteen

If Blue Flower had been feeling lonely before, she was now beginning to feel downright crowded. Surrounded by dozens of overactive robots, trees as far as the eye could see the likes of which she had never known, her mind was filled and filling more and more with half truths that had no proper nouns. She had a friend she could barely speak to and from the darkened tree line, two more Beings of that friend's species approached.

Each of those new Beings wore their own particular mask, complete with unique shapes, symbols, and color palettes. The one on the left's had a more cylindrical quality with two darkened but separate viewing holes (one for each eye). That full head shaft had a metallic, turquoise coloration. Two large coppery ears projected out on either side, though Blue Flower doubted they were actually meant for hearing. Protruding from near the chin, there was a small cylindrical snout with a mesh sort of interior... perhaps another way of syphoning out those harmful minerals from the air.

As for the second one, the Being on the right, it wore a mask that openly combined concepts from each of the others. Cylindrical, with turquoise splitting down one half and red down the other. The viewing hole occupied the majority of the face and at first formed a 'v' at eye level like her friend's, but as it lowered approaching the nose, the shape pushed out again into a square down to the bottom of the facade. Most prominently, there was a large nose that extended out and down like the snout of an anteater might.

Blue Flower had been wrapped up in the funny look of them and had to take a moment to notice that they were actually beckoning her to follow them somewhere. Almost as if in a trance, she fell in line. She recognized the two new Beings as her friend's remaining family and though she did not know the natures of their hearts, she felt the need to follow. Crow Mother watched her go, but remained behind to keep the Jomony active at their tasks. Blue Flower wished her friend could have joined her for she did not yet feel certain that even the Being's friends could be trusted.

Together, Blue Flower and the two newly met Beings walked between the gaps in the tall bamboo trees. The drum beat was still present, but became fainter the closer they came to the unnamed river. Then a new clicking sound licked at them from overhead. It was not a threatening noise. There sat a humble watcher in the trees, a crow welcoming the three travelers into the deeper places of the wood. They walked only a short distance, though with each passing moment, Blue Flower's sense of dread deepened. The crow rattled once more and flew up to a higher branch across the way as if sensing the girl's discomfort. Blue Flower wanted to stop, wanted to take a moment, a breath — watch the bird, the slow breeze in the trees, but she could feel the Beings continue to beckon her forward... softly, welcoming. She was welcomed, a guest, but to what?

After a time, the Beings stopped, stood in place gazing forward at a denser patch of trees cusping the river's edge. No, now that Blue Flower adjusted her eyes to the shade she could see it was not truly a tree line at all there; mossy as it was it had fooled her. She stood staring at the base of a mountain and plunging through the side of that mountain there were a series of perfect, linear cracks. Oddly, the more she stared at it, the more she understood that those cracks were not a natural formation. Something else had been here long long ago. Something ancient and ominous. Yet the Beings showed no fear of the place. They gestured for Blue Flower to approach.

"Is this meant to help my cause?" she asked them rather foolishly, "I fear for my safety if I'm expected to approach there."

But of course they did not understand. These Beings were just as unlikely to know her language as her friend had been. Blue Flower was about to reach for her kopa when the one with the anteater snout raised its hand and pointed directly at the largest crack. So Blue Flower resignedly approached what was increasingly becoming clear in her vision. The crack was a gate. As she stood at the entrance of the place, she looked back and noticed that the others had not approached alongside her. They waited by the river, presumptively.

"Won't you be joining me?" she asked.

The Beings did not respond. So she took one more step forward, pressed her hands against the mossy slab and the door peeled back until Blue Flower found herself standing against a seemingly endless pit of unimaginable darkness. She felt a sort of suction pulling her toward that blackness. Then another great breeze swept up from behind her, slammed the breath from her lungs, and shoved her forward toward her new fate.

Within only a few steps, the outside light had dissipated completely. Blue Flower brushed through a long, empty, and foreboding hallway made all the more eerie by her natural blindness. Droplets plopped and plunked all around her so perhaps the unnamed river had its own secret channel within this place. Blue Flower moved carefully forward trying to will her eyes to glimpse something, anything at all in that darkness. If there were a buried stream or a lake here, surely she would be able to catch a gleam on the rippling surface, wouldn't she? But she knew that her hopeful assumption still required some light source to exist somewhere.

She walked face first into a wall. At first she was shocked. She reached up and patted her nose, but there was no blood.

Then she wasted a moment feeling foolish and sorry for herself. Blue Flower swallowed those feelings, remembered her pride, and raised her hands slowly to press against that stone wall which stood in her way... it was not stone at all, but a stinking, degraded material — harder than any stone — like the stuff from the Being's shuttle but older. She wondered if this was as far as the "cave" went — if she perhaps felt along a moment to find an opening could she find her way back? Well, she wanted to trust her companion. It had not given her reason to be afraid. Why would the alien send her off to her doom at this point? She laughed at her own stupidity and the sound of it echoed and bounced along the corridor, giving her some faint hope of finding the correct path. It had not been long, but her ears were adjusting to the dark even as her eyes had given up hope. She could hear all the little sounds in this state — could follow the drips if nothing else. The hallway did continue to her left, she realized. So Blue Flower turned her hips and carried on.

Around another corner, she was surprised to find her eyesight restored. A single lit torch goaded her toward the center of a massive cavern. She did not want to be careful anymore. There was light there and she so wanted to reach it. She threw caution to the wind and rushed — unthinking — toward that center. Quite suddenly, her legs gave out. There was no ground beneath her. Blue Flower gasped as she felt herself slipping, falling into an abyss.

Quickly, she reached out her hands and caught hold of a ledge. Her knees smacked hard against the rock and she winced at the pain. Blue Flower wondered how much damage her body had taken these last several days. At least she was no longer falling. Still, she was in a rather precarious situation; a dead hang. To make matters worse, she could clearly make out the roaring of that river far below her now. She did not wish to be pulled away by the invisible tide. So she leveraged her weight pulling her feet one by one into separate divots. Her back arched and she felt a hard protrusion against her shoulder blade. Taking a small but necessary risk, Blue Flower pulled one of her hands free and dangled out hoping to find a grippable stone on the adjacent wall. It was there. She freed a leg and crabbed her way back up until she once again could glimpse the lit torch.

Blue Flower forced her body back up onto solid ground and brushed the sweat from her brow. Just another ridiculous thing she had somehow managed to survive.

She approached the light cautiously, cognizant of each slow, purposeful step. Fortunately, she found no more pitfalls before her. *That one had been the test... if I am being tested,* she thought conspiratorially. She reached out with caution to brush the backside of a finger against the torch base. It was cool enough. She grasped it with her whole hand and pulled the fire from its post.

Thud! The noise shook her from somewhere deep in the cavern. Had she awoken something? Blue Flower peered around her hoping to see if anything had changed. Not in her immediate vicinity. Perhaps she had activated something else she would have to meet along the path. Briefly, she considered replacing the torch in its podium, but the thought fluttered from her mind. After all, she had managed to get this far already and the idea of having regained her vision only to lose it again without this prop did not sit well with her.

Instead, Blue Flower wielded the light within her hands and began turning, walking in circles around the soilless ground she had felt beneath her feet already. She took a good look at the cliff behind her — the same pit into which she had fallen. It was shaped awkwardly, as if someone had intentionally cut and lifted several boulders of varying size from that place. The leftover hole certainly did not appear natural, almost taking on the outlines of the mountain golems from Mother Tree's creation myth.

Blue Flower would have shaken that idea from her head completely, but as she turned and walked past the podium toward the side of the space she had not yet visited, her eyes caught sight of a wall cut with similar, albeit smaller holes. She raised her hand to the closest one and realized the stone was soft to the touch — springy — not just stone, but stone with a thick layer of foliage skirting it around those holes; ivy of a plant she had never seen before. Then she felt the heat of the flame expanding, licking at her arm. Before she had understood the nature of the substance which had covered the walls, she had allowed the torch to come too close and the leaves of the ivy were catching afire in a rapid trample.

Blue Flower did not have time to consider rescuing the plants on the walls. She rushed back to the podium at the center of the chamber and lingered there in fear and anxiety. She imagined herself fleeing to the pit and leaping down into the water far below where she might die drowning, but at least she would not die on fire. Yet, somehow as she sat huddled beside that podium, she understood that she was not in immediate danger of either of those fates. Sure, the flames were moving quickly, but they were not approaching her position at the center of the room.

With her eyes opened wide, she could finally see the whole of the chamber for what it was. Those cut out divots in the walls were everywhere. She knew their shapes. They were the crude outlines of the clay dolls she had met outside. And it occurred to her that the mountain in which these chambers ran had struck her as odd for a number of reasons. It began to gain a new shape in her mind's eye — the tree line, the New Mountain, whatever it was — the caves within — these chambers and holes

— this place was the remains and wreckage of a great interstellar spacecraft; one that had at one point housed the entire remains of a flesh and blood species as well as those robot workers who now lingered on her planet without true masters to direct them. This ship reminded her of the one from the Being's story, but it was most definitely not that one. An ark ship meant for a different purpose. Something the primitive girl wished she could more clearly understand. The scope of the journey this thing must have made in order to reach her world — the length of time it had been here to allow the world to grow over it in such a way — the girl's mind raced with a new sense of imagination and wonder.

Still, regardless of the spacecraft's origins, Blue Flower knew she had not seen any clay dolls the size of that hole in the cavern floor. She audibly gulped as she contemplated what such a large "worker" might be needed for.

That's when the drumming started; strange, mechanical, and very loud. But drumming — a new rhythm — it clearly was. Blue Flower watched the flames making their way in a morbidly beautiful sort of pattern along and through another hallway across from her. She picked herself up, regained her confidence, and approached the newfound passage.

As she raised her eyes to address her surroundings something struck her as funny; the walls of this new room were still afire, but the flames themselves no longer moved wildly or licked out toward the girl. This fire felt somehow contained, pinned to the walls, moving with a purpose in the direction of a sort of smelting furnace where metallic liquid gooped and oozed down into a press. Blue Flower had no frame of reference for such a device. She tried to ignore the sting of the fire, the aching pain that was beginning to reverberate across her flesh. Intently, she rose to her feet and carefully pushed forward, the sound of the drums blaring and constant in her ears.

The shape that formed within the press was difficult to interpret at first. Strange, round with winding, patterned lines manipulating the slowly solidifying texture. A shield perhaps, heavy, in the shape of the sun. "Is this..." she thought aloud wondering at the purpose of the piece.

Behind her, another thud rattled the room much closer than before. It sent a jolt up Blue Flower's spine, and she turned to face the inevitably large thing that lingered there. *It is,* she thought, *one of those great rock beasts. Mother Tree's Golem come to life. Standing before me. Approaching me.*

Instinctually, Blue Flower fled back toward one of the walls, but of course the flame was there and she had to stop and control her childish emotions. The ground shook beneath the Golem's massive feet as it approached. Yet it had an invertible face like its smaller clay doll kin and it did not attempt to look her way at all.

She watched the Golem as it approached the furnace, lifted the new formed metal from the heat of the press and, with several swift and concentrated motions, it emphatically crunched and shaped new elements along the surface until the object began to resemble a sunny, red, and golden iteration of the Beings' protective masks.

Blue Flower's heart leapt and she asked, "Is that one of their breathing masks?"

The Golem stopped applying pressure to the thing and turned its head full circle to face Blue Flower for the very first time. Then, without looking, it applied an additional coat of color using a small spray spout attached to the inner end of its wrist. It turned its body to match the direction of its head, faced the girl fully, and held this new sun mask out for Blue Flower to take.

"For me?" She asked, licking her lips with a new anticipation she had not expected to feel. She lifted the piece of art from the Golem's hands and studied the contours and winding, beautiful patterns. It had three eyes, though the third one sat vertically inverted and would rest against her forehead just above the bridge of her nose. The mouth was a perfect circle allowing just enough room to fit the end of her kopa within it should she choose to play the reed. And tendrils of feathery metal shaped out from the top and sides of it like rays of sunlight.

The Golem spoke rather dryly after a moment, struggling to formulate the words in the language of Tetset. "Use." It said. "Speak."

Fourteen

Putting out fires as it went, the Golem led Blue Flower back through the hallway — which felt rather broad now that the flames were being extinguished — and into the larger, cubby-filled chamber. Each spray of mist from the giant's appendages risked sending the girl into a coughing fit which she struggled painstakingly to keep down. *Better this than burning to death,* she thought and nearly laughed setting off yet another round of awkward wheezing.

When the Golem stopped at the center of the room where the podium stood, it stooped slightly, collected the torch which Blue Flower had mindlessly left on the ground there, and replaced it in its stand.

"Thank you!" Blue Flower was surprised to hear herself say the words, but after all, she did not wish to appear ungrateful.

"Welcome." The Golem said in its unassuming manner. Then it raised a hand and pointed toward the first passage; the way back out. Blue Flower nodded. She patted at the thin remains of her clothes just to be sure she would not be reentering the world in complete nudity. Then she felt a little silly, what would the aliens care if she was naked? Just another foolish thought. Blue Flower wanted so badly to be done with her foolishness. She was a survivor, more mature than when she had set out from Tetset, more capable of understanding the true nature of things.

She nodded to the Golem and walked along, avoiding the gaps in the ground. As she turned the corner, she looked back to see the giant let out one more massive spray of exhaust which coated all the walls of that space extinguishing the rest of the flames all at once. The drums stopped. As Blue Flower was about to turn her head to continue up into the light, the torch reignited. One lone flame in a world of darkness.

Daylight surprised Blue Flower as she ascended into the world of morning. With one arm she shielded her eyes from far too much brightness. With the other, she cradled her new prize. It took her a moment to make out the shapes of the others waiting for her by the unnamed river. Their numbers had grown while she was inside the New Mountain. Dozens more had arrived, but before she could even make them all out, she knew that her friend was not among them. She could hear the Being's distant drum from here and she very much wanted to get back to her.

Still, she took the moment with pride. Several clay dolls had joined the other two Beings as well as a small group of apes and crows clicking playfully; a sound that seemed increasingly like giggling the more she heard it. The animals hopped and fluttered around each other attempting to interact with the Jomony who, of course, could not change their general expressions. Yet somehow even they wore a sort of pleased bewilderment in the movements of their little bodies. Blue Flower understood that they were celebrating her achievement, that this group had chosen her for something, and she was at last ready to join their dance.

Blue Flower raised her new mask into the air and the crowd stopped playing around. They stood still and watched her, their anticipation lingering on the air. So she did not delay. Blue Flower placed her Sun Mask over her shoulders for the very first time and the crowd cheered.

From within the Sun Mask, Blue Flower could see and hear in a new way. She was no longer using her own eyes and ears. And the machinery inside was pumping and turning, clicking and clunking away implying that the Golem's smelting and shaping had only been the final stage in a much more intricate process. Yet, even though she was suddenly very aware of these inner mechanisms, they took an immediate back seat to the newfound depths of clarity and color she could now prize from her surroundings.

A field of pollen frolicked before her and she found she could hone in on each individual tuft, discern the most minute of details from the greater field if she wanted. She stepped down from the gate to follow the microscopic stuff, passing a hand through it and watching the particles bound and swirl around her. Then it occurred to her that the crowd had once again stopped what it was doing to watch her but the beat of the Being's drums took precedence in her mind.

Swiftly, Blue Flower walked through the waiting crowd to return to the gully where her friend could be found. The group followed her as she went passing by the water which made a more musical sound through the filter of the mask. They crossed through the bamboo trees and she heard some small chatter from the animals that sounded surprisingly similar to speech. She put that from her mind until, all together, the group converged upon Crow Mother's location.

That Being stopped playing her drum and the gully went silent. Her mask stared deeply into Blue Flower's own. Then a light, wistful melody came from the alien. The sound of the Being shaped itself as it swam through the air toward Blue Flower until the notes became words. The words said, "Can you understand me now?"

The apes and crows seemed to whisper and it occurred to Blue Flower that even those primal grunts and caws and clicks seemed to make some kind of sense to her. Statements swirled around her from every side. Statements like, "Did she?" Or "Can she?" Or "Do you think she can hear?"

Blue Flower felt a surge of pride. “I always could.” She said it at first in her own language. Then she reached around and found her kopa dangling precariously from the few threads that remained of Mother Tree’s pouch. She raised the instrument to the opening in her mask and played those same words in the language of The People, knowing at last and for the first time that her words would be understood.

And the crowd was pleased and sang her song with her.

Fifteen

Deep within the shadowed folds, the spaces between the spaces that encompass all matter in the universe, imperceptible by human senses, lay the realm of the spider. Not unlike another dimension of space-time, it lingers like a network of web, somehow always intertwined with the reality that man has come to know. A spider could fold itself back into that realm and seemingly disappear. Or that same spider could reach out into the network across the voids of time unmoving to commune with its own kind and read distant messages in whatever form another spider may have witnessed and transcribed them. Such activity could be sensed from any location or moment in space-time, so long as the spider was connected to that realm. That is what the Spider Woman was doing — communing with the others — hearing their tales of timelines past and future — that same day when Silent Wolf dreamt his terrible dream of Blue Flower and her newly formed aggression.

The Spider Woman had already by that point tied such a link to the boy's id that he was practically just another — albeit weaker — representation of herself. Of course, Silent Wolf knew none of this was occurring and the Spider Woman had been musing to herself about how easy it had been to take hold of the human's mind — of all humans she had met so far. *It shall be easier to take this world than I imagined,* she was thinking and laughing.

A blue-black, almost liquid orb the size of a boulder hovered before her at eye level and she stared into the void of it, caressing the surface of that sphere with her long, gangly fingers which sent ripples of her own desires deep back into the realm of the spider.

But as she laughed and mused, she began to receive a signal. One she had manipulated away into the fabrics of her temple long ago hoping never to have to witness it again. Yet there it was, staring her in each of her eyes. The Mask! The Mask of the Sun! It became brighter, stronger until the Spider Woman began to feel powerless before it. She did not often sweat in the strange body she wore, but she did in that moment under the intense pressures of fate. Escape was impossible! Impossible! Still, she turned her back from the orb; the waiting, watching, hungry eyes of all her kin throughout all of space and time. She dropped wholly to the floor, and in that same moment the orb separated, crashed in waves against the mica. Just a messy puddle of sticky liquid after all.

The Spider Woman took a moment after her fall to catch her breath. She had hoped she had managed this version of fate well enough — that the Sun God would not have had a way to come into being, She had hoped she had nipped it in the bud with the capture and destruction of Tetset. But something had gone awry. She knew it then, the error that had occurred, had come from her disconnect with her boy Qotle. It must have been that severance, the disappearance of the girl in the teosintl, that had allowed and would always allow this thing, this god, this version of reality to exist. She had been helpless after all to stop that moment from occurring — the timelines had jumped. She would have to be more careful — could not afford to be so helpless again.

She picked herself up off the floor flashing her usually well concealed lower legs — six of them if you left out the arms — to the empty room. In a huff, the Spider Woman rushed out onto the crystalline pathways at the highest points of her tower. Those pathways were a physical extension of her network, her great web that she had made to leak from the darkness of her realm into this reality. Usually, walking the pathways gave her solace; confidence. Not that day. The Spider Woman was becoming filled with a mad fury.

A cleaning fentium clung to a wall before her polishing the stones there as she approached. She paused before it, attempted to rebalance her mind to better communicate with the large insect. "I have made a mess in my chambers," she said as faux-innocently as she could make herself sound, "will you clean it for me?" Ordinarily her link to these creatures was so clear, she need not even finish her sentence before they would be on their way in obedience. But she was cross, and the stupid fentium bent its stupid head troubling itself to understand her. The Spider Woman sighed with frustration and winced, vexed by the humble idiocy of the creatures of this planet. "Well?" She said a bit too harshly. Apparently this last jab was enough to reconnect the sad creature to her mind. The fentium took the hint and crawled across the wall, scuttling sideways through the doorway to her inner chamber.

The Spider Woman lingered in that spot a moment clearing her mind and reasserting her dominance in the minds of her servants. She felt a pang of recognition; a memory of the other thing — the good thing — her great and feeble weapon... the boy that had come from Tetset was weak and she had gained his trust through the equally feeble presence of the Hen'Bon'On people. For people trust people, she knew. People let down their defenses in the presence of that which is familiar. She felt Silent Wolf letting down his barriers now.

With a new curiosity, the Spider Woman turned and approached the ledge of a pathway. She wanted to see this sight down below in the main hall at the base of her temple. She wanted to see Silent Wolf in this reality separate of their mental link. She wanted to see Silent Wolf with all of her eyes in this conversion of Space-Time. But most of all, she wanted to see Qotle whose mind she could no longer access.

She spoke then to herself and whichever of her kin could hear her through the echoes of the network, "These humans, their resilience seems only a byproduct of their stupidity." She said it aloud in a faint echo that any of her brothers and sisters might hear should they care to listen. She would grow to regret the statement in time, for more of her siblings were listening from the depths of that place at that moment than she would have liked to know.

Sixteen

Finding himself conscious and genuinely cognizant for the first time in many days, Silent Wolf sat up in his cave-like sleeping chamber in the heights of the tower. He tried not to focus on the dream; a vision of the girl he had played with as a young boy, the same girl who had shown him just enough kindness as to draw out his affections only to put a wall up against him. She was angry. He should, he felt, be equally so. Yet something about his extended slumber had instead left him feeling numbness rather than pain. No. He would not think of it anymore. That was enough.

He resolved himself to rise at long last and experience more of this tower that was to be his new home. Nearby he found some beautifully woven and stained and patterned Hen'Bon'On clothing. He recognized that they had been set there for him. So he got dressed and made his way from the room, down the long, sloping pathways, and into the lobby of the main hall.

Several layers of mica benches rounded off toward the center of the large space and Silent Wolf selected the end of one of those adjacent with a protrusion of crystalline spires that jutted up from the floor all the way to the very apex ceiling of the great structure. He sat and waited and watched the daily comings and goings: Hen'Bon'On women bringing produce in heavy bunches from gardens he had not yet seen, fentiums crawling across any surface that would bare them en route to one mindless task or another, children... well one child at least was in view. Shi'Yun, the friend's sister. She was not in the temple, but only occasionally visible through openings in the outer walls. She hopped about and played with a smaller fentium, an offspring of that race, in the arcade. The open front door to the hall framed the best of the scene, and Silent Wolf let all the other white noise drip away as he focused his vision on that place. For Shi'Yun was smiling, laughing, genuinely happy. Silent Wolf had forgotten about happiness. This reminder of the emotion hit him harshly. He knew he wanted to feel something like it again. But there was a new voice in his head clearly and constantly telling him to forget about it. Joy was not a man's fate, not his lot in life... It had certainly not been the fate of his people. *Don't think of it.* Silent Wolf tried to reflect on his newfound savior instead; numbness. Yet, all the while, he could not convince himself to look away from the girl; the simple reminder of joy through the open door. He thought he felt a tear begin to form in his left eye but —

"Mind if I join you?"

The question was a jarring thing in that moment. Silent Wolf turned abruptly, working with some difficulty to bottle up whatever emotion it was he had just been feeling. And all at once his mind was a blank thing. Amazing. He was looking up at the proud form of his friend (and captor), Qotle. The man was smiling, though the expression was meaningless to Silent Wolf then.

"Please." Silent Wolf said offering up the seat beside him as common ground.

Qotle joined him there and sighed with comfort. He looked off in the same direction as his companion and caught those same glimpses of Shi'Yun. Again he smiled. *Why does he keep doing that with his mouth?* Silent Wolf wondered awkwardly.

"I know what you must think of us." Qotle began speaking, "That we are a strange bunch. Insects and men living together in this way."

"Honestly," Silent Wolf spoke without thinking — his words not his own, "so much has happened to me this last week that I have struggled to even consider past the current moment.

Your 'culture' is surprising. Yes. But no more so than the shock and pain I have felt. This drowning feeling my sorrow has pierced within me."

The girl was climbing up onto a raised platform and roaring down at the fentium child as if she were some great beast and Silent Wolf shook his head at the sight.

"I used to think myself a powerful young wolf," Silent Wolf continued, "a member of a great growing pack that could hunt on his own or rely on his family if times became harrowing. Now I have only the one option."

"I get your meaning." Qotle responded thoughtfully, "Though I would like for you to understand, the Spider Woman asked that we bring you here for a purpose." Of course, Qotle was at that moment struggling himself to recall what that purpose was, but he did not give up this information to Silent Wolf. "I would not have done this," Qotle continued, "if not for the promise in my heart that you would find yourself a willing member of our own community... our own wolf pack."

This offer was too much for Silent Wolf and he stood up suddenly. He did not understand it, did not want to think of it, did not know why in his mind he called this other man a friend. But it hurt him greatly to try and deny the thought — that Qotle had somehow betrayed the Spider Woman. Better to remove himself from the situation altogether. "I thank you for this attempt at kindness." Silent Wolf said it atonally, "Though my wounds are still too fresh, perhaps in time I may call you brother." None of this rang true to Silent Wolf, but he could not control the words as they flowed out of him. He reached his hand forward and grasped the other man's own in a forced sign of friendship.

Seventeen

Qotle was taken aback. That man, Silent Wolf, was walking away, weaving his steps between a traffic of fentiums as if he had been living amongst the creatures all his life. Silent Wolf's words had presented one mind, but his eyes betrayed something adversarial within him... as if the man was not wholly complicit in his own behavior. Qotle wanted badly then to remember something which he could not quite grasp. It was there, but it wasn't — on the tip of his tongue, then gone again in a flicker. For some reason, Qotle felt as though he were being watched from afar. So he looked up and immediately spotted her, the Spider Woman, a small dark blip peering into him from all the way up top.

The urge to scream struck him like a hard spear. But he quashed that. He did not know why his looking upon her made him so suddenly angry. Yet he felt... Qotle felt that this was an honest emotion. Their mission had turned into something sour and terrible and he did not wish to compartmentalize it any longer. That being said, the Spider Woman had saved him and his sister from certain death those years ago. He remembered, at the time, having felt a sort of eminent benevolence from the lady. And she had shown him — had it been love? He wasn't so sure any more. He remembered —

Eighteen

The sky had been growing darker by the minute, even though it was not past midday. Qotle, hardly a boy of twelve, had been out walking above the canyon, in the dry lands with Elder Gon'Ki, a wise woman who knew the many uses of the dry land's strange fruits better than most. She also happened to be Qotle's mother, though Hen'Bon'On adults did not marry or take on parental responsibilities; rather, all the adults of the clan shared in the joys and pains of child rearing as one large and cohesive unit.

Qotle was one of fifteen children conceived during a particularly blessed moon orgy. His baby sister, Shi'Yun, had been one of only three during her own ceremony. The other two had died amidst the drought and she would always be a child apart. So the elders said. Gon'Ki wore Shi'Yun in a wicker pack on her back. Ordinarily a child her age would not be able to see the dry lands during monsoon season, but the drought had lingered and Kyun'Bon'On was still giving way to the easier path up from the canyon.

So the three of them walked the dry lands collecting medicinal pok'yu fruits each one the size of Shi'Yun's head and exceedingly high in healthy fats if one could get past the dense and spiny husk of it. But the clouds were coming in swiftly as they collected, something Gon'Ki had clearly not anticipated, and she was growing increasingly concerned.

Qotle remembered Gon'Ki asking him to pick up the pace as they hurried back along toward the wider, easier path to Bo'No'To. He remembered the dense, foreboding clouds reaching across the once blue sky. He remembered the unworldly shadow enveloping the land. There was a crash that sounded like thunder but so much louder, like something massive had tried to elevate into the atmosphere from behind them... he did not remember what the elevating thing looked like... but he sure remembered the crash, the vision of the crater forming behind him as Gon'Ki grabbed him by the wrist and forced him in the opposite direction.

Then, after three years of little to no new waters, the clouds decided to break. The monsoon rains his people had prayed for all that time had chosen that moment when they were unguarded and ill prepared to come upon them. It should have been a joyous time of celebration. But the little family was trapped above ground in the wet of the storm with only an impossibly dangerous path available to get them back down to Bo'No'To. Gon'Ki tried to find another route, but of course, in the dense rain, any recognizable paths would not be visible. So she decided instead to take a risk. She led her children to the dam; a weak, wooden structure that skimmed the upper outskirts of Bo'No'To at the time. It had served where it stood those last fifty years protecting the city from the usually consistent, predictable, and mild rains the region was known for. And perhaps, if they were lucky, they could use its wooden exterior to make their way down. But they were not lucky on that day. None of Hen'Bon'On was.

Gon'Ki carefully stepped out onto the wooden structure. Hopeful until the last, she lashed a rope she had been carrying to the end of a large, protruding log. Qotle remembered the look on her face as she gestured for him to join her and his sister; calm but purposeful... almost soothing. It was the expression he had always remembered her wearing. Tenderly, she knotted the rope to his waist and leg.

A cruel wind rushed in then... unnatural... but Qotle had never taken the time to consider it had not been just another aspect of the storm. Why had he never before considered it? Now that his mind had regained that sense of freedom, for the first time since that day all those years ago, Qotle could see the other emotion forming across his mother's face... the one he was meant to forget... the one of fear, of recognition of something truly horrifying.

Gon'Ki was looking past the boy, over his shoulder. The wind was sweeping her off the dam. The dam itself was being swept away by the tumult of Kyun'Bon'On white water below. Qotle was reaching out for the elder that was his mother. She was suddenly holding Shi'Yun out for him, and rather than catching Gon'Ki's hand in that moment, Qotle was instead holding fast to his baby sister. Dangling from the rope that managed to stay taut to the small patch of dam that had not yet collapsed. He watched her fall — watched her hit the water — watched her disappear beneath the torrent.

Qotle and his sister dangled there, fifty feet below where they had started. Qotle in shock. Shi'Yun crying. The white water smacking against the canyon walls beyond. He could see the flood raping the shallow caves where his people had been living. He could remember the drowned corpses smacking over and over against the far rocks and then eventually, mercifully being pulled under into the secret river beneath.

A light glared harshly upon him after that. The Thunder Bird had come at last. At least, that was how he had liked to imagine the thing the Spider Woman had used to rescue him and the tattered remains of his people. She was there, standing atop it, like a raft that sailed through the air, like... like the shuttle he had signaled destruction upon so recently.

He thought about what came next shaking the sudden knowledge that he had done so so many wrongs since that day. He remembered the Spider Woman pulling him to safety... telling him of the dream she had had about him… how she had needed him to survive. She needed his people too. *But apparently she did not need my mother,* Qotle thought for the very first time… *or perhaps she intentionally did not want her.* That pain in his heart, that was new. He was angry. He could not prove it, but he understood the truth. That the Spider Woman had been responsible for the storm… that the wind that took his mother's life had come from the jets of the Thunder Bird. He had always assumed that the Spider Woman's craft had been destroyed by accident as she attempted to rescue more of his people from the flood. He had never before considered that she might have intentionally thrown the thing away to conceal her misdeeds.

And now that he was grown and somehow had loosened his mind from her bitter grasp, Qotle finally realized how many times over she had manipulated him to do her evil deeds… yes, evil. He felt it. He felt the anger boiling within him. He wanted to feel it as he stared up at the terrifying thing at the top of the tower looking back at him. *Does she know,* he wondered, *that I am no longer her man?*

Nineteen

Of course she knew. The Spider Woman had always known it would come to this with Qotle. But she had grown attached to him. It then occurred to her just how many of her kin had been aware of her weakness; her mortal affinity for her human boys. She had shown them all that she had become capable of something so foolish as affection. And then she knew that her brothers and sisters were laughing — laughing at her. But why should any of that matter? She remembered herself. She alone had survived. She alone was the strong one. She turned her gaze away from the prying stare of that failed experiment named Qotle. She thought deeply, so the others could feel it too, about the other boy, the path she had planned for him, her new success story.

And she spoke aloud so her kin would know that she had everything right where she wanted it, "Yes." She was gloating, "It is as I have known it would be. The boy named Silent Wolf will forget his past, wash away his sorrow, and join us in our purpose."

After all, she could see the future... well, patches and versions of the future. And in that future she could see the way and moment in which she could deal with Qotle. It would be so very easy to rid herself of that one.

The Spider Woman returned to her chamber. She stood over the puddle she had left there when looking into the other realm. The cleaning fentium she had summoned to it had become stuck there in the gooey liquid, and not by accident. It squirmed, but only a little. She liked when they squirmed. It made her feel like the apex predator she was.

She spoke again for the benefit of those others who might be watching, "I will soon be strong enough to summon you all to me. I will soon be stronger than any of you, my kin, have ever seen." She felt them tremble across the epochs. She felt them crafting, making plans for her world. And she was pleased. She wanted them to come — wanted to bring them — to summon them back into existence.

Then she clicked her inner jaw open and crossed the sticky pool to at last enjoy her prone fentium meal; her quick reward. She could still hear the drums of the New Mountain, could see the Mask of the Sun. But she ignored all of it. The luscious fentium blood trickled down her lips. She would be ready when the time came.

PART III - THE PEOPLE

One

In the gully, Blue Flower sat in communion with her three alien friends, the apes, the crows, and the clay robots called Jomony. She was learning, enjoying her newfound ability to understand all of these creatures and their separate languages. The music in the gully was joyful for this time as words of greeting and mutual appreciation were exchanged. Blue Flower held her kopa to the mouth of her new mask and played a literal interpretation of what a blue flower looked like on this world. She saw it as the others would, forming in that same vacuum of darkness where the Being had so frequently taken her. Only now, she felt a new sense of pride. Finally, she was not the viewer, but the shower; not the taken, but the taker.

Her friend, still playing a steady drum beat, sang the notes that said, "You are called Blue Flower. We know this."

Blue Flower had not expected the Being's voice to be so playful and funny to her ears through the mask, like hearing a child singing some kind of hopscotch chant only through a filter of wood and water.

The friend continued, "Yet you do not know our names." So the Being flared up the feathery appendages on the back of her head, and the image of an aged crow flew between them. "I am best known on this planet as Crow Mother, for the crows have often followed me since we arrived here two years ago." Crow Mother then lifted a hand away from the drum to introduce one of the other Beings, the one with the turquoise mask and large copper ears. "She is called Morning Singer." And a crooning armadillo raised itself up on its hind legs and howled like a rooster toward a rising sun against the song void. Crow Mother pointed to the third Being, the one with the mixed mask and the anteater nose and carried on, "And he goes by Eldest." Against the dark of the mind, an elder human male bathed itself in washing oils and smiled. "Our race is known as The People. You know our songs. And we, yours. Perhaps now we can begin to harmonize as one."

The human girl thought back on Crow Mother's earlier song. The death of one world, the dying of another. She became firm in her decision. "Perhaps now," Blue Flower played, "we can decide what is to be done with the Spider Woman."

"Yes." The one called Eldest responded with a kind of anguish in his song. "The Spider Woman must be done away with. I fear no peace can ever be made with her."

"Who sings of peace?" Blue Flower's tone was confusion and frustration. She understood that there was still a great deal she did not know about the customs and conceptions of The People. Yet it dug into her mind that a peaceful resolution obviously would not be reached.

"Long have we hoped for peace amongst all creatures in the universe." This last bit was sung by the one called Morning Singer. Blue Flower felt she understood the name better after hearing her, for her voice was the sweetest of all the group.

Eldest chimed in once more, "We sing of peace and have done since before Eratta's destruction." For the first time in their conversation, Blue Flower did not understand the sound 'Eratta' — what she thought she heard was 'Green Thing' but the implication of the sound felt greater than her mask's translation.

She asked, "Eratta? Green Thing?"

Crow Mother tried to help, "Our world, which you have witnessed through song. We knew it as Green Thing. Your ears hear the language because the word is too simple. So to call it Eratta in your words is justified. We would just as quickly refer to your Blue Thing — this world — as Orotti if that translates."

Blue Flower smiled at the simplicity of their language, the lack of requirement to directly name anything. Or perhaps the description of the thing as the name had in fact been more direct than her own people's use of proper names handed down to children or objects. In no way, so far back as she could recall, had her own name described anything about her. She was not some dainty little blue flower that could simply be plucked by passersby. She was stronger than that, more capable of escaping, surviving. Then she thought of Mother Tree, wondered if she hadn't in fact changed her own name to better describe herself as the years went on. Were her own people so like these aliens? How little she knew of what was now gone.

She returned her thoughts to Eldest's statement. "Your world... Green Thing... was destroyed. Is this where peace has taken you?"

There was a lag, a pause. The People did not wish to respond to the question. And Blue Flower struggled to find the notes of passion she required. They seemed to pass then before her eyes, the mask seeking to help her to translate.

"I cannot ignore," she forced out the obscure sounds, "that in my heart a great evil has been created... one of hatred and vengeance. I wish to remove the Spider Woman from this life before she can do more harm. You sing of peace, but I cannot believe that you do not truly feel the same as I."

Then it was the apes barking and she understood their words of assent, "Yes!" "The human is strong!" "The girl will show us the way!"

Morning Singer responded with a loud, hollow, high note that forced the creatures into abrupt silence. Her own anger shown harshly through the movement of her body. Yet her song was still sung with a sour beauty and precision. "Do not think, young human, that we have not felt as you feel. Indeed our ire has led us to take difficult action in the past. But you do not know all. We heard Crow Mother's song as we approached you here before your mask was earned. She is young. Her memory of the death of Eratta is biased."

With a mastery of the song unlike anything Blue Flower had yet, or would ever again experience, the girl's mind was pulled back to that green world once again.

Two

The details of Morning Singer's Eratta were exquisite. Blue Flower saw and learned how the technology of The People coexisted — lived in harmony — with the vegetation of that distant world. She learned of small friendly birds and sprites — pollinators — that added to the overwhelming beauty that had filled every corner of the globe. She even knew — and genuinely comprehended — the concept of that world as a globe. An odd revelation since the idea was never presented to her as something to consider before... well, at least not until Crow Mother had taken her up above the atmosphere, but Blue Flower had not had much time to think then.

With fluidity, Morning Singer pulled Blue Flower from the natural spaces of Eratta down under the crust to a place harboring something called The Nexus. It was an odd place — something akin to a nuclear reactor — situated underground as to not interfere with the natural progressions of the world above. Blue Flower was able to understand all of this almost instantly. This dense collection of information about Eratta's makeup was so clearly presented by Morning Singer's ancient song that packing the girl's mind with recognizable comparisons seemed somehow the easy part.

But then, Morning Singer had to change her tactics in an instant. The next part of her story was built in the world of the abstract and this "simple" presentation would not fairly impart the necessary information.

"We summoned her," Morning Singer's words were filled with remorse, "The Nexus was an incredible achievement for our species, a way to reach across the voids of space to connect with other beings capable of complex thought. We hoped to no longer be the only People in our universe. And our space ready vessels had not been able to find any life-sustaining worlds within the reach of our feeble bodies. Mind you, our species can live as much as ten times the length of yours, but even a thousand of your years, using our common physics, would not have been enough time to reach your world or any others that may have promised other advanced lifeforms... Not bodily."

Blue Flower's mind was processing advanced conceptions of physics, astronomy, biochemistry... concepts she had never hoped to dream of in her before-life. She was digesting the ideas through a steady chain of examples like water boiling over a fire and the particles then thinning and wisping into the air as vapor. Flip. She was as small as the molecule. Flip. She was the size of a star. The music could tap into an area of her brain that was capable of processing, conceptualizing, and understanding seemingly anything and everything. Though it was beginning to feel like a great burden and Blue Flower was not so certain she would be the same person she had been going in by the time Morning Singer's song was done.

"From the Nexus," the female Being continued, "we reached out, contacted something. The signal was very faint, but it was present and most exhilarating for all The People of Eratta — an accomplishment to beckon in a new era. Of course, our Green Thing had only ever known peace. The idea had never crossed our scientists' minds that someone out there might be... hostile... might wish to deceive. That simple optimism — and a bit of bad luck in that the first Other we made contact with was a Spider — that was our undoing."

The core of the Nexus alighted and vibrated, protruding out in a bubble from its previously stable and fixed location. Blue Flower witnessed the scientists within the chamber as they checked and rechecked their calculations. They were all expanding their plumage as if the vibration of energy had somehow begun forcing itself upon them. And then the scientists each turned their eyes up to the ballooning pillar of light, staring with the same choreographed expression of awe as a silhouette began to accelerate and forcefully pulse out from the beam. The silhouette, the extra appendages, the face and many eyes of the Spider Woman revealed themself, corporeal and lucid as a hunting predator.

At first the Spider Woman seemed surprised, though the group of scientists did not waver... could not. They were not themselves any longer. And Blue Flower felt a shiver run through her as she watched the new alien smile, breathe that atmosphere heartily, and then manipulate the scientists in unison, bend them against their will into a single file line with the strange, twisted motions of her long fingers.

"She came from the other dimension," Morning Singer persisted, "the one we had not considered. The Nexus itself. It was so much bigger than we had known, a vacuum of seemingly nothing, not perceptible to anyone who ever lived in a world with light or matter. But it was there, a dark place where only dark things know how to squeeze. The Spider came from that place. And our scientists were responsible."

Blue Flower was back on the surface of Eratta watching a huge gathering of People — watching their uncharacteristically far too controlled behavior — watching them watch the Spider Woman as she sang aloud one of the songs of The People.

"At first, The People trusted her... trusted her songs.. none of us could recognize the manipulation, that the Spider could not actually sing, could only reach into our collected consciousness... she could make us see what she wanted us to see... she could make us do practically anything."

Blue Flower saw what Morning Singer meant. That the vision of the Spider's singing had only been a facade. The Spider Woman almost appeared lazy when viewed from this perspective outside of her mind manipulations. Blue Flower was made to turn her head then to see a mob of... something else entirely... converging on The People. Smaller, more primitive, but still spiders of a sort. These new creatures overtook the hypnotized gathering — sank their teeth in — and gorged themselves on the blood and the flesh of The People.

Crow Mother's vision appeared then. The naked and free herd of People in that zen paradise of love and song. The manipulation of the world the Spider Woman had made the Beings see.

"She wanted us,' Blue Flower could feel the tears and pain in Morning Singer's voice then, "she wanted us for food."

And the herd's orgy returned to what it had always truly been, the feasting field for the Spider Woman's children. The end of a civilization. The end, perhaps, of an entire universe should those things learn to spread further.

Blue Flower watched as some of The People woke up from their trance in the midst of the feasting. Those who awoke, awoke in horror and trauma. Some ran. Others did not have the chance to do so and were torn and eaten with ravenous abandon. Then Blue Flower recognized Crow Mother in the group — awakening — quicker to react than the others. She fought off the closest of the spiders and pulled another of The People and another and another from the fray. She had single handedly saved a pack of her own kind and they ran and ran but they had nowhere to run to.

"We have perceived the truth too late.
The damage is already too great.

And now we are left with only hate."

This was Crow Mother's voice. The words were sung long ago. Blue Flower knew her friend had voiced them on Eratta before the end. Crow Mother had felt then as Blue Flower did now. She had harmonized revenge... a strange and terrible kind of revenge and Blue Flower did not wish to hear more... to see the act. She felt sick even thinking of the thing she knew was to come. She felt claustrophobia tearing at her and she wished to be out of the memory, to be breathing her own "Orotti" air. But she fought against this weakening. The story had not all been told, the song not yet completed, and she would have to hear it now or in the near future. She decided now was as good a time as any. Blue Flower had to know if what had happened on Eratta was somehow avoidable on Orotti.

Three

"Darkness took our hearts then," Morning Singer continued, "Terror, sorrow, and ire. It was an ire felt so deeply and on such an instinctual level like The People had never before known ourselves capable." Herds of Beings rushed forth, blood shot eyes perverting their usually kindly dispositions. Thousands, perhaps millions, of the Awoken — those of The People that would fight back against their aggressors — formed up in ranks. "There was a survival song. A deep resonance that we created, could feel and hear all across the world. We sang it together as one — all of The People — a super entity intent on that ire — the unlikely ideal known as purge or vengeance. We waged war against the spiders."

Blue Flower stood there, amidst the fighting. All around her, spider murdered Being and Being murdered spider. She felt the hatred soaking into her blood, her own mind buzzing with The People's war song. But as she listened, boiled and brooded, something else within her was forming up a new sort of wall. It was something she could not yet put words to, but she understood what her own mind was trying to tell her... what she wished could be true. She hated... what was it she hated? The overwhelming hypocrisy... she hated the Hate even though she felt it as The People had. Perhaps that was the message in a strange way. Morning Singer hated the concept of Hate but had known that it was necessary. Blue Flower would have to come to agree in time, to feel the cruelty of the failures of vengeance in the same way as she.

All of a sudden, Blue Flower was floating in space. She stared down at the green world of Eratta. She watched as the green was overtaken by fire, smoke, and deep blackness. In macro, she could perceive that blackness as the crawling, oozing bodies of trillions of the spiders.

"We had lost the surface." Morning Singer's voice trembled within her. "So we took the fight off world." A space craft floated out there above the planet. And Blue Flower remembered the scene of Crow Mother leading the others to a ship. But this was not that moment. This was a different ship, one made for war. Blue Flower felt a pang of concern; uncertainty. Why had her friend omitted so many details? Was she worried that Blue Flower would somehow not understand? That she might wish to run away? These images did not make her want to run. *But* — she felt the sadness of the thought before it worked itself out — *perhaps the act of omission would.* She bit down on the inside of her cheek until she tasted blood. And she watched the warship begin to fight. It blasted the surface of Eratta on repeat, clearing swaths of black spider bodies, leaving in their wake only scorched earth. "Once we had been so in tune with our world. The Spider changed us, made us heartless, made us lose ourselves."

Blue Flower found herself in another underground lab. Large, clear pipes projected steam along through vents, and magma followed, curdling upward through the man-made tunnels. Eldest, eyes ablaze, operated a massive computer with a monitor which indicated where the magma was heading. As he clicked away, Blue Flower found herself lingering on the fire-beaten surface once again. That was when the magma turned to lava, rose up through those vents and began to cover the crust of that world with abandon. Blue Flower wondered what Crow Mother had known of this part of the story and when in the timeline she had been apprised, for Crow Mother, in her earlier vision, had been genuinely frightened and surprised by those eruptions. Blue Flower would have to ask. She needed to know.

"Ultimately," Morning Singer's song drilled on, "we had to do anything and everything within our power to eradicate this threat from our universe, lest it spread and overtake everything. We finished off the surface ourselves... but the Spider finished off the world.

"She had managed to develop her own warship. The spiders are very capable of working together when they wish. They were able to harness the energy of their realm, the Nexus, into a terrible weapon and the whole of Eratta — Botto... Black Thing at this point — was ejected out of its own orbit, atmosphere-less, and fragmented."

The Spider Woman's ship lingered in space where Eratta had once been. Blue Flower understood this as that moment Crow Mother had shown with the other ship, the escape, the explosion. She realized that the delicate balance of her own world might be at stake in this same fashion. It made her angry to see what these others had done about the problem — how they seemingly gave birth to this threat. Wondering if The People had accidentally lead the Spider to Orotti, Blue Flower finally willed herself back into the conversation playing the notes that said, "You destroyed your own world! How the damn did you end up here? Why?"

Morning Singer's song lurched to a halt.

Everyone was back in the gully. The music did not return for a time as the Beings considered the girl's emotional outburst. Blue Flower found herself near to hyperventilating. Now that she had the power to understand, she found she did not want to hear more. She did not want to continue watching one race attempt to destroy another. She did not want to experience the sacking and burning, the defecation, the eradication of all of natures countless beauties. The People had asked her to watch as they showed — as if it were happening here, now, this very moment —

the desiccation... the demolition of an entire world. And she wanted to be sick. "Why..." Blue Flower forced her notes back up again, forced herself to play out to Crow Mother, "Why did you leave these things out earlier?"

Those Jomony nearest Blue Flower reactivated as she played and lay silent once again after that thought. The new silence was harsh; awkward. Crow Mother had to study the girl's behavior. Blue Flower understood why. Crow Mother knew she did. But Crow Mother also knew that Blue Flower deserved the full truth as immediately as it could be offered. This dance they did, tiptoeing around that sensation of hate and powerlessness would not serve them any longer.

"I needed to show you," Crow Mother began, no longer allowing hesitation in, "that you were not alone. I needed to show you that I too shared your same emotions. Your sorrow and mine are as kin. We are the same, you and I. I needed to show you this even though I knew you could not understand all the details of my song. So I simplified. I am sorry."

Blue Flower began to pace. Her head was pounding and fresh tears were working their way down thinly between the metalwork of her mask and her skin.

"There is yet more we must show you child." The one called Eldest spurted out. Blue Flower watched Crow Mother shoot him a frustrated glance. These aliens were not on the same page.

"You still have your people." Blue Flower choked out a lazy tune for this.

"We are a small few." Morning Singer tried to help.

"I am alone. All of Tetset is dead. I have no one." This song from the human was practically inaudible.

But Crow Mother understood. At last, she rose up from her post at the tree stump and galloped the short way in order to be within touching distance of her friend. “You have me.” Crow Mother sang this with a deep sadness in her voice. She reached out, grasped Blue Flower by her naked shoulder, and embraced her until there was not fight in the girl. Together, they cried behind their masks, forming a heap on the ground with their bodies.

They sat a while like this before Eldest felt the need to sing again, repeating the sentiment a little more gently this time, “There is yet more to share.”

And while Crow Mother was feeling her own frustrations with the elder, she knew that he was probably right. “I am sorry,” Crow Mother whispered to the girl. “It is urgent or I would not ask you to hear any more. We have wasted much time already.”

Blue Flower tried to shake it off and put on a brave face. She sniffed out the last of her tears, letting go of Crow Mother and rising to her feet. “I am ready to listen.” She played it plainly, without emotion, but clear enough for everyone to hear.

Four

Eldest took the vacant post at the tree stump and began to thump a much slower rhythm out of the wood. He was clearly not as strong as Crow Mother and he tired easily and often. But he did not allow the song to stop once he started and his sound had a mathematical kind of precision to it that Blue Flower had not anticipated. Again, Morning Singer's voice pulled them backward into the distant memory.

They were in the large escape ship from Crow Mother's song. At first Blue Flower wondered why The People had taken this one and not one of those vehicles intended for fighting. But in the back of her mind, it occurred to her that this vessel was substantially larger than those warships had been — that it housed many more People than those other ships could — that the, perhaps four hundred, living people aboard this ship were all that remained of their race and world.

Through the myriad hallways, the memory took Blue Flower, showing her the sorry living quarters those survivors had to occupy; the subpar food they were disgustedly forced to ingest; the utter lack of personal space and privacy they had to endure.

And then the ship lurched.

Once again, The People were under attack from the Spider Woman's warship. She no longer wanted to harvest them, utilize them as slaves or food, or anything else. At that point, all she had wanted to do was snuff them out. Worse still, The People had been so visibly changed by the ongoing threat of genocide that they too had forgotten all thought of peace. The People wished the Spider gone as badly as she wanted to be rid of them.

The two vessels traded blows back and forth across the vacuum of space. The spider ship would launch harsh beams of

Nexus energy. The People would shoot back ejected matter; used up encasements of that gross food and excess fuel pods which had apparently broken amidst the various barrage of attacks and were now made useless for their original purpose.

"We attempted to evade her many times. She only attempted to evade us once." Morning Singer sang as the spider ship appeared to jettison a larger amount of energy from its engines than it had done previously. A hole tore in the fabric of reality... blacker than space. "She stole away into the Nexus. And we desperately... foolishly took chase."

The People's ship plunged dramatically into that fresh sea of nothingness. They free fell for a long time. Being after Being stepped away from their posts and ran with panic. Some would smack painfully into a wall or a door... Blue Flower could not tell which, the space was becoming so confusing. But she did know that the energy of the ship was failing in this realm. Nothing was working as it was supposed to. The lights flickered and stabilized at the wrong color. The monitors scrambled, died, then revived only to die again moments later.

"We do not know if the Spider intended us to follow her into that space. I suspect now, she did not even realize the matter of our universe was capable of making such a journey. And at the time, it seemed a trap that we had fallen into. The Nexus... the Spider's Web."

Blue Flower noticed the younger Crow Mother among the crew in the cockpit... the only Being not actively fighting the experience of falling endlessly through that void of absolute nothing. No, Crow Mother's viewport had not been a monitor or a board of technical components. She was not stuck to the broken technology of their universe. She had been stationed with her eyes pointed out a sort of window. Crow Mother had never loosed her focus from the target.

"What did you see Crow Mother?" The song had intentionally left an opening wherein Blue Flower could ask such a question.

And Crow Mother was pleased to respond, "I saw the ship of the Spider, frozen before us, splayed all at once everywhere and nowhere. No free fall. No time. Such occupations of our beings do not exist in the Nexus. Therefore, we could not have been falling... it occurred to me that we could not truly be doing anything in that place. We shouldn't even have existed there. Yet our collective consciousness, our ability to communicate deeply with one another beneath the fabric of our own reality — our most primal songs held us together. Gave me the... I say time, though the statement is inaccurate... Gave me the opportunity, more like, to study their ship and find and understand its flaws."

"We need only wait," Morning Singer retook the lead, "and unfortunately force ourselves to bare the madness the Nexus had induced within us. Indeed, many of our numbers did not survive that place.

"And then," Morning Singer sang on, "it could have been a second's time, it could have just as easily been a thousand years — then we were out of the Nexus like nothing had even happened."

"We believe now," Eldest found a natural opening in the song, "the spider ship had been jumping back and forth between realities all the time we had been running... under our very feet. It was a mistake... I believe it to have been so... that ever we left this universe. That is my opinion. Though I do have a more apparent fact to offer... to perhaps explain your earlier question... you know the one Blue Flower? How did we arrive here at Orotti?" His moments of vocalizing within the song were slower, heavier, but not without a sort of charm.

Before her eyes, Blue Flower could witness his analytical prowess working within that charm. Thin, abstract lines formed and knotted with overwhelming complexity until the image of the two ships began once again to take shape. But the fabric of everything was odd, scribbly, or incomplete. Blue Flower watched, enthralled, as the knitting carried on and on. At one point, she raised her own hand and noticed that even there the stitches were threading, the universe and her own body, never content, never satisfied with what was; everything across reality always manipulating, growing, and changing. Perceived norms were becoming obsolete, lost to her, and any purpose behind it all was becoming only a muddled guess... but she found herself agreeing deep down. Something within her knew Eldest's representation of the universe was more than just conjecture or opinion.

Eldest continued, "Do you see what the Spider had done? The mistake she had made?"

Of course, Blue Flower had no idea what he meant. She had been distracted by the new spatial relationship the molecules of her hand had been forming with the air around her. She had not yet looked back up to see the thread, taut and a bit too hardy compared to all of the other threads that had formed.

"The Spider," Eldest almost seemed to be laughing at the idea, "she had intended to jump into the Nexus, retool her own battered ship, and use a harness connected to our vessel in our own universe to return to the same location where she had left us in space and time." Blue Flower's jaw dropped and Eldest laughed again... or for the first time... she did not know which.

"The Spider had unwittingly towed us through the Nexus into some unknown corner of the galaxy," Morning Singer must have been laughing as well, Blue Flower decided, for her sounds had a silly sort of joviality to them at that point. "Once we returned to our universe, Crow Mother explained her findings to those of us who would listen. We formulated a plan and took chase of the enemy's ship."

By now, only ten People remained in the cockpit, the other fifty or so remaining after everything were too sick or senile to occupy active work stations. The place felt morbid, empty, uncharacteristically silent due to the absentees. And then even young Crow Mother rose up and left her viewport post. She made her way decisively toward a wing of the ship that housed shuttles docked along the walls. And she climbed on into one... perhaps the same one the Jomony were now repairing.

In space, Blue Flower watched Crow Mother's shuttle depart and sail slowly but methodically, breaching the apparent distance between it and the spider vessel. It perched along the blind, windowless hull of that ship, tucked and docked there with a precise silence. Then Crow Mother got out. She was floating around in space wearing a heavy suit of material that reminded Blue Flower of a chrysalis or a worm or one of the massive armadillos of Orotti. She grew flush within her cheeks because she wanted to laugh at the silly way Crow Mother had to finagle herself around given all that extra bulk. But her friend was eventually able to get herself into position. Crow Mother planted three small canisters at various points along the exterior of the craft in an unavoidable triangular formation. Then she rose up and bounded just as silently back into her own shuttle which promptly disengaged from the enemy warship and flew away.

It was not like anything Blue Flower could have expected, the way the side of the spider ship burst open,. It erupted some foreign atmosphere, as if through a funnel, out into space — like space itself wanted to suck up that bizarre, smoky air — a crude, gaseous snack for eternity to enjoy and then forget about.

And then the spiders each in turn were being torn from their harnesses, sucked out to die quickly in the cold void. Blue

Flower watched them die. She wondered if all life, even that from another reality, might so easily be destroyed. She had so many new questions to ask of the universe, but of course the universe would not answer. But then she watched as the Spider Woman too was pulled out into the black, a look of desperation and surprise on her face. Of course, Blue Flower was acutely aware that the Spider Woman had not died in this way even if her offspring had been too weak to bear it. Still, her eyes glazed over within the memory, her body perfectly still as it hung in the void.

"We thought her dead." Morning Singer insisted, "We thought our universe was rid of this threat, that we had outlasted it, overcome it." She lingered on the thought, savoring that brutal memory, "Yes, in violence. Which was not our way. But this virus had to be removed that the body could survive."

"Obviously," Crow Mother interjected in discomfort, "we were wrong. The threat remains still. All of our efforts to this point have been for nothing."

Still, the vision of the two ships lingered before them. And Blue Flower felt the music lending her another opening. "You followed her to Orotti? When you realized she had survived?"

"No." Eldest chimed in. "We did not realize the Spider was still alive until the two of you arrived here in the gully."

Five

The few People healthy enough to operate their large ship trickled in and out of the cockpit; an extremely tense regiment of work — eat — sleep — work — work — work — survive — no time to think of anything but the work. Blue Flower watched the dull period speed by before her eyes. She watched as the population of healthy and capable People continued to diminish. Only a handful, maybe twenty survived in all. She listened as Morning Singer sang the last of her song.

"Floating through space with a skeleton crew, we had too many provisions and not enough manpower to operate our escape vessel. We hoped to find a world where we could once again thrive."

A huge, gaseous planet swirled into view before the group. It had three great rings banding around it and a great staring eye — a massive storm. Blue Flower decided instantly that she had never imagined anything so compelling, so beautiful, so terrifying as this. That this world of clouds could exist in her universe implied to her that anything and everything was in fact possible.

"We found a pattern of planetary formations we associated with the building blocks of life," Morning Singer added on. "The Spider had accidentally dropped us in an area of space that might lead us to our original goal and our salvation... New life... New species and civilizations to bond with... we simply followed the crumbs left behind by whatever great explorers had come before us. Another species we will likely never meet. Those that came before. They had left world after world in a state of almost livability... some so cold they would freeze your bones, others far too hot with atmospheres that would turn your insides to porridge. But always, we could see those worlds had been tampered with in some fashion by them... by The Others."

Orotti appeared at last before the travelers, its blue oceans and pristine, tree-filled forests enveloped the viewing area of the cockpit. But just as Blue Flower began to feel that sense of homecoming she had been craving, Morning Singer ended the visions. The gully returned to normal. The song dwindled.

"The Spider survived," Morning Singer was sullen, "and unfortunately, she arrived on your planet some time before we could find it."

"We were not aware of her existence on this earth until you and Crow Mother met amidst her scouting mission." Eldest repeated himself as he was prone to do. He was troubled and his body language became that of a fidgeting child, "Now I feel we are to blame for your woes as well as our own."

Six

It occurred to Blue Flower with a pang of surprise and perhaps regret that the small group of aliens had felt uncomfortable since her arrival, guilty even. She may have been made upset in her own right by the tales of war and destruction that the aliens had been singing to her, but she felt then that she had been given a precious gift from the Beings as well — the gift of honesty. She did not wish to repay that gift with spite. They did not deserve that. Nor did they deserve to feel guilty on her behalf. The hundreds of years distance in time and space between the Spider Woman's summoning and the death of Tetset were very clear to her. These People that sheltered her now and sang to her were not the originators of the events, simply players in a great bout that was larger by far than any one individual among them.

Blue Flower then played this, "I would not blame you for the death of my tribesmen. It would appear that this universe is greater than I had ever understood. And I would never have known it had it not been for all of your courage."

She removed her mask to make her eyes visible to each of them so that they may see the sincerity within her; the tumultuous honesty she wished to express to them in the way Tetset had taught her. She touched Crow Mother's mask lightly with her fingertips. And Crow Mother obligingly removed the apparatus. Their eyes locked. Crow Mother was noticeably struggling to breathe in the Orotti atmosphere as before, so Blue Flower had to simplify the ceremony she was to explore. It was the Tetset ceremony of naming, usually reserved for babies of the tribe after they had survived their first week of life. Hoping to have her closest friend act as giver, Blue Flower took Crow

Mother's hand in hers, raised it to her own human face, and guided Crow Mother to tap first her forehead, then her left cheek, and finally her right.

Leaning over, Blue Flower then lifted Crow Mother's mask to help her put it back on. The Being accepted with some anticipation. As her breathing restored to normal, Crow Mother reached down herself. This time she collected Blue Flower's Sun Mask and returned it in kind to the girl. She had understood the significance of the unsung ritual.

Blue Flower was ready to drop the self that had accepted the words of her tribe. She was no longer willing to accept her own death as the first answer. She could do more than simply be told what to do or how to do it. Now she could be the one to give the orders. Blue Flower placed the mask over her shoulders again and she played a new song:

"I am not a precious flower,
To be trampled underfoot,
Ephemeral as the passing moonlight,
A child lost in dumb regret.

"I am like the sturdy cactus,
I take each season all the same,
Pricking hands that try to harm me,
I'm a woman thriving yet."

She took the kopa from her mouth then and raised her hands toward the sky. The Beings moved to do the same... and then the apes copied them and hummed a tricky chant in coda to her cactus song. The girl smiled for now that they had said their piece, they would hear hers, "I am reborn."

She took a new name that night in the gully beneath a waxing gibbous. She would be known as the Grand One; a name reserved in Tetset for the oldest living cactus in the valley. She was akin to that idea, the oldest living member of her tribe.

"It remains," she played then as the Grand One, with an instinctual raw power, "that the Spider Woman still lives. She continues to wage war on the many tribes of Orotti. I cannot turn a blind eye." The Grand One looked to each of her companions. Her heart beat to a slow but hungry rhythm. She felt all at once the agony of defeat, the pride of purpose, and the regret that such crude action should be the source of that pride. "I must ask for your aid in removing her from our realm."

The crows began to snap at one another then. At first, the Grand One thought them angry at her request, but as the largest of them scuttled down between her and Crow Mother, she realized they had only been squabbling over which of them would get to do the honors. The bird approached her first on its scrawny, branch-like legs. It clicked at her and she could hear the click as a layer of their song saying something like "Yes Yes Yes Yes" or "No No No No" to drive a particular message home. She hoped this bird's click was the "Yes" one. The crow approached Crow Mother, its head bobbing loosely as it shook out a rough patch in its foliage and bit at its inner wing. It whispered then into the alien's ear, and Crow Mother seemed to bob her own head in the same fashion the bird had done.

Crow Mother sang then, "We have held to hope in the face of too much destruction. It would seem that with this most recent massacre, yet another tipping point has been reached." She held her palm to the forehead of her mask and waved her arm out in a sweeping motion as the crow's wing might spread and added, "I will join you in this task... Grand One."

The herald crow beside her repeated the gesture. It whispered so that the Grand One too could hear the words, "And We." The other crows lingering in the trees above sang the same words in a unison, a great collected caw that echoed far beyond the unnamed river. The Grand One saw that she was meant to lead. Crow Mother had given her command. She could at last perform a task of genuine purpose with the means at her disposal to make real, lasting change.

Eldest abruptly ended his drumming and the Jomony stopped their tinkering as if dead to the world. The elder Being raised his voice in a ticky-tack chant, "Then let it be that Crow Mother and her team of black birds will join the Grand One, this woman born of Orotti. Together they will lead the charge against our most terrible of enemies." One Jomony awoke again to the percussive nature of his chant. It signaled him, spinning its head full circle and presenting a high pitched whirring sound. And Eldest was pleased and howled loudly in his own rite, "Your shuttle stands ready. Your bodies are made strong again. Let your skill in completing this task be as a triumphant beacon to all in the universe who may find themselves under foot."

The Grand One was, of course, surprised by the statement, proud but surprised. She posed the question, "And what of you, Eldest? And what of Morning Singer? Would you not fight alongside us?"

"My age," Eldest's chant was slow again; quiet, "denies me. And Morning Singer lingers with child." Until that moment the Grand One hadn't noticed the bump on the other female's belly. "This little creature would be our future... should we survive this."

The Grand One found herself distracted by Morning Singer's now rather obvious state of pregnancy. But wiser than she may have been in years past, the Grand One breathed in a deep breath and did away with her sense of abandonment. She responded eventually, calm as the breeze, "Then it is decided." She turned her attention to Crow Mother and played a simple request, "Shall we?"

Crow Mother raised her plumage with pride, singing, "I have only been waiting for you to ask."

They approached each other then, Crow Mother and the Grand One, and made their way together toward the newly repaired shuttle. The Grand One teased her companion, "And this time... perhaps we could use a bit more caution?"

"That is not a skill with which I am equipped," Crow Mother mocked back.

They and their crows entered the ship. The door closed. The engines blared into life sending a burst of wind across the gully. Morning Singer, Eldest, and all of the apes stood and watched with pride as the shuttle zoomed up far above the forest canopy and out into the upper atmosphere on a direct path to the place from which that destructive beam had emanated before striking Tetset from the sky.

PART IV - A DIFFERENT KIND OF TRUTH

One

It was the great monsoon and all of Bo'No'To could feel the presence of the storm. The clouds raced across the skies sending hard thunder claps and a heavy rain down into the canyon. Thick water droplets drenched the shell of the great obelisk there and all of Hen'Bon'On safely closed their chamber doors once inside. But Shi'Yun and her young fentium friends must have become sidetracked for that night they were late to arrive within the main hall — the designated emergency meeting space for her and her brother.

Qotle had been distracted all that day with the newfound feeling of hatred for his mistress the Spider Woman. He had been distracted and had not seen where his sister had gone. And then regret and deep concern began to overtake his earlier aggressions. Where was Shi'Yun after all? Had she been climbing around the canyon when the rain had begun? Had she perhaps fallen? Was she trapped under a stone, the water preparing to submerge and drown her? Qotle could not stand to think of it. After all of these years to find himself once again powerless to protect his family. Why had he not been with her? Why had he not kept a keener eye? He shivered as the thought drizzled down his shoulders —

that he knew why he had been distracted so — that he had felt himself contemplating bloody murder.

Far above, Silent Wolf sat in his hollowed out sleeping chamber, mentally broken. He stared out a window, the pouring rain making it all but impossible to see the canyon beyond. Briefly, he saw a flash of lightning in the sky across the way and his ears rang with the accompanying thunder. And then a tree that lingered in the dry land above the canyon was ablaze. He had seen it catch and felt the death of that tree reflecting in his eye as the rain somehow failed to put the fire out. He wondered why he did not care — why the death of that thing which he might have grown fond of in his previous life suddenly felt acceptable... correct. He felt a pang of a thought of a fear that perhaps he was losing his humanity there in that tower. But in truth he felt nothing.

Rising from his sleeping place, Silent Wolf stepped out of his room and onto the high pathways of the inner temple. He looked down from there to see the little girl, Shi'Yun, arriving through the main door far below. She was soaking wet from the storm and her brother — the man — Qotle was rushing to her aid. Silent Wolf could see the worry in him — could hear what the nearby fentiums heard — the man saying, "Shi'Yun! You could have caught a fever..." — the girl saying, "I'm sorry Qotle. I lost track of time." as the man wrapped her shoulders in a woven blanket and brought her into his arms in a loving, sorrowful embrace.

And still Silent Wolf felt nothing. It ached to feel so empty, to know things one should not know and yet derive no satisfaction from that knowing.

Indifferent, Silent Wolf turned his attention away from that scene to another ongoing event along the pathways. It was another thing he should not have been able to witness. He did not even see through his own eyes. He was looking through the oblong viewers of an insect; another fentium. It ran along the highest pathway, the one that led from the Spider Woman's own chamber. And it ran, dragging with it the gooey, messy remains of a deceased member of its species. He knew it for what it was without having to climb up to that level. But he wished to climb there nevertheless. As he approached the chamber of the Spider Woman, he knew somewhere deep inside that he was not one of these aliens. But he had begun to feel like one. He wondered that if these creatures — the Spider Woman — the fentium — could take him in and he could somehow become as one of them... after all the things that had happened to him... He wondered — He wondered what he was to become. And, though perhaps the young man of old Tetset should have felt a sense of worry... alas, even that he could not.

Two

The Spider Woman had finished her meal. Routinely, this kind of feast would take her several days and often she might even lick the floor of her chamber clean of the residual fentium guts especially if the creature she had finished was a particularly minuscule one. But she did not sense that she had much time to enjoy such a practice and this worker had been large, strong, healthy, and suitably filling. Briefly, the Spider Woman wondered if, in her anger, she hadn't made a mistake in choosing that one. She had allowed her frustration to cloud her judgement and had accidentally selected someone useful. *No matter,* she thought, her bladder enlarged from the feast, *I'll just have to be more careful next time... mustn't lose my temper.* Her siblings listened to these thoughts freely from the dark place and they laughed at her, though she could not hear their laughter — her corporeal form was becoming too solid and she was losing her ears for the thoughts of that other realm.

Then the boy, Silent Wolf, barged in without knocking. *Rude.* For a brief moment the Spider Woman felt utterly naked, embarrassed, caught in a hideous act. It was an absurd feeling and she nearly laughed at herself this time for having felt it. She controlled the boy after all — body and soul. Why should she care if he saw her as she truly was? Shroudless, fattened, a god to him. She smiled showing off her inner mouth mandibles and many sharp, hairy teeth. "Silent Wolf," she said aloud, "why have you come to see me this night?"

Silent Wolf replied without emotion, "You have gorged yourself on a worker bug, Spider Woman." Not Silent Wolf saying those words at all actually. The Spider Woman was having a bout with herself losing track of the fact that she spoke through the human.

Well of course I have! It was a silly thought and an even sillier statement. *On the one hand,* she thought, *this boy might be judging me. But I know that is not how he meant it. He is my general. All he wants is to be certain I remain presentable in the unlikely event that we should receive visitors... he's right though, the time grows later than I realized.* Her disconnect was leading her down the path of insanity.

She wiped her mouth slowly with her whole forearm, elbow to knuckle, licked any final bits from her lips, and only then spoke for she knew he would wait, "He was a drone. He had no thoughts of his own and felt nothing, I assure you."

The boy gulped and she wondered then if he could still feel that one emotion the humans called fear. She rose to her first two feet, then deliberately extended the other four down to the floor to show off her true stature. She did feel a little drunk off the insect she had eaten and she needed to move without seeming clumsy. *Be damned if I should have to hide myself from this human,* she thought half-heartedly... and her siblings heard that too.

"You are afraid..." she spoke without care, "afraid that I might devour you as well." And she lowered her face all the way down to his own. It would have been uncomfortably close if she did not already occupy his mind, "I would never do this." She resolved at last to take this moment seriously, "You are my chosen hero." Again her siblings scoffed at her from the void. "And besides, you are a man... I wouldn't like the taste of you."

Silent Wolf stared deeply into at least two of her eyes. He did not fidget any longer. "How can you be certain?"

Well he asked. And she did want to make him comfortable. She knew how to be a good host after all and she said, "I've tried." She liked to make a show of this. Even a spider needed a little fun every now and again. She turned theatrically in a circle and put on a sour sort of face to feign something the humans called regret, "When first I crashed upon this planet, I was forced to resort to..."

And she presented him then with a vision. Her eyes had opened as she floated there in space. Her war ship lay empty and open to the vacuum. The dead and dying children of her own loins, frozen there. But aye she — at least — was still alive. Breathless and cold, she groped around her in the distantly empty space of this universe until she felt at a weak point in the fabric of existence where she could peel back the layers and burrow, not without difficulty, back across the dividing plains into her own cozy, beginning-less, endless realm.

The Spider Woman wanted the boy to really understand the way in which a spider might perceive the Nexus — the Realm of the Spider. Without a preexisting connection to the pathways within the void, it would be near impossible to recognize anything but darkened, still nothingness. The void. But with that connection, a spider could see and feel every piece of that reality at the same time. If one had the cerebral capacity to connect all of the dots, one could live in all places and all moments forever... truly a god. Unfortunately, even the Spider Woman did not possess such faculty. Though she was closer than most.

For that blink of an eye that the Spider Woman held Silent Wolf within the memory of that realm, it could be stated that she and the human really were there, back in that moment within the Nexus, and the Spider Woman remembered herself remembering the presence of the human she had brought there like it was a thing that had happened a thousand thousand years ago. And she remembered the pain of her dead siblings and children who had themselves no corporeal form again after the attack on her ship. She remembered their anger too as she returned to that place. She had assumed the first time she had occupied this moment that their anger was based on their recent defeat. No, they didn't care about that. They cared about the presence of the human, Silent Wolf — one who might be able to see them for what they truly were — one who might be able to see a way to destroy them. It was a bad precedent being set for this boy. The threads of versions of that other reality that expanded out from this moment were especially dangerous.

Awkwardly, the Spider Woman forced herself and the boy out of that realm. Her siblings knew something she did not understand about this human. But he did not himself show any signs of the reaction of which she now knew they had been afraid. So, she played it off with the continuation of the moment from the memory when she had returned to his universe and fallen to the planet in a new shuttle that could satisfy this next aspect of her destiny. *The most likely result naturally occurs most of the time...* she quipped to herself as she watched the human watching her hoping she had not in fact altered his path. *A strange race. I wonder if their probabilities in this universe are somehow different from those in my own.* She shrugged off the thought and decided it would not be worth the remembering.

Her shuttle fell through the skies of the human world. She crashed creating a crater in the South of the Dry Lands. This, she knew, the boy could understand without too much trouble. And her damned siblings could take no insult in her showing him events from his own universe. She pushed on, exiting the shuttle, trudging through that detestable desert land until eventually she arrived at the falls of a river — The Fingers of All, that is what the humans of Hen'Bon'On had named this place. Here Kyun'Bon'On, Antan, and several other waterways converged in a pleasant sort of family gathering. And the Spider Woman remembered how she compared the site in her mind to the pathways of the Nexus as she had understood them. At least she attempted the metaphor, but then her hunger had stirred up within her which had made it difficult to think.

Down by the base of the falls, a voice rang forth bouncing up the rocks so the Spider Woman could hear. Silent Wolf recognized it as a male human's voice, likely of Hen'Bon'On... But at this time in history, the Spider Woman had never seen a human before. She only understood the voice as the sound of supper. She slunk down the rocks quietly until the man came into view; muscular, hairy... very appetizing. She approached. He was not a very careful man and he had been drinking something that smelled of rotting flesh which clearly had made him slow and drunken. Nevertheless, when the Spider Woman finally reached him — touched him on his back — clicked her jaw to widen for the feast — the man still had enough savvy of the situation to scream. That may have been the most confusing moment of the process for the Spider Woman, for she had not yet figured out how to reach into the primitive creature's mind... had not been able to make the death seem hospitable as she had done on that other world... had not been able to dull the moment for the other. Well, what was done was done and she would learn, in time, the clearest ways into the brains of mammals.

"I can tell you from experience..." She spoke aloud to the boy in the room, "A bitter flavor... I could feel his fear the whole way down... and far too many bones. I nearly choked myself on his..."

She ended the vision. An odd expression, a feeling of confusion and discomfort had entered into her listener's mind. This too she had not been used to. Most species she inhabited would simply obey. She had so rarely met another people that could contradict this... the last species that fought assimilation had nearly killed her... Perhaps it was this universe then that was the problem. And the boy was still staring at her with that stupid expression.

"Have you never killed another creature for survival, Silent Wolf?" She asked it plainly.

"I... Why would you tell me this?" The boy stumbled before her.

She was somehow frightening him. She had not intended that. "I want you to trust me. To know that I will never lie to you." He was slipping from her as Qotle had. She could not allow this, must control him, must control all of them. "I wish to make you a king among men. I have seen it in your time stream. As I have seen the importance of you in my own." This was true. She knew this boy. She knew him better than she had realized. She could see him in that memory of the future like a beacon that would summon her siblings forth once again into this reality.

But then the shouting started. Ringing through the halls of the temple. Climbing up into her chamber. Diverting the boy's attention.

"What was that?" Silent Wolf was defensive as he asked, full of emotion. This just would not do.

But the memory presented itself then to her. It had always been there, a moment in time, a time that she struggled still to keep in accurate measure. The sun's phases. The moon's. The rainy season. The dry. The birthing and death cycles. The days of war to come. The night upon them now. Yes, this night. It was to be a beginning. And she spoke the premonition aloud, "On this night we will be under attack. You and I will win, but it will come at the cost of the humans of Bo'No'To. It has already begun."

Silent Wolf was floored by the statement. The Spider Woman was falling into a trance state that was giving him the separation he needed to step away from her control. He was finally, fully himself again and he could not believe what the Spider Woman was saying to him in that moment. "Aren't you going to help them?"

"I am." She replied. But there was no implication of action from the woman. Rather, she appeared to fade deeper into that trance leaving the boy flabbergasted. He did not know how to proceed. Where to go? What to do? Well it certainly wouldn't help for him to stay there with that sleeping goddess. That sleeping... monster.

Silent Wolf fled from the chamber out onto the upper pathways. He made it as far as the first ledge and stared down through the abdomen of the temple. There were other creatures there below. He knew those ones however — birds — crows. A whole barrage of the large, black beasts flew through the halls. But for what purpose?

Worse than the presence of the birds, the fentiums were becoming riled up. Their regular, calm demeanors and clear, black eyes were beginning to mimic that of locusts in a frenzy, their eyes grown sharp and red. They amassed and mobbed the walls forming links in the air to extend their reach against the invaders. Silent Wolf no longer saw them as fentiums in his terror. He saw swarming zombies in his midst.

Three

The tree had been burning above the canyon for some time now. Crow Mother's shuttle lingered beyond it, hidden amongst the stones of the dry land. And the Grand One watched from her own hiding spot. Somewhere below the shuttle, the beam of energy that knocked Tetset from the sky had emanated.

The Grand One looked down upon the pinnacle of that strange temple nested within the walls of the earth and wondered how long it might take the crows to perform their designated reconnaissance mission. But new lights were blaring on from within the structure and she and Crow Mother could see quite clearly that a chase and row had begun to stir within. The crows had been found out. There was no chance they could have gained much of an advantage in such a short time and the Grand One had to hold her breath in frustration. Not a good start.

"They were meant to do this quietly." The Grand One's song was dry and limp on delivery.

Crow Mother matched her tone, "Unfortunately, they are crows... they have minds of their own... and now I realize too late that they do not understand the meaning of quiet."

The Grand One's frustration bled out into physical form. She crushed her fingers in her hand and nearly broke her kopa. But resolve overtook that emotion in time. "We need to get them out of there," she sang.

"Yes." Crow Mother was already walking, "Come. I have an idea." She dropped down on all fours and galloped across the wet, rocky landscape hurtling right over the side of the cliff and out of sight of the girl. The Grand One had been following but she stopped several feet shy of the edge.

"Crow Mother!" The Grand One pulled her mask from her head in a misinformed attempt to spot her friend's body somewhere in the basin below. But the rain smacked at her eyes and she replaced the cover quickly resolving not to take it off again till better weather found her. She worried for her friend. *Had Crow Mother not realized how slick the rocks would be?* she thought. *Had she misinterpreted the distance?*

Of course, Crow Mother had done neither of those things. She had only briefly forgotten that the Grand One was not a member of her own race. After a moment, she rescaled what little of the wall she had already descended and popped her head back up above the side of the cliff for her friend to see. The Grand One breathed a sigh of relief as Crow Mother pulled herself back up to the surface and the alien intoned, "It is too slick for you to climb, I'm afraid. However, I can make quick work of it. Stay with the shuttle."

"But I can help." The Grand One did not like this very much. She came to be a part of the fight. It bruised her ego to be so nonchalantly relegated to the side.

"You will fall." Crow Mother grew very serious then, "I cannot have another human death on my conscience. Especially not yours. Stay with the shuttle, we may need to make a speedy escape." She reached out and touched the side of the Grand One's neck where skin was still exposed, turned, and leapt back over the edge without her.

The human watched the alien as she climbed expertly down the canyon walls. It was much easier to spot her now that she knew where to look and the Grand One bobbed her head to see as here the rocks jutted out, there peeled back, her friend making quick work of the myriad crags and slipping silently down and through the exposed upper window of the obelisk.

After seeing her friend disappear through that gap, the Grand One waited barely a heartbeat before turning her attention to the surrounding terrain. Surely somewhere nearby she could find her own access point. Cliff. Boulder. Ledge. There was a hint above the tower of a minor crevice she might be able to descend. It lingered in her vision through the rain like a perfect inverted teardrop not far above that same upper window. "That is my path." She spoke in the dead language of Tetset and took off at a sprint in the direction of the breach in the canyon side.

She nearly fell into the crevice not realizing how soon the mouth of it would arrive. Pausing in a stumble, she surveyed what little of the channel she could make out from overhead, but much of it was difficult to see, covered here and there with large, flat pallets of unbroken land. But water was pressing through and the Grand One knew there had to be a burrow wide enough for her tiny shoulders. She leapt.

Like a billy goat, she descended into the darkness. Hopping from wall to wall, rock to rock, always mud flowing in a torrent beneath her feet. She held her balance surprisingly well at first only needing her hands to help her once in a while. But those once in a whiles would become her downfall as, on a particularly slick stone, her fingers struggled to hold their grip.

Then she was fumbling, tumbling downward into the new formed river of mud pooling below. Waves of the wetted earth hammered her, crashing one after another until she was buried in the sloppy stuff. If not for her mask she might have drowned or suffocated then and there. But she was fortunate, managing to pull her head back up above the waves.

Her hand reached up and caught hold of a protrusion in a nearby wall. She lifted herself out. Heavy breaths. Sighs of relief. *No time to waste.* In that darkness, she thought she spotted the end point of the crevice; the minor hole in the cliffside that would take her to her goal. So the Grand One crawled her way, more heavily now that she was caked with so much mud, making slow but constant progress across the remaining boulders. At last, she reached the opening and pressed her head through.

As she peered down, it was apparent that she had badly misjudged the distance from this opening to the top of the temple. She could easily break both her legs if she calculated her drop incorrectly from here... or worse. If she pushed off too hard, she might miss the acute roof altogether and plummet the full way down to the base of the canyon... and obviously her death. She chuckled at her stupid pride. But she was not deterred. This thing had been put in motion and no one could get her through it or out of it but herself. *Well, here goes.*

Tossing her feet out below her, the Grand One dangled from the gap, mud trickling over her hands and head onto the roof in pats. If that stuff could land there, so could she. She held her breath and let go. Her feet hit solid rock with a thud. Her knees bent, but did not shatter. The ache and sting of the fall spread through her and then dissipated. And she breathed again at last, sighed relief. She was standing on the tower. She was alive. "That was very foolish," she told herself rubbing at her shins. Then the insane drive of necessity overtook her again. "Let's go!" She egged herself on and ran and slid across the roof until she spilled over the ledge. Her fingers caught and held firm to a small divot there and she performed a sort of acrobatic trick flinging herself out over the canyon then launching herself back in the opposite direction at a sharp angle. She slipped through the same window she had seen Crow Mother take and, just like that, she was inside.

Four

Soaking wet and muddy as all hell, the Grand One had landed right in the midst of a mini skirmish. Two of her newly claimed crow family were in a pecking battle with a corps of five red-eyed fentiums. The struggle appeared terribly violent to the girl as she witnessed the large insects landing blow after harsh blow against her friends, stripping feather from wing, mounting wounds upon their backsides, blood speckling the floors and walls around them.

But the blood coming from the fentiums' peck induced wounds was apparently worse. They were a large target and though they were rather dynamic in their range of movements, they did not have the ability to separate into the air as the crows did.

One of those fentium dropped dead the moment the girl arrived and she did not linger long to process the event before she reached out, tore a strange bespeckled stalagmite from the wall of the tower, and jumped into action smacking the pillar into the nearest bug and sending it reeling across the floor with a terrible crunch.

By that count, only three of those odd creatures remained in that stretch of hallway. The Grand One fought beside the crows trying at the same time to reach for her kopa. But that proved to be impossible for the moment and she needed a different way of communicating with the birds. So she took to awkwardly singing the notes with her exasperated human voice, "Where has Crow Mother gone?"

Apparently, through the power of her mask this method could work, because one of the crows quickly replied, "She seeks the Spider Woman."

"Alone?" The Grand One was nonplused. *How could Crow Mother be so foolish?* She asked herself. This was not yet the time. They clearly still required more aid to deal with the army of insects she had only just discovered occupying the valley.

The other crow cawed at her then, "We hold back this hoard for her."

"And for you." The first crow shouted, "Go!"

So this was how it would have to be then, the Grand One realized. Ill prepared, she and her friends would have to fight their way down the levels of this many tiered structure, fending off more warriors than they could possibly handle. She had witnessed her friend's carelessness before, but she had genuinely hoped the crash had been an anomaly. Now she understood with clarity why the Spider Woman had not been finished off before, why The People had failed to complete their own tasks. Their leadership had been careless in their planning, never following up to ensure their victory, never thoroughly considering the steps that were required of them. It had cost The People everything. She would not be so like them... assuming she could escape her current predicament.

Instinctively, she raised up her stalagmite club and flattened another fentium. But two more of those creatures entered the hall and she knew she had to get moving. The Grand One rushed past those latest insects swiftly avoiding each one as the crows swooped down to distract them.

Racing across the upper balcony, the Grand One could see the massive interior of the tower and the battle currently in progress throughout the entire body of the structure. A hundred crows clashed against a thousand of the terrifying man-sized stick bugs. *How could we be so careless?* Outnumbered. Outmatched. She watched an entire wall of her allies collapse within a row of the larger hoard of insects and she wanted to scream.

Out of the corner of her eye, the Grand One then saw something that changed her mood. She could see, amidst the fighting on the lowest level, a group of... humans... standing in a circle. She stopped dead in her tracks. There were elders and children among them. And there was a man... she couldn't be sure, but something in his body movement reminded her of... that night in the teosintl... when Tetset burned.

Of course he would be here, that man from the other tribe, the one who stood before her in the dark against the flames of her dying civilization. And she heard herself in her memory asking that stupid question, "Who are you?" She had said, "Why do you soil this celebration for us?" And she was shaken then by a pain she had hoped to never feel again. In that moment, she forgot where she was. She was blood. She was hate. Like a great fire. The flames of her village against the blackness of the night.

She began to understand and contextualize Crow Mother's behavior then as she herself weighed and ignored the results of her own attempt at rational thinking. If that was the man from the teosintl, she would have to reach him to do... what? To murder him? No. The Grand One was not like those people. She could not be so easily coaxed into the baseless act of... It dawned on her as she stood there that she likely already had, just a moment ago, killed that large insect... But was that the same? She did not understand who she was becoming. And she did not know who those humans really were down below. If it was that man, what would she do to him if she reached him? *Only what he deserves,* she thought not knowing exactly what she meant by that thought. But she did know that the other humans surrounding him were afraid. She could see it in their body language. Perhaps she could help... Yes! She would help... That was who she wanted to be.

The Grand One leapt then over the balcony ledge and slid down an oblong, crystalline pillar gaining speed at first, slowing at a groove, stumbling and then reasserting her will and balance into a treacherous but controlled hurtle. The material beneath her feet was so smooth and she was very light. Without delay, the Grand One landed flat on her feet all the way down at the bottom. The ground floor. She had become quite good at those kinds of maneuvers in recent days and she huffed with an odd sort of pride for she knew almost immediately what it had meant for her to get to the bottom level. She had changed her and her friend's fates by coming down here... *But Crow Mother can take care of herself,* she thought from someplace far in the back of her mind. After all, her alien friend had not even wanted her to follow on this leg of the mission. She knew as she thought it that this assertion was wrong. But she was already there. Below. The choice had been made and could not be unmade. *Move on. Hurry up. Be strong.*

Five

Qotle was in shock. He and a group of his tribesmen — not another soldier among them — had been caught in the middle of a surprise attack. Shi'Yun was back inside and safe from the storm, but then the birds had come. He had been busy batting away said birds with the blunt end of his spear, hoping to keep his sister and those other nearby Hen'Bon'On safe when he noticed the fentiums in the vicinity behaving strangely. And then he was under attack by one of them, a bug he had known and thought of as a friend. But its eyes were bleached with red and, if it did recognize him, it must have hated him. So he swatted at that fentium with his spear as he had done the crows. And then there was another fentium and another all coming for him and the other humans, not even caring for the presence of the birds. He fought those off as best he could, but he was only one man and there were so many... enemies. The thought came to him in a moment of panic but that hadn't made it any less true.

The fentiums were the Spider Woman's pupils... no... her soldiers. She had somehow found them living in the subterranean caves that burned and oozed miles beneath the crust. They were likely calm, placid creatures down there, but she had not brought them to the surface to remain as such. As Qotle found himself fending off bug after bird after bug he gained a sick kind of clarity within his own mind. He began to remember more and more of those lost memories which the Spider Woman had hoped he would forget and the puzzle began at last to put itself together for him.

He swung again at an approaching crow, exhausted and losing hope. And he was struck flush against the belly by something else — something even harder. A piece of the tower had come undone and sent him reeling to the floor. Another alien stood before him. A strange, beautiful, terrible Sun God. It stood above him as he knelt there, breathless, the wind knocked from his lungs.

"Why... why do you attack us?" Qotle struggled to say the words against his choked up gut pain.

And to his surprise, the alien spoke back, "Why do you run when you do not know?"

The alien's voice sounded like that of the girl's from the teosintl. The circle was completed. Qotle was suddenly aware that he could remember the moment when he had been freed from the Spider Woman. That girl in the field. She had... she had freed him. How? What did it mean?

The alien raised its mica club, seemingly prepared to finish Qotle off. He did not shy away from it. He was ready for this death. It seemed somehow fitting to him and besides, he was far too tired to fight any longer anyway. But another thing formed a shadow over him then. Shi'Yun had intervened, covered her brother's sagging head with her whole body, hugged him and held him shouting, "No! Please don't hurt my brother!"

Six

The Grand One looked down upon the little girl holding steadfast to the man. She felt the pangs of regret deep within her. For she and this child were so very alike; hopeful, strong willed. On the day Tetset was destroyed, Blue Flower had promised her ancestors vengeance. But the Grand One was not a murderer. In that moment, she did not even wish to continue swatting away those large insects anymore. She did not want this war that had been forced upon her and she felt a keen frustration in the knowledge that she would still have to see it through. But — she decided, hoping it would not be her ultimate downfall — not at the expense of more human life.

The girl on the floor was still crying, yelling, “He is a good man! He protects me!”

A moment passed. The crows kept the fentiums from reaching the circle now that the Grand One was there and she took her time digesting the situation before her. She had not truly wished to kill this man, even in her rage, she decided. She had wanted to make him feel helpless as he had done to her that night. She had accomplished that thing and now it was time to take the next step.

She lowered her stalagmite club and allowed her shoulders to sag. “It is not safe for you here,” she said. The Grand One was ready, at last, to lead.

Seven

Silent Wolf had not made it far from the Spider Woman's chamber since the attack had begun. He had intended to... He wanted to get away from that place. But one thing after another had distracted him from the growing realization that he had his own mind again. Those damned birds for one thing! They pecked at him and flew out of reach. So, he had gone to get a spear of his own from the upper reserve armory in the hopes of scaring them away from him.

Once within that room however, he was surprised to find the bloodied bodies of several dead Hen'Bon'On warriors... some of the men he had met on the long walk from Tetset. They were still warm to the touch, so this event had only just occurred, and not a one of them was breathing. He wondered if the crows could have made it into this windowless closet of a room and been so brutally efficient with these men... but when he checked them further, the marks left on their bodies did not remind him of the scars he had seen left by beak or talon in the past. He grabbed his spear and left the dead men untouched in the room, shuttering as he went.

The crows did not scare easily. And Silent Wolf was getting very annoyed as he swatted haphazardly at another incoming group of the birds. He knew he needed time to think, to process everything that was happening, but the opportunity was nowhere in sight for the boy.

Something else, however, was coming into view. Silent Wolf had reached that point along the upper pathway where he could see all of the levels of the tower below. And as he swatted at the birds, he watched as the little child named Shi'Yun led a masked Being toward the front entrance of the compound. He watched Qotle following them as well as a small group of other Hen'Bon'On citizens. And deep down he wanted to go with them. He felt awful because he did not see an easy way to reach them... to help... or to fight.

"Silent Wolf. I am in need of you." The Spider Woman's voice tore into his mind with a jolt of pain.

He lost control of himself again. His emotions, ripped from him like a decaying tooth tied onto a string. He turned from the scene, not seeing the last of the humans as they left, and he walked directly across the long balcony to the Spider Woman's chamber batting away the occasional crow without losing stride.

Eight

The Spider Woman had been squaring off with the creature called Crow Mother alone for too long in her bloated and drunken state. She had known its kind from the last planet, and she despised its presence in her new tower; a reminder of her failure to protect her children. It was such an insignificant nothing when compared to her greatness, yet as they stood there circling each other across the room from one another, she found she did not yet wish to destroy it. Something rattled around within her mind, the thought that perhaps she had been misinterpreting her visions of the future. She had seen the humans as the new vessels that would help her to reunite with her sibling-children. But her future self had not made it clear to her that one of these other creatures would be so close at hand. She wondered that the pathways of reverse time and reality could so imminently fluctuate in her favor. For this was one of those same beasts that had allowed her the opportunity to bring her family into corporeality the first time. Even if it had ended in failure, she knew that this Being could provide the necessary properties. She could channel its life energy from it, and with that failed Hen'Bon'On experiment behind her, she only need remove those pesky birds in order to peacefully propagate.

But in her current state she still desired that one human general by her side, the one who's meek but handsome face she had been dreaming about all these years. She wondered if, after the latest incident in her chamber, he would respond to her call. His mind was not so strong as Qotle's had been. He should come to her aid. He would, she decided. The Spider Woman had seen enough of him in her visions to know he would always come if she asked him to.

The beast across the room was singing at her. *Damn their singing!* She had never cared for it. Still, it did not attack her and she kept her arms raised as if prepared to strike back at any moment should the thing come any closer. With her mind, she reached out to the boy. And then he was there, Silent Wolf, he did come as she knew he would. He was standing right there in the doorway waiting for her to make her commandment known. This manipulation was becoming a tricky business for the Spider Woman. She still wanted the boy's trust. She wanted him to love her as she loved him. Strange that she should feel such a human emotion toward the boy, but she could not help herself. She had studied his face across the epochs; the cold, loud, and lonesome eternities within the Nexus. She had grown attached to the idea he represented for her, the opportunity to own this universe... to spread across its many worlds, to feel this luxuriously light mass around her, not that heavy blanket of extreme density within her own realm. Ease of movement — a body to move with — time that could move along and not remain stagnant or boring. Silent Wolf's humility represented that for the Spider Woman, and yes, she loved him for it as she had briefly loved Qotle for his own mortal stimuli. And her siblings laughed and laughed and laughed... all but perhaps the strongest of them; that one that worried after the thing that none of the others seemed to mind. But it was not that one's turn to make its voice heard. Not yet.

"This Being murdered your people." The Spider Woman presented the thought to Silent Wolf and she knew what he saw then, the vision of Tetset falling from the sky. The moment of death. The splatter. Though the memory was neatly missing that one other detail which the Spider Woman did not want Silent Wolf to recall — the laser from the turret.

Nine

Silent Wolf lingered in the doorway a moment longer. His mind was again at odds with itself and he was revisiting that terrible day in his memory, uncertain of how to proceed. The Spider Woman was reaching out to him, pleading for him to act. And damnit, he wanted to. If that other alien was in fact the same one whose shuttle had captured and then dropped his people then it was a monster far worse than his own lady and it must be made to pay for its crimes.

Fortunately, the Spider Woman's mind speech had not tipped the other to his presence in that room. In fact, it was still singing a pained melody that the boy found oddly beautiful, but could not understand. The Spider Woman scoffed aloud at the song. In his mind, Silent Wolf again heard her say to him, "It is vermin and should be caged, humiliated, and killed." He saw her long, sharp teeth expose themselves to the Being as she continued, "Now Silent Wolf. It must be done. It must be you. My champion."

This last statement had a powerful, stirring effect on Silent Wolf's equilibrium and he shifted his stance just the slightest bit. Did Silent Wolf love the Spider Woman as she loved him — she freely presented the information to the boy unafraid of the power of his own consciousness? And to be fair to the Spider Woman, he was so wrapped up within her, he could not have known it if he did. Regardless, Silent Wolf was certainly willing to accept this particular order, even if his mind were in conflict with itself on so many other items. He raised the sharp end of his spear ever so quietly knowing what the Spider Woman wanted him to know — that this beast was responsible for the death of Tetset — and he plunged the blade of it deep into the singing alien's body. It tore through the Being's shoulder, flesh — muscle — bone, and extended out the other end.

Ten

Crow Mother was in shock. She did not understand how it had so suddenly come to this. Her mental faculties caved in around her until all she knew was sharp, searing pain. She scrambled to get to a wall taking the whole of the spear with her. It was a part of her now... it always had been. She had born this pain for so long within her, not knowing the moment would become real. And she climbed like a frightened animal, too quickly for her own good. She made it about halfway up the slick chamber wall before her fingers seized and she came splashing in a heap down to the floor. The sound that rang from her beak was not so much a melody like she had been raised to produce all her life long. Rather, the sound that emanated from her then was a scream like a human would make when all things were lost to them.

That unnatural sound echoed through the halls of the temple. Crows swiftly ended their battles all throughout the building and flocked en masse up to the heights to find their leader and, as a cohesive unit, they breached the threshold of the chamber where they knew Crow Mother to be. This created a haze of innocuous confusion for all within that place. Innocuous, but only to a point...

Crow Mother forced her eyes open as the swarm surrounded her. She could still see the Spider Woman through the crowd. She saw that evil one swatting at her friends. She glimpsed those long, dangerous legs as they shot up from the floor and impaled several of her closest allies. She saw the terrible smile on the Spider Woman's lips and she cried out with what little sense she had, singing for the birds to disperse, to save themselves.

The crows waited a moment longer, not wishing to heed her warning. And in that time, at least two more of their ranks were murdered. The Spider Woman greedily stuffed them down her elongating throat as if they were mere berries being plucked from a bush. She could eat anything. The birds began to figure out what was happening to them in that cloud, that they had made things somehow worse for the Being by sacrificing themselves so foolhardily. They dispersed with fear and regret in their hearts taking whatever windows or doors they could find nearby, though none of them crossed that large glazed window that draped the back wall of the Spider's chamber. Crow Mother watched them go and wondered if she should ever see them again. She hoped that the Grand One had stayed with the shuttle. Given her painful new injury, this would have been a fantastic moment for her friend to decide to come crashing through that massive glass surface... the girl could scoop her up and leap out in a moment and they would be free once more. Unfortunately, that fantasy did not come to pass.

Silent Wolf approached the fallen creature and pulled his spear from its torso with a great deal more force than was necessary. He felt a new sense of pride within him. He had accomplished something he had set out to do for the first time in a very long while. *People go on losing streaks all the time,* he thought, *mine is finally over.* Of course, he was losing in that moment more than ever he had been in all his days, but he could not know that sad fact.

He spoke to the Spider Woman not aware that she had defeated him, "There was another of these beasts in the great hall. It took the humans."

"Then we will have to capture her as well." The Spider Woman told him. Silent Wolf was not cognizant enough to catch the word 'Her' in that statement. He only heard in his deluded mind that there was a new mission for him. Something else to conquer — to dominate. He was not alone under foot... and perhaps now at last he truly was the right man for the job.

PART V - THE GRAND ONE

One

With effort, Qotle and the others trudged through the muddy roads of the lower canyon beyond Bo'No'To. Fortunately, the rains had let up just as the few remaining Hen'Bon'On moved to make their escape. It was Qotle, Shi'Yun, Fubiok (an older woman who had badly been losing her vision these last few months), Hi'Ni (the medicine woman who had been looking after her when the attack started), youngsters Birdo and Genk (both of whose current elders had gone missing early on in the assault)... and the alien who had agreed to help them escape the dangerous war zone. Qotle had become distracted by that one. She was practically all he could think about as the mud rose all the way to his waist — how she had spared him — how she had been capable of feeling empathy for his sister and her words — how this alien was not at all like he expected. Qotle was cold, dirty, and far too exhausted from the unexpected journey, but he also knew that if he felt this bad — he being the only trained soldier of the bunch — the others must feel so much worse. Though if the alien was feeling that same strain, she did not show it.

Qotle watched the alien out of the corner of his eye as he and his sister led the small party. She seemed impatient with their speed. At least something in her body language presented him with that idea. He could not see her face beneath that weird bucket on her head, assuming she had a face... assuming she was a she or even a living creature like those of his family from Hen'Bon'On in the first place. He thought about the words they had said to each other back in the temple — how she had spared his life — how they had come across the bodies of many of his tribesmen and women all across the arcades and apartments of Bo'No'To as they made their way from the Spider Woman's temple. Those people had not been so lucky as he and his sister — had not been spared from the terrible madness of the fentiums. Why had they killed so many of his people? Why had they tried to kill him? Why had this alien helped them so in their hour of need?

For some reason, at that point in the repeating thread of his exhaustive thought cycle, he would begin to think about that night in the teosintl again. The girl there and those same words they had spoken to each other. He had been lost then, but when she struck him with that... that liquid that had burned his eyes... when she did that, he must have broken through the web enshrouding his mind. He had reawakened because of her. He wished he could find that girl again and thank her. He wondered, each time his eyes fell on the alien in the group, if perhaps he already had.

Five hours passed in that way, their steps slowed by the mud and the company that traveled with them. And he finally decided to ask the question that had been feverishly bouncing around within his head, "You are her are you not?"

The alien thought a moment as they walked eventually asking without commitment, "Who?

"The girl," he tried to say the words with a decisive air, but he knew they ultimately had come out weak, "the girl from the teosintl." He waited, hating that stupid bucket on her head. He could not guess if she was thinking or angry or even laughing at him. And she took her time leaving him to wait in obscurity... but he shook away his own aggressiveness. If it was her, he owed her patience — an explanation for his actions — an apology — more apologies than he could probably account for in an entire lifetime... if it was her — he knew he was overthinking and needed to be patient.

"No." She responded too quietly. The tide of the lower river Kyun'Bon'On nearly took the word with it. The alien was louder and clearer with her next statement, "You are mistaken. I come from another, more peaceful world than this one."

Qotle felt a sort of regret. He did not think he was wrong, but he did not wish to force the alien into saying things she did not wish to say. He owed her everything. She owed him nothing. The conversation would have ended then and there were it not for his little sister.

"So you are like the Spider Woman?" Shi'Yun asked with a fresh excitement, "You are here to protect us too?"

Then something odd happened. The alien's body seemed to sag into a shape of uncertainty. For the slightest of moments, Qotle swore the veneer of strength slipped from the alien. Something in Shi'Yun's question made her as uncertain of the facts as he had been. He wondered if in time he couldn't manage to get the full truth out of that one after all. He would have to make her trust him — show her the good man he knew himself to be.

"I..." the alien spoke with hesitancy, "No." and her voice had a bite of sass to it, "I am not like the Spider Woman."

"Oh." Shi'Yun was disappointed.

But then the alien stopped for the first time since the party had set out. She turned to Shi'Yun and lowered herself to the girl's level and spoke with a motherly tone, "But I do hope to protect innocent ones such as yourself."

Shi'Yun burst into smiles then. She leapt up and hugged the alien at her midsection shouting, "I knew it! I knew you were good!"

It made Qotle smile to see his little sister had not lost her positive energy this last night. He actually laughed when he realized how little the alien had anticipated the embrace. That was Shi'Yun for you. He remained watching with that jolt of happiness as the alien awkwardly attempted to reciprocate with two stiff pats on Shi'Yun's shoulders. The hug broke and Shi'Yun skipped ahead having forgotten her own tiredness. His sister had never much minded the heights and she genially picked up speed as it occurred to Qotle to what point they had come along their path; he wondered if the elders Fubiok and Hi'Ni could still handle the sheer wall climb — if the children Birdo and Genk who were both younger than Shi'Yun by three years had even had a chance to train in the climb. *Too late now,* he thought, *we have no choice but to leave the canyon and escape the Spider Woman's domain altogether. The farther away we can go, the better.* Qotle felt a heat on him then. He was being watched. Not by the Spider Woman (and he was glad to know it) but by the alien. She watched him and he wished he could know what it was she was thinking.

Two

The Grand One looked upon the man named Qotle — the man she had hated when she still wore the name of Blue Flower — but she was not that girl any longer and she wondered if perhaps she had been wrong about her path... These people. If the girl, Shi'Yun, was any indication, this tribe had once been not so unlike her own. She wondered about Qotle's actions that day in the field. She had been so certain he had wronged her, had committed inexcusable offenses against her. But then, with a new sense of maturity, she decided to look back on those events with an objective eye, as now she was a different, more honorable woman called the Grand One and not the foolhardy girl known as Blue Flower.

Blue Flower had been under great duress. She had been right not to trust the terrifying presence of a strong man she did not know out in the silence of the teosintl as her native lands burned. But it occurred to the Grand One in her contemplation that the man had not set his hands on her. He had remained relaxed through the whole encounter, only moving slightly in that moment when the girl had reached into her satchel for the vial of Lidolia; the hot liquid which had struck Qotle like pepper spray. The man could not, in fact, have been among the killings she knew had transpired within the town of Tetset. He was out there in the teosintl. Alone. Too far from the town to be a murderer...

She contemplated whether or not Qotle's actions, limited as they were, should ever be excused. Then she raised her kopa to her mask for the first time since the fighting had begun and played a song of sorrow and frustration, of remembrance and of letting go. Everyone stopped. Everyone listened. Awe saturated the faces of the three Hen'Bon'On children. Tears came to the elder women's eyes.

In a blind panic, the man named Qotle shouted over the music, "The crows are back! We must hide!" He turned and began to run, riling up the tired group.

It was then that the Grand One realized that they still did not fully understand what had transpired back in the tower. That the crows had come for the Spider Woman and the fentium had turned against the Hen'Bon'On peoples. "No!" The Grand One shouted briefly pausing her song, "They will not hurt us!"

"But — " Qotle tried to argue.

"I will speak with them." That seemed to shut the man up for the moment and the others reluctantly waited as the birds closed in on their position. The Grand One returned to her song as she awaited her foolish allies' arrival.

Three

Qotle wanted to run. He wanted everyone else to run too. It took everything within the man to control himself and do as the alien instructed. His heart rate shot up and he felt a sort of over saturation in the backs of his eyes as the crows came, overtook the group, flew past a ways, and turned back with a frightening but elegant precision. He closed his eyes tightly then as the wind of the beasts grazed his cheeks and exposed arms. There were the sounds of fluttering feathers and the taps of talons skipping along stones followed by a moment of seemingly mourn-filled silence.

Shi'Yun tugged at his arm and Qotle opened his eyes again. The crows had not touched the group as the alien predicted. Actually, they had sensed the discord amongst the humans and given them a wide berth as they settled down on the other side of the odd companion.

The alien's song carried on. Qotle felt the sadness of it... almost understood the meaning of the notes. He was eased from his fear of the birds. Enchanted by the mystery unveiling itself from within his heart. He felt the alien could have been playing his own story. But he knew that was not the case. It was deeply, passionately her own tale being told and told again on repeat. That is, until the birds began to chime in with their own oddly harmonious caws — singing — actual music that played beautifully off of the alien's own song.

"Are they singing to each other?" Shi'Yun asked her brother, fascination flowing across her lips.

Qotle could only nod his head a little in response. The surprise he felt was overwhelming. Had he been so wrong about the beasts of his world as to have missed this? They shared an ability with mankind. They could sing together. And suddenly he felt ashamed, for he had killed for sport so many creatures such as these... never once had he thought to share a song with them. Never had he imagined that they would listen.

"What do you think they are saying?" His little sister chimed in once again.

But Qotle could only shake his head dumbly. He had been so wrong for so long about so many things.

Listening in anguish, the Grand One received the crows' scattered message against the backdrop of her own music.

"Crow Mother has been wounded!" The one crow insisted.

"We burned our feet!" Another cried.

"Crow Mother has been taken!" Sang the third bird.

"Crow Mother suffers!" Replied the first.

"And we cannot help her!"

The Grand One had not wanted to hear of these events. She had been told emphatically to stay behind. She had been relegated to the second team and she had found a way, nonetheless, to serve a purpose. She did not wish to be made to regret her own decisions. She loved Crow Mother. But Crow Mother had asked for the impossible without applying the lesson of restraint to her own person. The Grand One shook the pain away, played the words, "She told me to stay behind. She told me she did not need me. I came all the same."

"You abandoned Crow Mother!" One of the crows spat it at her.

"But I found people who needed my help!" The Grand One understood their insinuations. She knew the birds were defensive and confused. She knew to take their aggressions with a grain of salt. Still, she wanted them to sing their piece, to work through their emotions as a child might. Cry it out. There there.

"Someone must help Crow Mother!" They were saying. Many of them singing on top of each other. "Someone must help!" and "The Spider Woman kills us!" or "The Spider Woman will kill Crow Mother!"

Damnit, the Grand One thought then, *I had hoped Crow Mother could hold her own and escape if need be. She insisted I stay behind. She insisted. So, I found another way to be useful.* The realization hit her like a wave, that she was Crow Mother's only real backup, that she had allowed her friend to become stranded in a dangerous place.

After she felt the crows had said enough, the Grand One bit into the din of the crowd with the highest note she could reach on the kopa. Then as a new silence filled that gap, she followed it up, insisting, "Then I will return to save her."

And this managed to at least calm the crows back into a more single file approach.

"Yes save!" Sang one.

"Save! We will follow!" Came another.

"We will die!" One crow scuttled back; fearful.

But the other crows pushed in around them. They were fighting with each other then, knocking the afraid one back into line like some rude gang ritual. The Grand One did not like it. She did not wish to see such hierarchies at play among her allies. But she also knew that they would need all the help they could get on their next mission. One crow really might make the difference and that fearful one seemed to calm down after a moment and remember itself.

"But still we will follow!" The frightened crow sang sorrowfully knowing it was the right thing to do. "For Crow Mother!" It sang this last bit emphatically and the rest of the crows joined the call — "For Crow Mother!"

The Grand One turned then remembering the humans. She approached the group, huddling together in fear that another attack might be imminent. Yet, the crows remained behind her, pecking awkwardly at the mud and pruning their feathers. For they were terribly afraid of the thing they had just requested. Even they understood how little they could help against the creatures within that tower.

Five

It was Qotle of course that spoke for the group as he had done these last hours, "What do they say?"

"That I must go back to the tower." The Grand One said the words matter-of-factly.

"Go back?" Qotle was stunned. Not in a million lifetimes could he imagine ever returning to that place; the place of his birth, yes; but the place of his family's death as well; the place of his imprisonment; the place where *she* lingered. He never would see the Spider Woman again so long as he drew breath, he had decided. And he was not wrong. But the alien wanted to go there again. Why?

"Someone I care for has been snared within that place," the alien responded as if she had read his mind, "and I must go back for her."

"No." Shi'Yun blurted out, apparently understanding the fear on her brother's face, "You cannot!"

The alien did not hesitate however, "I must."

Qotle remembered something the Spider Woman had once shown him — many years ago, perhaps when he had first been taken... he had not seen another of those Beings in the temple last night... but of course there would be more, "Is the other one..." he asked rather awkwardly, "like you as well?"

"She..." and this time the alien did hesitate, but only for a second, "Yes."

"Then my sister is right." Qotle recalled that feeling of rage filled hate the Spider Woman had made him feel toward this species though she had always liked to think herself the very model of 'calm' and 'compassion' — but the hatred toward them, the Beings of that earlier world often bled through from her thoughts into his own mind. He continued, “You cannot go back there. The Spider Woman teaches that your kind is a sort of beast without consciousness or purpose.” He reflected looking toward the crows, “Clearly she has never seen what I have just witnessed.” And that sense of shame crept back in, “You can speak with the crows. And they speak back... If crows can speak back... What does that mean?”

“All living things have emotion and purpose big brother,” Shi’Yun stated. “Did you not know this?”

His sister’s childish wisdom surprised the man. He tried to remember more, “The Spider Woman teaches...” but his tank was coming up empty.

The alien that did not look so like an alien propped him back up — helped him out for the third time, “Well the Spider Woman is obviously mistaken... dangerously so.”

“I’m sorry.” Qotle meant it. He wanted only to do the right thing for all the rest of his days, “But I also cannot in good conscience see you return to that tower. I—”

“Do even the fish speak?” Shi’Yun interrupted again. And damn her it warmed his heart further to hear that question asked. His sister really was a one of a kind intellect.

In fact, the alien seemed to agree with that sentiment. She was chuckling, responding with a sense of genuine amusement, “I have not yet tried to speak with a fish. Though I would imagine so. At least, there must be a kind of creature within the great oceans that sings. I have heard things on my journeys over water that sounded of music. Though, at the time, I could not understand the words.” That satisfied Shi’Yun’s curiosity for the time being and the alien returned her attentions to Qotle, “Why can I not return to that tower? What do I not yet know?”

He surprised himself by gulping so everyone nearby knew that he was nervous... something he could not recall ever having done before. But this was an uncomfortable thing. "The Spider Woman will be..." he began, stopped, started again, "She will be tinkering with your friend... to see how it... how she works. The Spider Woman will be looking for a way to control her... your species... once again as she did on that other planet. If this proves an impossible task — if she cannot control her... bring forth..." Qotle ran into a mental block again. Something the Spider Woman had definitely wanted him to forget. He had not wholly done so, but his mind was reluctant to search too deeply for the memory. So he too gave up and spoke only the bit he could get to follow that missing patch, "She will likely kill her."

This, of course, had an adverse affect on the alien who instantly jumped into action, "Then why are we still talking? I must go." She ran in the wrong direction, backwards toward the crows.

Qotle could not let her make such a terrible mistake, "Wait!" He cried after the alien, "You would need an army to take her!"

"I have crows!" She shouted back, lifting one of the birds up between both of her arms. The bird was very large though and it blocked her entire upper body from view. Worse still, the bird itself did not seem to wish to move by itself at that moment. None of the birds did. They all just pecked about and cleaned their feathers lamely.

So Qotle walked toward the alien and the birds, no longer afraid that they may try to harm him. He needed to make her understand. So he took her gently by the forearm and helped her place the heavy crow back down where she had found it. He scrutinized her bucket of a mask trying to see into the eyes of the Being within... and for a moment he swore he had found them; those same eyes staring into his from across the days. "I mean an army." His voice was strong, purposeful... loving. "You know... an *army*. Some bunch of crows will not be enough."

Six

The Grand One stood there with the man named Qotle still holding her forearm in his large, dirty hand. She felt the warmth of it. Different from the warmth of the child's embrace. Different from the touches she had shared with Crow Mother in the gully. There was something else there. Something... she would forget about it. It was not important. She pulled her arm away, but not too harshly. He had been looking so strangely at her. Not like the boys had looked at Blue Flower when she was just a girl back in Tetset. It was different. She pulled her eyes from his, hoping he could not see past the Sun Mask but — she looked off to the crows as he had done a few moments before. They looked stupid, the man was right. A poor army; something they had already proved the night before.

"Then I am at an impasse." No sooner had she said the words out loud than the actions of her brain began ticking and turning. She had a thought — a ghost of a thought — that if only they could go to one of those meeting places — could find other creatures of her world to join her cause — Yes! "You spoke to me of a field of teosintl."

The man had clearly not wanted her to mention it again for though he could not truly know who she was behind her mask, it clearly made him feel a sense of embarrassment to know that he had behaved so poorly. She had to ignore his emotions. They had so little time to make this work... but she also knew how far that field of Tetset was from their current location. They would never get there in time... not without the shuttle... which she had left behind.

"Are there other crops that grow in such fashion nearby? Would you show me where they are?" Her words seemed to sigh relief into Qotle's lungs. He turned and looked off toward the sheer cliff ahead of them. The way they had been walking. The Grand One wondered if she could run it unaware of the extreme change in the landscape to come.

Seven

In Bo'No'To, the sun had cusped the high canyon walls. It blared down senselessly on the Spider Woman's great temple and the extent of the damage from the evening siege was all too clear. Fires burned around the hardening muddied terrain; fires formed from the ashes that had fallen from the blackened tree above. All around, outside and in, carcasses lined the grounds — fentium, crow, and human. Bloody, smashed, and beaten — streaks lined the walls of the once vibrant canyon city. There were still plenty of living fentiums around and they worked intently at those spots that had been hit the hardest trying with a new sense of desperation to clean the mess away and return the place to its former beauty. An impossible task. But the Spider Woman had shown to them the terrible ways in which she could activate their own inner monsters. Where once they had obeyed her will complacently, now they did so with a sense of terror in their hearts. The insects knew now the extent of the Spider Woman's power — that at any moment she could force them into a mindless and bloody rage.

For Silent Wolf, the human presence in that land had been completely extinguished. Still he stood, as he had all that night, within the Spider Woman's personal chamber. The other Being remained captive in that room, strung up torturously, each limb of the creature held fully taught by web-like crystalline appendages that shared a minute but uncanny resemblance to the larger pathways and pillars of the rest of the temple. Silent Wolf had watched as the Spider Woman trapped the beast, pulled those crystals from the very air around them, and fixed the then mushy stuff to the Being's hands before the material could harden. It reminded him of something being trapped within a cobweb, a thought that had always made his skin crawl back in Tetset. So he closed his eyes as she performed a similar task on the Being's feet. When he reopened his eyelids, he could see the pulsing energy moving backward in varying stages of blues — deep and pale — deep and pale — outward from the creature's body and into the walls of the chamber. With each pulse, the alien weakened a little more.

The Spider Woman wore a harsh, wicked grin all that time. She remained at the center of the room watching her captive — playing with it — filled with a terrifying glee Silent Wolf had never seen from her before — the facade fully lifted. He was now a full-time member of her inner circle and apparently she no longer had reason to waste her energy hiding from him.

She spoke to her alien prize, "Where have I seen you before? Oh yes, that despicable little prairie planet. You welcomed me to that world once. You practically forced me to come. You opened the gate to my realm and pulled me to you. Of course, I knew this would happen, I stand in all times. But if I'm being honest, which I promise you I am, I never really wished that day would come. I used to be happy in my realm. It was quiet there, comfortable... Only whispers with my family. I never wished to become this form. But to gain corporeality in another universe, one really must adhere to the rules of that place. You trapped me in this form. Did you know that? Though I must admit, I have grown to enjoy its..." She raised her slender fingers to her eyes and then caressed the cheek of the Being's mask, "... peculiarities. I think my family had grown to like this realm as much as I. That is, until you murdered them all."

Silent Wolf understood this as an oversimplification. But then, the wounded alien began to sing a tense and tormented song... and he... began to see the darkness. Not like the Spider

Woman's visions, it was not someone exerting control over him, it was simply a telling... and for what it was worth, he found he preferred the new form of communication better in that moment. Even though the message was rather bleak.

The core of the alien's world was erupting out in bulbous, volcanic ejaculations. The alien peoples ran in fear. Their eyes shown a truth of that fear to the man and he knew that emotion as he had known it in Tetset. Those creatures were not the offenders, but —

The Spider Woman's caress turned sour. Roughly, she tore the mask from the alien's face and tossed it across the room. The song ended, the alien's breathing became erratic, and Silent Wolf returned to himself... at least, the version of himself the Spider Woman had been making of him.

"Why do you brood so on what is already done beast?" The Spider Woman began again, "We cannot change what is past. You see, you have done as much wrong to me in our time together as I to you. Can we not at least agree that the nature of our relationship is..." Oddly, the Spider Woman leaned in again, rubbing her naked underbelly against one of those crystalline appendages. Silent Wolf wanted to be sick as she rolled her eyes back in a new state of euphoria. The blue energy bled from the prisoner into the appendages and up into the Spider Woman's undercarriage and she shivered and climaxed out the final word in a trembling whisper, "...mutual?"

Silent Wolf left the room preparing himself to wretch over the balcony. After some time, the Spider Woman became aware of his absence.

She felt great pleasure. It had worked. She had caught the one she needed... it was not the girl of this world she had been hoping to sample, the human girl of Tetset who had always appeared such a scrumptious option in her dreams... but it was the one that she was certain would get the job done, a creature of that other world, the proof in history already on her side. She no longer knew why her visions had shown the human girl if she was not ultimately the one that would fill this role. But she was happy nonetheless to receive life-force energy from this Mother of Crows. Unfortunately, just as she reached the height of her joyous success, the Spider Woman felt her general, Silent Wolf, disconnect from her. *Pesky thing.* He never seemed to stay attached to her in the way she hoped. These humans were becoming a more difficult species to control than she had realized.

Silent Wolf had stepped out onto the upper pathways. So, the Spider Woman wiped her gooey excretions from her hands and, with difficulty as she had grown exponentially in those last few moments of conception — her torso greatly widened — her many legs now exposed and similarly fattened to a state of gross morbidity — she shoved her way out across the threshold to join the boy.

"Why do you run from this?" She asked with feigned compassion, "You have seen the destruction brought upon us by that creature. I have shown you as much."

"I..." the human was having trouble speaking. Something had clearly snapped within him, and the Spider Woman no longer knew how to help, "Yes. I have seen it. I still see it now." Silent Wolf was not looking at her, but down upon the mess of corpses accrued amidst the violence of the previous night. The fentiums were doing a terrible job of cleaning it all up.

Still, the Spider Woman wanted to help. To convince the boy rather than force him, "Then why do you reserve yourself? I wish for you to be open with me. To help me decipher that creature's true intentions. We can harness its inner strengths together for the mutual good of our two kinds. There is enough energy within that thing to complete my connection back to the greater communion. To bring them all —"

"Greater Communion?" Silent Wolf interrupted her... he really interrupted her. That made her terribly angry. "I... I'm trying to understand... but..."

He must have been pulled too far in the other direction, she thought, *I will have to force the issue this time.* "Yes." She tried to tell the human, "Have I not shown you that place where my siblings wait for us?"

But Silent Wolf was somehow so lost in his rambling that he was not even listening to her any longer. "You told me it was like your drones..." he yammered on, "that it had no sense of self... no feeling. But that is not what I saw in there."

Damnit! "Ah, I know what that beast exudes may seem some crude form of our own consciousness. But I assure you, it is a trick of the mind." The Spider Woman felt the heat boiling under her skin. *This boy would waste our moment and never know how close we had come to perfection,* "What you witnessed in there is more akin to a reflex than a true, sentient reaction."

"What is the difference?"

Well, she was done with this. "Consciousness." She blurted it out. Then she raised her poorly cleaned palm to the boy's forehead for the last time. A last resort that she had not intended to come upon. It did hurt the Spider Woman to have to do this, but it was clear to her now that the minds of the humans of this world were not fit companions for her ultimate purpose. They could not break free of the concept of empathy. So, she would have to force this one past the foolish emotion.

Nine

Silent Wolf was standing in space. Floating. *How did I get here?* he wondered, the world he once knew a distant memory. That breach in the fabric of reality tore open before him. *Why?* From that tear, thousands of tendrils extended out, reached for him. He grasped it at last, saw the silhouettes from within the place, the other spiders reaching for him... reaching out to take his universe. They sewed their tendrils together, sewed and stitched and reformed themselves as the man that was Silent Wolf. Silent Wolf was the spiders and they were him.

He knew their names then... all of their names: Vicaltorbissus, Sacarrentio, Husceratti, Dongojio, and countless thousands more. He knew them as if he had always known them. Torn between so many different minds, he both loved and hated each of them as if they were at once his own self and that of his bitterest rival.

The one currently living in his universe, the one the boy had known — the Spider Woman — Eccioporte stood before them all, their collective consciousness feeling the fabric of this other universe around them again. They looked to her engorged body with anticipation. Their eyes filled with blue Nexus, the energy of the beasts within them. They were ready to be born.

Their name was Silent Wolf. And this was the day their humanity was taken from them. This would become the day of the spider.

Ten

Crow Mother hung from those heavy appendages, limp and in pain. She could hardly breathe without her mask and she suffered, cried, and choked. Why had she done this to herself? She knew the answer of course. In the moment of action, her decisions had all seemed perfectly logical. Once the crows had given themselves away she had thought it best not to waste the element of surprise that would only have existed for that one night. Of course, in hindsight she understood that 'surprise' meant nothing without good reconnaissance.

She was humiliated, dripping with the excrement from that hideous, evil creature who had raped her of so much of her life force. She choked again and attempted to see her mask across the way. Could she reach for it? Did she have any power left within her to break herself from this bondage? Well, she did have the Grand One. She had left the girl there above the canyon with the shuttle. Perhaps... perhaps she would come for her. The Grand One. Yes. She would rescue her. Crow Mother was certain of it and beneath the terrible duress of her humiliation, the daughter of The People gave herself to the Calm State — a world of the inner mind — of quiet reflective song and meditation. She slowed her breathing, relaxed her pained shoulders, and waited for her opportunity, her own beautiful mask never too far from her thoughts.

Eleven

The Grand One had not expected the path to be so difficult. She remembered the pain in her shoulders as she sprinted toward her destination, sweat spreading across the view plate of her Sun Mask. She had convinced Qotle to deposit the exhausted elders and youngsters of his tribe in a safe annex above the place he referred to as The Fingers. He would show her the way to a cropfield he had known of with as much haste as he could muster. And of course, Shi'Yun had insisted on joining them. The Grand One looked to her left and was pleased to see the younger girl was not holding back their progress, keeping pace the whole way... or just a few steps behind. Actually, Qotle was not particularly far ahead himself. He had a soldier's training, yes, but he was one very weary soldier.

After what was about a three hour marathon with hardly a break to sip at or even collect water from upper Kyun'Bon'On... and a brief (and likely intentional by Qotle) circumvention of an aboveground crater, the three travelers could at last see the strange crop rising from the soil ahead. The Grand One slowed a pace, stopped, finally caught her breath... she was so thirsty. All this way she had only taken a small sip of the drink, and that could only be accomplished when she had known her companions were not looking.

"Excuse me a moment." She said the words sternly as she approached the stuff called pok'yu and tucked her whole body between the cactus-like stalks of the larger plants. There she felt safe to remove her mask and drink a full quarter of the canteen she had been weighing herself down with since they had reached the mouth of the upper river. *What a day.* She wished she could eat and sleep as she wiped her human brow. But she did not have long to enjoy the comfort of her own skin. The crows had been following them. They landed far enough away from the humans, but the Grand One did not wish to see any new disputes between what she could not help but see as separate factions of her nascent coalition.

The Grand One stepped out of the pok'yu with her mask reestablished on her shoulders. She reached for her kopa before anyone could ask her some new, likely unanswerable question. She would simply have to show them all why they had come this way. So, the Grand One played a powerful, winding song that spoke of summoning those that were near, could hear, and understand the message. She played with all the strength of breath she could manage after such a long, restless period.

Qotle and Shi'Yun looked on with a new kind of surprise prevailing over each of their faces. They still could not understand the strange song, but they could sense that the air was changing around them. Yes! Something was coming. Something large that made the great fields of cacti sway and snap behind the Grand One.

From the edge of those fields, those megatherium — the giant ground sloths — emerged. Fifteen giant, bear-like creatures with long snouts that munched on vegetation and huge claws meant for tearing at tree bark and digging holes in hard-packed soil. They stood before the humans and crows, an imposing force even in their minuscule numbers. Together, they opened their mouths and barooed, harmonizing heartily with the Grand One's song.

"You!" They sang. "You speak!"

The voices were so similar to one another that the Grand One at first had trouble picking out which of the group was saying what. Instead, she continued to address the whole herd as simply as she knew how, "Yes. I speak. I need."

One of the megatherium with a rather noticeable cavity in its blackening front tooth stepped up and sang so she could single him out from the group, "We do not know you!"

Another buried deeper within the group tagged on the earlier thought as these creatures would tend to do, "But you speak!"

The Grand One knew that she would have to convince them that she was a friend. She felt fortunate that these massive creatures could understand the words of her song. She set to work.

Twelve

The melody was odd to Qotle, beautiful but unattainable. Quippy, with strange guttural huffs frequently snapping off from various megatherium throughout the herd. He wanted to love the sound. Wanted to be welcomed in, a part of his world in a way he had never before understood a man could be. He could no longer recognize himself or any of his people as gods like the elders used to say... separate from all other beasts. No. He had discovered that he was more akin to the beasts of his world just as all those who came before him had been. His own sister had known this basic fact of life — had told him as much. Why had it taken him so long to grasp it? He knew the answer, of course, but he so desperately wanted to forget about her...

Thirteen

"Why do you speak?" A member of the herd asked.

"I speak because I need." *Keep this tone,* the Grand One thought. *They will trust you if you make it easy to understand... do not make the same mistake as The People... always say the truth.*

The one with the bad tooth barked the most important question, "What do you need?!" He was clearly the leader.

"I need your help to rescue my friend." *To the very heart of the issue. Stay calm.*

"But we do not know you!" The leader reiterated the thought on each of the others' minds.

How to convince them? The Grand One couldn't help but make it into a sort of game for herself. *What will it take? Have I not already done the impossible by calling these megatherium to me?* That was what she would have to gamble with. *Keep it simple. Easy to understand.* "But I speak."

And from the herd independent voices seemed to contemplate the truth of that statement, "She does speak." and "True!" and "She does!"

The leader was working it out diligently in his own mind. He huffed a few times letting his nostrils clear of mucous. He dug at the dirt and he seemed to connect with her assertion on some base level. "Very well! You speak! And you understand!" He came closer to the woman and sniffed at her. "Smelled you before! When the valley cried with fire!"

"I once lived there across the lands where the valley cried." The Grand One had hoped for this, that these creatures might remember something of Tetset and her mad dash through the distant crop... that one of them would be that same gentle creature she had come across the morning after the fires on the far side of the teosintl.

Again, the leader sniffed her, "Perhaps!"

And the herd echoed the thought, "Perhaps!" "Perhaps!"

"Perhaps..." The Grand One felt it, the moment of ascertainment approaching, "You will help?"

"Perhaps we will help!" Sighed the megatherium, "Where do we go?! Who do we fight?!"

The Grand One raised one hand back in the direction of Bo'No'To. For a moment, the eyes of the herd watched only that motion. Silence lingered around the field. As she brought that arm down, she returned her fingers to the kopa and its loose song. "We go to the canyon beyond. We fight the Spider Woman. We save the Crow Mother."

A single voice rang out from the back of the herd, "The Spider Woman?!" There was a period of unease as all the megatherium sniffed around themselves, a desperate appeal being made to their leader, left unspoken. The leader studied the large murder of crows as if he recognized an old friend among them... or was it an enemy?

"For the Crow Mother!" He yowled at last, bereavement in his voice, "Yes! We know these ones you speak of!"

"We fear the Spider Woman!" One of the other sloths blurted out.

"Yes! We fear her!" The leader replied matter-of-factly.

This was it. The Grand One would have to make her firm push at this moment or she might lose them, "Then we must put an end to that fear."

The concept struck an obvious chord. Again, the leader lingered. Those sloths were incredible specimens in their day. Not slow at all as their smaller, tree climbing offspring would ultimately become. But their leader was also not hasty. He would allow his wisdom to process the meaning of the human dressed like an alien's request. He chewed at cud and began at last to truly register what such a victory over fear could mean for his species. "Mmmm..." he intoned more quietly than before, "Perhaps."

The half-huffed whispers began then bouncing around the herd. The Grand One could hear that now too familiar word repeated over and over there, "Perhaps." "Perhaps." She had heard the damn word so many times it was beginning to lose all shape and meaning to her.

"Show us!" The leader shouted over the crowd and then let his voice lower once again, "And perhaps we fight."

"Thank you." What else could she say that would make them a definite rather than a... perhaps? She did not know. Perhaps — she wanted to laugh at the word — she would have to convince them again before they reached Bo'No'To. As it was what it was, she turned from the herd then, hoping she exuded a sense of truth, power, and trust with this direct action. She approached Qotle and Shi'Yun.

"What do they say?" The man asked.

The Grand One knew the odds were not great, but she could will this thing to happen if she continued to play the decisive general, "I believe they will fight." Not quite a lie. She would make it known that she still had concerns, "They are an ornery bunch, but they boast physical strength. Will they be enough?"

"If they can get beyond the turrets," Qotle's gaze became distant, "they would last longer than the crows."

"The turrets?" The Grand One did not know that word.

Something in Qotle's gaze told her that this was something he would rather not discuss, as if it hurt him to do so. Still, she had to know and waited with a patient sternness for his response. "Those two gigantic rigs outside the tower." His voice grew weak then, what was happening to this man? "They shoot massive energy beams... formed from... another..." He stopped speaking. Frozen. Odd eyes.

She would help him along, "Like the beam that struck my shuttle..."

Qotle looked away, but regained enough composure that his words could return, "Yes."

"I see." That was all she was likely to get from the man at that moment, so she pushed on, "We must make haste. I have a plan." Purposefully, she turned and again approached the megatherium herd. They were patient, and their state of calm helped her to silence the overexcited thoughts bouncing around her head. She made a b-line for the leader and placed her palm flat on his great, furry shoulder and scratched there allowing the calm to run her actions. She sang rather than played, "Do you have a name, oh, leader of the sloths?"

He liked the scratches and his tone lightened a bit more, "I am Toothache of the Dried Fields. How shall I call to you?"

"I am the Grand One. That is my name." The Grand One dug deeper, scratching and finding a scabby patch on the great beast's back. He sighed out a relief-filled moan, and she sensed she had found a real friend in him. So, it was worth asking, "Will you allow us to ride you and your kin, Toothache of the Dried Fields? I believe we would get there more quickly on your backs. And our time is short."

"Ride?!" The idea stirred something primal in the megatherium and he raised his head sharply as if to buck. But the Grand One found another patch a little farther down and scratched more vigorously. And Toothache succumbed, his tongue plopping happily out the side of his mouth, "If you must!"

She whispered the lolling tone into his ear, "Thank you, my friend."

Without removing her scratching hand from the megatherium's backside, the Grand One waved the other two humans over to join her. They were of course reticent, but they came all the same. The Grand One found a balance-able spot on Toothache's shoulders and pulled herself up mounting the giant ground sloth's upper spine where she could hug his neck if he turned out to be a particularly wild ride.

Shi'Yun apparently loved this idea now that she had seen it done. She wasted no time picking out another, smaller sloth in the herd, greeting it with a goofy hand wave, and leaping up to the same mounting place that the Grand One had found. Qotle, unfortunately, had a more difficult time with his riding partner. His sloth, the Grand One realized, had been the one in the back of the pack which had been most vocal in its fear of the Spider. Together, they struggled to get comfortable with one another. At first, he tried to mount it as the others had so easily done, but the weight distribution was wrong and the creature behaved as if burdened by his presence there so close to its head. So, Qotle pushed himself back and nearly lost his balance. The two were embarrassed, but no one said anything outside of a few under breath giggles.

Toothache yowled again so all, even the crows, could hear, "We will need more than just this group if we wish to defeat the Spider! We will get others!"

"Others?" The Grand One spoke this last word so the humans could understand. And the herd of megatherium took off at a dash in a new direction to round up... well the Grand One did not yet know who else they would round up. But for the first time in the last few days, she felt like someone had finally given her good news. She would welcome this with gratitude.

They rode across the dry lands recrossing Kyun'Bon'On and passing the Fingers. The megatherium were very quick when they wanted to be and rather adept swimmers as well. When they pulled themselves from the water onto the northern bank, they did not take time to shake themselves of the soak. The humans all relished the cool dampness after a day of high sun. The monsoon clouds had passed them the night before and a new nimbus had yet to form.

As the megatherium herd stampeded across the northern landscape, the Grand One began to glimpse something else moving... tumbling in the distance. Great creatures wrestled in the dirt up ahead. She had heard stories of those beasts from Mother Tree some years ago, she realized. But she had been made to think them extinct since the ices thawed. Yet, clear as day, there they were. The glyptodons; the giant, shelled armadillos of old. Wrestling one another into submission, those glyptodons — perhaps twenty of them in all — did not notice the incoming megatherium until the herd was almost upon them.

Toothache shouted in his strongest of voices, "Brothers! Join us! We go to fight the Spider Woman!"

The glyptodons did not take even a moment of deliberation to form up ranks alongside the great sloths. It was written on their bodies, the armadillos' purpose to shield and protect. To defend themselves and their world. And it occurred to the Grand One how glorious her Orotti had been to provide other beings with such a powerful, natural purpose.

She leaned in toward Toothache's big ear and sang, "Thank you for this my friend." Toothache merely grunted his approval and the Grand One raised her eyes up to see her crow friends scuttling along against the winds. She had three species by her side and she wondered if they would be enough. They would have to be, for Crow Mother's time was running out and this was all the army they would be able to put together on such short notice. So be it. This scrappy band would make up the body of the Grand One's Army.

Fifteen

Arriving at the upper crest of the canyon, the Grand One's Army yielded before the Fingers of All. They stayed there staring across and down at the lengthy, wide path only made available to them by a fortuitous end to the rains and an unusually scorching star above. The Grand One wondered if they could trust this path that Qotle had only mentioned in passing over the night. Surely the glyptodons could not climb as she had been forced to do earlier that morning.

"Why do we stop here?" Toothache huffed at the girl.

"This is where we must convene." The Grand One sang back to him sweetly, "I have been to the Temple of the Spider Woman and I do not believe it wise to simply rush in headlong." The sloth appreciated her candor and so it was time. "Let us turn and address our army, Toothache." Together, they about-faced, the Grand One not ready yet to descend her steed. She would have begun her new song to the army then and there, but... Qotle was dismounting his reluctant megatherium. He approached Shi'Yun and helped her down as well whispering something to the little girl. The Grand One had been under the assumption the two humans would be joining them in their march against the Spider. Qotle clearly had different plans.

Sixteen

"This is where we leave you." Qotle felt odd as he spoke those words to the alien. He was torn. One side of him had vowed to never see the Spider Woman's terrible face again. However, he had just been through the darkest of tunnels and come out the other side. He had awoken and in this last, most eye opening of days, he had realized several unavoidable truths about his world. A part of him wanted to be stronger for these gathered creatures who had proven themselves sentient, had borne him and Shi'Yun safely across the harshest of lands. Part of him wanted to be stronger for this, the Grand One, who had helped him when he had not deserved her help. And part of him wanted to be strong for Shi'Yun, but that is where the reality of his predicament settled in. To be strong for Shi'Yun did not mean fighting in a war. It meant surviving to help her so she may grow old and wise someday. He loved his sister. She had to be his priority even as his heart had begun to lean on the alien like a needy child. Qotle wanted to cry out that his heart was pulled like a wishbone. His new sobriety stirred in him more than he had bargained for.

"You would not fight beside us?" The Grand One asked him, "Restore humanity's good name?"

That struck him hard, "Up until last night, the Spider Woman cared for us, gave us shelter and purpose." Qotle's mind was not on the Spider Woman as he said that. It was on the Grand One wholly. How to convince her that this... what should so obviously have fallen to him... that the burden of this war could not be his. The words began to taste bitter in his mouth as he addressed the lie head on, "I would not have considered myself her enemy. But for the truths I have only now begun to understand."

The Grand One was angry with him then, "Would you consider me your enemy?"

Again her words wounded him. He was developing something that felt like love for her. Wished to make her proud... Instead, Qotle became defensive, "I would not have ventured this far with you..." And he faltered. "I... I believe I owe you a great debt, whether you would admit it or not." He tried to search the Sun Mask for the eyes he had spotted there previously, "I recently wronged someone... My entire tribe was in the wrong actually. We did irreparable harm to a peaceful people in search of..." His mind nearly locked up again, but perhaps this was how he could be strong, by fighting back the shield the Spider had layered across his memories. He blurted out the rest of the thought, "... two children the Spider Woman believed to be of particular importance. We brought one back. He was... controlled by the spider as I had been. As for the girl..." He had to say it again even if she would not hear him, "I believe you are her — that same girl I found in the teosintl. I believe you are human." There. He said it.

"I am a being of the skies." The Grand One spoke the words like some great oratory, as if she had rehearsed them over and over again. They were too clear. Too precise.

Qotle wished to rouse her, to make her slip, "Yet you wear human hands on the ends of your human arms." He snapped, "Your legs stand vertical as mine do. And you speak with words I can understand. If you are of the skies, I have never before laid eyes on such a being as you."

The Grand One took a moment. She scratched at a spot on her sloth's head beneath her. Such a strong connection they already shared. Then she spoke and Qotle knew before the first word of this that she had already won, "If you believe that I am this... woman," she said it far too calmly, "if you believe you owe this debt..." and Qotle felt the dagger twist, the absurdity of it all, "why would you attempt to leave me in my hour of need?"

"I..." but Qotle could not. He had to go. But he could not. He gazed backward in the direction of Shi'Yun. He remembered how important his sister was to him. He took that breath. When was the last time he had really allowed himself to breathe? Felt the air expand into his lungs? "My sister is young. She cannot fight in a war. She will not survive this next stage without a guide."

Then something changed in the Grand One. "No." She agreed with him. She was a generous host. She listened. Was willing to listen. And she understood.

Qotle felt it in his throat that just as his victory had been assured, in that moment he did not want it anymore. He did not wish to let this alien girl who had rescued him and his sister down. So out of that new sense of obligation, he reversed his words, "I cannot speak for the few other humans remaining from my tribe, but should you demand it, I would fight for you."

The Grand One lowered her head at that. An action the Spider Woman would never have taken, "I do not demand," she said. And then, as if reading his mind, "I am not the Spider Woman."

With that, as the girl in the field had freed him physically from the Spider Woman's grasp, this alien on sloth's back freed the last dregs of his mind from Eccioporte's manipulation. He gasped. He could remember the Spider Woman's true name... he could remember everything and the words came out freely like white water through a broken dam, "Then let me tell you a secret before I go."

The man said so many things of importance in such a short span of time, the Grand One felt as if she were back in the gully with the Jomony and The People. All these things Qotle had known, had kept buried within him. She understood then that he was trusting her with his entire being. She watched his mouth move, his tongue snap the thoughts out word after word after word — and she, understanding them all as if she had always known them... the origins of the crystalline pathways she had only ever seen for the first time the night before.

Morning Singer had already explained a great deal about the Nexus, so the principles that guided their tangible, physical threads of linear data were simple concepts for the Grand One to digest. What worried her, however, was the nature Qotle described as inherent in those turrets. They harnessed that same eerily beautiful energy of the Nexus and manipulated it into something awful, an eruption of those same communication receptors outward creating a brutal, precise nothingness — the inverse of thought; emptiness; destruction.

Qotle's voice returned after a moment, he had never actually stopped talking during that time, only the Grand One had been lost in the minutia of the moment forgetting that he was in fact a human speaking human words. She had become so used to the songs of the non-humans.

"Eccioporte chose this canyon because it housed a natural opening to the void of the Realm of the Spider. She knew what could be birthed here. The energy of this place need only be combined with a few key ingredients and she would have the means to reach across realities, manipulate the matter of this 'verse, and bring forth others from her race to join her here on this world. If these others seek to harvest life in the way she has, I now believe our entire planet would be at risk."

The Grand One remembered the spiders from Morning Singer's song. *But how did they come? Could they really come again?* The Grand One did not truly wish for war. She had known this definitively in her bones. But what if things had already progressed beyond a simple rescue mission. Indeed, her hands were forced. And in pressing the issue with The People, in once so badly wanting bloody revenge for Tetset, she herself had done the forcing.

She remembered a strange poem Chief Tetset had once spoken when he thought no one was listening.

Oh to lead,
Oh to lead and to be lost.

She had to ask, "You say the right key ingredients could align to make this happen. What are they?"

Qotle's eyes were so clear then. It was like a shroud had been lifted from his memories and now he could fully recall his time spent under Eccioporte's spell. He impressed the words upon her, "Two she already has in her possession. First is the structure she has built at the end of the canyon. Hen'Bon'On has been calling this the Temple, but it is really a massive power generator. Second, a lovelorn, sentient male of this universe who has been bonded to another creature of this realm through a mutual tragedy. This boy will be the vehicle through which she can awaken the combined consciousness of her family. She already has him..." The man was ashamed then, "I delivered him to Eccioporte myself and he has already begun to walk the path of attainment as I now walk the path of freedom... for which I believe I have you to thank..." He blushed. She blushed too, though he could not see it. "I apologize for my role in this particular matter as I apologize for my many other crimes."

"Noted." She felt embarrassed, but what else was she supposed to say when he treated her now with such reverence. "What is the third ingredient?"

"Have you not guessed?"

No. She had not. "Say it so I have been told."

"Third is a girl... I should refer to her as a woman..." He was not actually awkward here, though it could have been a fumble. It was an attempt at respect that made him change his wording, "one whose heart rages with vengeance for the suffering of her entire world." Check, check, and... was he talking about her? "She is the ovum, the birther by whose life-force Eccioporte will be able to manipulate the matter of this 'verse. The Spider Woman's womb will yield such power as can reap a whole new age upon this world... she can create... and her creations can destroy. When I came for that tribe — Tetset — I sought the woman — the ovum — as my most important target. By comparison, the boy was a pittance. At one time, even I could have played that role." Qotle shook his head realizing just how close he had come to being the greatest traitor his world had ever known. The Grand One watched that regret again pass to a solemn joy as the man pressed to speak further, "But to my elation, you... I mean... the woman eluded me that night in the teosintl. Though I now fear what will come to pass should you, the Grand One, return to that temple."

"I see." The Grand One's mind raced through his words. What he had said to her just then was certainly disconcerting. And something in his explanation of that third ingredient left a vacant hole in her heart. Crow Mother had been captured. Crow Mother was a woman of this universe. Crow Mother had wished for vengeance after the destruction of Eratta. She was at least as ideal a fit for the role so defined as the Grand One had been. "Could a Being from another world fill this role of ovum?"

A shadow crossed Qotle's eye. He nodded. "So long as she is born of the matter of the stars of this universe."

At first, the Grand One was angry after the buffoonery of her friend. Then she wanted to cry, for she had equally instigated this new threat with her own hubris. But she could not linger in self-abasement for long. The threat itself was far too imminent. "I shall consider what you have told me, Qotle. Thank you and I wish your family, little as it may be, a safe journey wherever you feel you must go."

"I..." a lump caught in Qotle's throat. Clearly it pained the man to leave her side, "I hope you win." He turned away, collected Shi'Yun who had been petting her megatherium friends, and together the two of them walked off toward the place in the Fingers where the other few remaining members of clan Hen'Bon'On had been left.

Eighteen

The Grand One watched them go. A part of her wished she could also take that path and walk away with them into the peace of a different life. But this was to be her lot and she would rise to meet the moment. She turned back to the crowd of animals, raised her kopa to her mask, and blasted out a song of preparation: "We will break off into factions!"

As if anticipating this order, the glyptodons formed up two ranks — one on either side of the megatherium. The crows fluttered into a saluting position at the front. That left the megatherium to separate into three neat rows of four and five — Toothache still bore the Grand One on his shoulders, so did not yet join the middle row.

The Grand One's song continued, "I do not expect we will surprise them this time! Heed the turrets at the mouth of Bo'No'To! They can reach us from a great distance! Drones will be many! Heed their numbers, heed their bite! Should you find yourself facing panic, hear me now and know as I now know, we do not only fight to rescue the Mother of Crows... We fight for the fate of this entire world!" The Grand One's Army exploded in shouts of praise and adoration. She had thoroughly riled them up. Now she would aim them at their target. "Forward! We march!"

PART VI - THREE FEASTS

One

The Grand One's Army traversed the wider path of the canyon in single file formation. She and Toothache led the long line, the anticipation of the ensuing fight filling the woman's mind completely. That is, until Toothache decided to whisper up at her in wonder.

"That human," he huffed, "seemed to pine for you. I imagine he would have had you journey with him instead of leading us to war."

She heard this, thought on the megatherium's intimations — wondered if she hadn't made another mistake. She had made the wrong choice for the right reasons... or rather had made the wrong choice for herself, for the woman she had become. But you cannot escape your past, even if you have become a different person. She had to do the right thing for her world... for her friends... because she had already done the wrong thing once before. She had to clean up the mess she had helped to make. That man had little bearing in her decision. He could not. She had made him free whilst trapping herself in this web. Her role in this matter, she knew, would be central. She did not know what would happen, if she or any of the creatures she had gathered would survive. But she did know she had to be there... owed it to them all... owed it to the megatherium and the glyptodons... Owed it to The People and the Jomony... to Tetset... to Mother Tree... to Crow Mother... She owed it to herself... to the girl she had once been... Blue Flower... to see it through. And that man named Qotle could not take precedence.

"Yes." She merely whispered it to Toothache, "I imagine so."

The air of the canyon changed then. They had dropped in altitude and her ears popped leaving her with a moment of clarity. Her body felt clearer, fitter than it ever had before. The ache within her muscles was a welcome old friend. The tedium within her bloodshot, sleepless eyes broke before her. And on the wind, she heard the sound of a distant song, melancholy, sung with purpose from one she cared for. She really did hear it in the echoes of the canyon. It did not make her cry. It helped her to steel her heart, to know that Crow Mother was still alive.

Two

Crow Mother knew she would die soon. Too much time had passed since her mask had been removed from her head. The strange mineral compounds of Orotti's atmosphere would soon build up within her lungs and fully suffocate her. The Calm State could only help her survive like this for so long and that time was nearly passed. She heaved her breath all of a sudden and spat out a choked patch of blood. She had been so focused on her ability to breathe in this atmosphere, she had nearly forgotten about the pain from the spear wound in her shoulder. It had missed her vitals, but just as time ticked away on her ability to breathe, so too did it tick on the blood that occasionally dribbled from that hole... and what presently came from her beak.

She decided with that sense of clarity that it was at last time to sing her death song. It was hollow, but precise. And it was sung loudly enough as to permeate the air of the temple, of Bo'No'To, and of the canyon paths beyond.

"Blue Flower," she sang, briefly forgetting her friend's newly taken name in her senility, "I am sorry I did not trust you. Where do you reside now? Have you forgotten me so quickly? Do you abandon me to this fate?" She changed the rhythm suddenly. It was not good to die on the note of feeling sorry for herself and she knew she had not been betrayed in truth, "No, I cannot blame you for my own folly. You would have fought beside me had I given you the choice. I am sorry, Blue Flower. I am sorry, friend."

Three

Their name was not Silent Wolf. Their name was Vicaltorbissus. Their name was Sacarrentio. Their name was not Eccioporte. They did not know why she had brought them here again, to this awkward 'verse of solidity and bad memories. They stood here in this odd body that had been naturally formed of this world, the boy depressed back behind the distant wall of their collective mind. They wanted to tap into the pathways, but the matter of this place would not let them.

Why has she brought us here again? Vicaltorbissus asked the others from within the confined mind. Husceratti laughed heartily at the question, the body of the human laughing along with them.

Sacarrentio was annoyed. They said so. Said, "She is a fool in this state. She cannot learn her lesson until she has returned to the Realm of the Spider."

Dongojio, overcome with the strange emotions of this universe, spat out from the same mouth, "She will not know the error she has made until she is returned."

Vicaltorbissus breathed deeply through the human body they had been forced to inhabit. He wanted to bite Eccioporte's head off... wanted to slowly feast on her entrails. She was no leader of theirs and this had proven to be no worthy home to their species. This was a prison of war for them and they would find a way out even if it meant killing them all once again. Such a death was nothing to Vicaltorbissus. They had returned to the Realm of the Spider the last time Eccioporte had called them to this verse. They had come willingly that time. This was different. They had seen what she had considered paradise. And they greatly disagreed. They even went so far as to consider a forced abdication.

The others had been following Vicaltorbissus' train of thought for that last stretch. That is, until the Mother of Crows' song cut through the spacious air of the region. They heard that one's song. Remembered the sound of her voice, of others like hers. A war not worth fighting the first time on that other distant world. Yet here they were being asked to fight it once again. *It must be stopped this time. The pain is not worth the struggle.*

Then their attention was turned once again — piqued by a new sound. Something much louder. A song of war! It was coming from the canyon beyond and several fentiums rushed by in a flurry, fully under Eccioporte's command. They wanted to laugh, but this time, as they approached the nearest window of the tower, they found they did not have the heart to crack jokes. She had awoken them in this human body... directly in the heart of the next terrible onslaught.

Dust rose from the mouth of the canyon. The battle of this place had already begun. And they collectively felt that stupid emotion toward Eccioporte that was intrinsic to this universe alone... the one they understood to be called anger as they tapped into the human's memories to help translate the feeling.

Four

Yes! Yes! It is time! The Spider Woman watched the canyon road through the waiting eyes of her fentium hoard. She had the insects line up in legions preparing them for blood. And she ramped up their aggression once again making the fentiums' eyes burst with a crimson complexion. She wanted them fearsome and rabid for what came next.

Oh yes, go to the turrets. She thought it sending two of the fentiums to arm the large guns. Those two would die in her service without ever becoming a part of her physically. She regretted that. But it was necessary to use the weapons as they had been constructed. This she had seen in her visions even though much of the rest was difficult to unravel after the birthing was to be complete. She needed the fentiums to keep the forces of this world out of the mirror room until that time had passed. For that is where she sat now, filling her body with the masses of the bodies of the dead, transforming that mass through the energy she had sapped from the Mother of Crows. *Yes! The time is near, so very near.*

Five

Vicaltorbissus took Silent Wolf's body down the physical pathways of the temple rounding floor after floor until at last they reached the main hall at the bottom. From there, they sensed after Eccioporte. She was in the sacred space. They knew it immediately. They would go there to meet with her. To voice their complaints against her.

Within the mirror room they found her feasting, a strange juxtaposition between the serenity of those waters — so like the Realm of the Spider — and the violence of her mandibles chewing through the flesh of the dead. She had become a massive creature and they could see the bumps moving around within her abdomen and throughout her inflated backside. The process had already begun. They knew it completely as they knew this feeble body would not be strong enough to take her. They would have to wait the birthing out until the first separations occurred. And then... well they would have to decide what to do with Eccioporte when their minds were oscillated again.

"They are upon us." The voice of the human felt odd to them, but it was the one they had been given and in their new emotional state they would use it.

Eccioporte didn't wait to finish chewing, "Yes. I feel them." She spat flecks of insect flesh out as she spoke the words. A terrible smile on her face. She gestured oddly with her arms forming a floating, wispy image of Silent Wolf — the boy they occupied — out of the water. The face of the human rose up to fill the empty face on the mural set beyond the gelatinous waterfall. She was still trying to convince the human they were wearing that she was somehow looking after his interests as well. Many of them wanted to break out in laughter, for the woman was clearly demented. She did not at this moment seem to comprehend who it was she was actually speaking with... who she had already summoned to this form. Vicaltorbissus quashed the sound that nearly rose up from within them. The 'Haw Haw Haw!' Instead, he smiled forcefully, allowing her — if she so wanted — to plainly see the malice they now bore her.

They left that room. Walked the length of the main hall to the front doors of the temple. There the fentiums lingered, hate upon their brows. Vicaltorbissus raised their arm knowing the role they were being asked to play.

From the canyon mouth, the dust began to clear revealing the army of this world; sloth and armadillo and crow and... and one more of them... those creatures from the other place that had forced them back the last time. Sacarrentio still bore an uncharacteristic distaste for those ones and said so so all their minds could sense it and agree or disagree. Torn between eliminating Eccioporte and getting revenge on the creatures of this universe, most of them agreed with Sacarrentio. So Vicaltobissus gave the signal, swiping their human hand down in the violent motion of the general.

The two fentiums prepped their respective turrets, aimed, and fired those strange beams burning their own bodies away in the process — the anti-Nexus always required a sacrifice in order to be utilized. In synchrony, the lights smashed against the opposing walls of the canyon blasting rock and rubble down over the incoming forces. Sacarrentio relished the opportunity to see that masked one out front disappear beneath the mess. Again the others agreed. And that loud song of war the opposing force had been singing to the wind was ended, the new made dust pluming forward covering Vicaltorbissus and the fentiums in a shroud of silence.

Six

The Grand One had expected this. She did not allow the animals to hear her cough and thankfully her sun mask shielded her from the worst of the dust. Regardless, she had not been crushed by the falling stones which meant at least some of the glyptodons had managed to get into position in time. This recognition calmed her heart. She was the Grand One. They followed her believing in her message. And the first stage of her plan had worked, had kept them alive for at least another moment.

Her lips parted. She began to whisper a chanting song, "Fly crows. Fly on your feathers. For it is your turn now."

The crows rushed in through the pluming air and struck out at the blinded fentiums they found within, striking an early and critical blow before the dust cloud had a chance to settle and reveal the true numbers of the Grand One's Army. But the crows could not find their first targets — the fentiums that manned the turrets. Those two were already gone. How odd. The report came back to the Grand One via a scouting crow and she did not know what to make of it. But the dust was at last settling. She would have to worry about that later... if there was a later.

The air was still. At the mouth of the canyon, the glyptodons formed up two rows holding the large stones that had collapsed from the walls on their spiky shells. The Grand One could see that none of her team had been harmed in the explosion and she was proud. Toothache gave her a sideways look knowing the moment was upon them all.

This was the time. And the Grand One said so, "Now!"

Vicaltorbissus watched with a sense of collective foreboding. Among their many minds some recognized this possible branch of the timeline and they barked their frustrations up through the ranks of their mind. *Eccioporte has placed us in this of all timelines. That manipulative Bitch!*

They turned around and walked back through the doorway saying, "Inside! Inside!" Though the fentiums posted there did not follow.

Vicaltorbissus walked calmly through the rows and rows of fentiums that waited within the main hall of the temple. They did not look back as they said, "Bar the door."

Some fentiums managed to get the large door shut just before a group of crows could make their way inside. Those same insects lifted the large securing pillar there and propped it up in its slot so the door would be even more difficult to breach.

But Vicaltorbissus could hear from those of his family that remembered this time branch that it would not be enough. The door would fall. They would come in short order. Vicaltorbissus asked them if this timeline had any other possible branch they might be able to leap onto instead. Those that remembered did not know. Dongojio would look into the matter... perhaps there was a way... a way they could keep their new bodies once they arrived. Vicaltorbissus did not think they would want that, but some of the others were already beginning to change their minds; hoping to see Eccioporte's plan through to universal dominance though they knew neither side could win this struggle. Madness had taken their minds.

Several crows were flying in through the open windows in the heights above. *They have done this before* — Husceratti informed them. So the boy's body climbed the pathways to meet those birds, to stop them if it could. Now that the spiders had started to split their votes, one way or another the new bodies would have to be born.

Eight

The megatherium galloped forth to meet those fentiums still standing in the yard after the crows' assault. They trampled over the insects, a pain filled crunching sound reverberating from the red eyed things under the massive weight of the sloths. They were already winning.

Toothache had just rushed several of the fentiums planting them firmly into the muddy pool that had lingered by the main steps of the tower. The Grand One had a front row seat for that charge. She tried to shake off the terrible feeling that all of this violence had been made real by something that was meant to be beautiful and full of peace; a song — the manipulation of something pure and gentle. She imagined that she was no better than Eccioporte for this manipulation.

As she looked away, she instantly regretted the place she took her eyes to. Several insects had managed to swarm one of the smaller megatherium and were forcing it down screaming. But some of the glyptodons had removed the shrapnel of boulders from their backsides. They reinforced the sloths, two of them goring away at the mound of fentiums covering that littlest one. It was free and fighting again and the Grand One sighed her relief. Clearly, this leg of the battle was on the side of her army. Though she wondered what lay in wait for them behind the great door before her.

She dismounted Toothache as the path up the steps cleared. Nudging at the entry, she felt the weight behind it. So she pushed harder. It would not budge. "They have barred it," she sang back to Toothache.

The ground sloth approached her and huffed, "I will try!" He rose up on his hind legs and slammed the full weight of his upper body against the door, but again it would not give.

The Grand One looked out across the battlefield behind her. Sloths and armadillos cut into and trampled the remaining hoards of insects... insects who had begun piling up on each other now, lumps of dead and dying things. Again she shook the image away trying not to see in her mind's eye the mounds of broken corpses of Tetset. She returned her mind to the task at hand, "We need more pressure Toothache." She sang that thought as she reached down and pulled the kopa to her mask to play a louder song of summoning.

Several megatherium turned at that new sound leaving their piles of defeated fentiums behind them. They ran to the player of the song — to their leader.

Nine

As Vicaltorbissus ran the pathways of the temple, they smacked crows down from the air, their human hands bruising, bloodying with both the boy Silent Wolf's body liquid and that of the injured or dying birds in their way. They heard a new song play below, more like the song from the canyon than the one from the chamber. *Have the enemy forces breached the main hall?* They stopped in place looking down to see the door, but it was still firmly shut. They still had time.

A particularly annoying crow came at them then tearing a layer of flesh away from the boy's upper cheek. This pain was not worth their time in this body. They reached out at the large bird and, feeling its beak attempting to bloody them further, they broke the thing's neck. It collapsed to the pathway floor, wings squirming for a moment longer before it finally succumbed to its obvious death. "It was not an important lifeform," Sacarrentio spoke through them coldly. But Vicaltorbissus was not so certain. They turned from the dead thing and continued their journey up through the heights.

Eventually they would reach Eccioporte's personal chamber where the prisoner was being held. They knew they must hurry to that place as the majority of crows were evidently moving through that room freely now, coming and going as they pleased. A quiet, moaning song was within earshot at this point. The prisoner had apparently not stopped singing its death tune in all this time, it had simply been drowned out by the much louder events outside. Vicaltorbissus pushed through to the chamber.

Inside, the crows were crazed, smacking their beaks into the imprisoning pillars holding the alien in place. Then they noticed Silent Wolf's body standing there in the doorway. The human form collected its spear, which had been propped up against the wall just outside of the room. And Vicaltorbissus spoke the message they all wanted to speak, knowing begrudgingly that they did not have the capacity within this limited body to translate it into the alien's musical language, "Your friends are here. They think they are winning, but it will not be enough." It was the message Dongojio had formulated in the hopes of leaping them to another branch of the timeline. If they could connect their minds to this beast as Eccioporte had done on that other world, if they could make it hear them, break through that language barrier, remove the last vestiges of hope from the thing's subconscious, dying mind... Some of the lower voices within them had begun declaring that they were overthinking this.

All we need do is kill the prisoner, Husceratti assured them in that moment.

But its energy has not been pulled in full, Dongojio argued back.

Frustration reigned! They were not in agreement... and one of those crows had not stopped smacking against the pillar holding the alien's left arm tethered. Sacarrentio took control of the body without Vicaltorbissus' approval and swatted the bird away with the boy's spear. Then Sacarrentio pulled the whole human body forth, mockingly close to the prisoner's bowing head. Sacarrentio was out of line and Vicaltorbissus tried to tell them so. But the moment was upon them, the moment they had meant to avoid. The alien's song became louder, not just because of their proximity, it had heartened, it remembered its power, it morphed its sad song into the one of war, the one sung by the animal forces invading from outside. Tiny cracks formed across the left-hand pillar like ice preparing to shatter. But Sacarrentio was not paying attention. Sacarrentio was angry and manipulated every facet of the body against the complaints of all the others within. Sacarrentio spoke only for Sacarrentio, "Why do you insist on singing? You have no words, your sounds are meaningless, like a bird lost in an empty ramble."

The alien's song became even louder then. Vicaltorbissus saw what was coming, but Sacarrentio would not let them in. The world fell into blackness. What was this place? Surely they still stood within that chamber at the top of the tower, yet this felt more like the Realm of the Spider... until the message came through. Unlike what they had seen in their spider forms with their superior mental faculties. *Damn this human body! Damn Eccioporte! Damn this Mother of Crows!* They all watched. They could not say anything while they were in this. They had lost control of the body. It was slipping from them, the boy somehow taking it back. The boy trying to understand the alien's message. The boy confused, angered.

Vicaltorbissus forced Sacarrentio aside at last and regained control over the human. This was becoming far too difficult. In the Realm of the Spider this would never have happened. They did not squabble so pettily in that place. They were free there, not made so foolish by all of this matter. But as Vicaltorbissus thought these things, Husceratti took control of them instead. *This is mutiny!* Husceratti raised the spear without the consent of the others. Why were they all so willing to break ranks and take these matters into their own hands? Vicaltorbissus had listened. Vicaltorbissus had done what the majority had asked. But the majority could not hold sway so long as so many others among them harbored such ill will.

Ten

Crow Mother had done it! She was certain she had broken through. The human stood prone holding the spear above her, but his face seemed to say that something else was going on within that head. He was openly arguing with himself and the crows had given her a chance she had almost believed would not come. The Calm State had gotten her this far. She would use her breath again even if it meant choking to death. Crow Mother put all of her weight into her left arm sending the imprisoning appendage shattering across the room. She reached her arm out and grabbed the boy, Silent Wolf, by the throat. He struggled, his own breath quickly running out. *This is how it feels,* she thought with malice in her heart but she had to get through to the human within him — to make him one like the Awoken violence would be required. She met the boy's eyes. He looked terrified by the sudden shift in power. She raised her voice even higher and sang that song again putting all her strength behind it.

She showed him the darkness. She showed him the turret beam shooting. She showed him the shuttle holding Tetset prone in the air. She showed the turret beam shoot, shoot, shoot. Smack into the shuttle. Her, powerless to save the falling tribe. She showed him her desire to save —

Something struck Crow Mother in the face. When had those fentiums arrived? Why didn't Crow Mother's friends stop them before... Her head sagged again as she began to lose consciousness. She had put everything she had left into waking that boy to the truth. Had it worked? Had he —? She caught his eyes as the insects dragged him from the room. He was in shock, utterly defeated. She hoped — she wondered if it would be enough. Then, Crow Mother succumbed to the darkness.

Eleven

Back at the locked doorway to the temple, four of the megatherium had come forth to help. They slapped their weight against the surface until the frame began to buckle. When they struck again, the bracing log split and the door collapsed into the main hall careening a ways across the smooth mica floor and smashing into the crowd of onlooking fentiums waiting inside.

The Grand One stepped within singing, "Thank you," to the sloths who followed her. They immediately went to work on the stunned insect crowd. The fentiums could not hold up against the Grand One's Army, their dense numbers dwindling exponentially with each passing attack. So the Grand One was afforded enough time to raise her gaze to the pathways without the fear of an insect reaching out to take her. A single crow buzzed about with a hurt wing up there. Where were the rest?

"Where are they keeping her?" She played up to the crippled bird.

It was out of breath. Yet it was pleased to see she had made her way into the inner structure, so it clumsily flew down to meet her.

"The top of the tower!" The bird's guttural cry was weak but concise. She was grateful for this one.

Turning toward the ramping pathways, the Grand One stoned herself for the presumable gauntlet to the top. But as she approached in the hopes of ascension, something peculiar froze her in her tracks.

Behind her, there was another small, stone-slab door beneath two huge, plunging stalactites jutting through the upper wall. Strange energy was flowing down those formations and the door itself had begun to pulse outward at her. Odd since it was made of such firm material. “What is—?” She wanted to ask the question, but the opportunity had already passed her by. The door exploded.

Twelve

From within the broken mind of Silent Wolf, the spiders were drained — reaching out to their yet unfinished forms within the womb of Eccioporte but unable to connect. They desired to kill her, to rend her flesh into ribbons and overtake command of the war.

Vicaltorbissus disagreed. They argued as one by one the other spiders tried to link their threads to the tower's center. They wanted to keep the other spiders from doing more harm than good. Without Eccioporte, Vicaltorbissus could not see a way to win. Without true leadership, the corporeal spiders would descend into petty quarrels... but that's what they had already been doing. Vicaltorbissus had been stripped of command. Was become as useless as — the boy had felt. Vicaltorbissus was connecting to the boy, Silent Wolf's, emotional center rather than linking back to the tower. They wondered if this was the right path for them.

But then the others were slipping away. Siphoning out from the defeated form. Vicaltorbissus should let go. Should join them to stop them from making the mistake. No. The mistake would be made. Vicaltorbissus could see it clearly from within the boy's mind. Eccioporte had gifted him her own future sight in the transference. She was blind to what would come next. *It's for the best she does not see*, Vicaltorbissus thought. Though none their kin remained any longer to listen.

Thirteen

The Spider Woman was ready to give birth at last. One by one the new bodies meant for her siblings slipped from her womb onto the wetted floors of the mirror room. Hybrid forms of spidery legs and teeth and eyeballs that could live in this realm. Black and furry and made to grow so they could one day take on a similar form to the one Eccioporte now wore. They were just mindless husks, but soon she would pull the collected consciousnesses of her brothers and sisters from the body of Silent Wolf. Soon her siblings would live again in all their glory as they had on that world. *Yes! Come my family!* She thought. *Join me here again! There is much work still to be done!* And she felt their presence. She felt their minds reaching out through the temple's pathway — reaching for those new bodies. She felt them coming back to life all around her, filling those tiny spiders that would grow and grow and own this universe.

Sacarrentio came. She could feel that one's presence, so filled with passion. And Husceratti. And more and more of them filled the vacant forms seeping through the fabric of the temple she had built for them. Reaching out for her mind. Reaching out for her spent body. Crawling toward her... Birthing was never an easy task. But this time they were touching her. Grabbing her. Biting at her flesh.

And for the first time since their deaths in that awful pocket of space, she realized her siblings were angry with her. Had she so wronged them? There was a pain in her arm... No! Her arm had been torn from her. They were eating it, all of her little children. *You must stop this foolishness! Give it back!* She wanted to say it, but for some reason she could not speak. Several of the children were on top of her, crushing her windpipe.

Where was Vicaltorbissus? They would listen to Vicaltorbissus. But that one had not left Silent Wolf's body. Why had they stayed inside of the human? Why had they not come with the others?

The little children were slipping through the openings behind her eyes. Feasting on the pathways within her head. Her skull collapsed in then, a pain she had never imagined possible. She had not foreseen this moment. The birthing had always been foggy to her, but... she never thought...

Her consciousness disintegrated. She fell back through the Nexus. She was alone... again... the inverse. She was the only mind in the Realm of the Spider. She had lost her matter. They had killed her. *Damn them!*

The Grand One stood there, shell shocked. One moment she had known where she was heading, the next that pulsing door had sent her crumpling to the ground. She had managed to help herself back up with her aching arms and found she had trouble seeing what had become of that strange entry. The room within was utterly black... A moving sea of velvet... writhing, entangled. She did not know these things. They burst forth from the entry; thousands upon thousands of slick, black, crawling monstrosities. They were like the Spider Woman, but smaller. They were the newborns yet to form the full-sized enemy army Morning Singer had informed her of in the gully. The Grand One had come too late.

"You have got to be kidding me." She said and braced herself. She lifted the kopa to play, "Look out!" to her unsuspecting friends.

Megatherium and glyptodons turned their attentions to that new threat, fending them off to the best of their abilities, but those new enemies were crowding in, overtaking — smaller and nimbler. It was like trying to fight the white water on a fierce river... from beneath the rip tide.

The Grand One could not stay in the main hall waiting for those spiders to swarm her. She had to move. Her feet propelled her and she made it up onto the first pathway. Running blindly, she passed fentium after fentium, their eyes returning to their original black. Odd. She slid past the confused drones and grasped at a spear that had been propped up against a wall. The insects had not reached out for her yet. But she pressed the spearhead toward them to keep them at a distance just in case.

Unfortunately, as she made those motions to defend herself, she caught a glimpse of the swarm behind her.

The spiders were eating everything they came across. Fentiums were no exception. They filled the main hall, the lower pathway, and all the reflection of her eye.

Sudden pain spread along her abdomen. There was at least one fentium the Grand One had not convinced to stay off her, and it too was out for blood. She shook the pain of that gut punch away and nudged the butt of her spear firmly up against the large insect's chin, sending it off balance and backwards where it was instantly swallowed up by the oncoming maw.

The Grand One turned again and put all of her energy into outrunning that madness... but to what end? What fate could she hope for for her world now? *Don't think of it,* she told herself, *keep on fighting until you can fight no longer.* She turned one corner and then another, sweat glistening across the shield of her mask, lungs near to bursting. The altitude shift came on her again. Her ears popped. Her equilibrium reset. She turned another corner and found that injured crow was waiting for her.

"Here!" It cawed, "Over here is Crow Mother!" She would at least see her alien companion one last time.

Through the threshold, she stumbled into the chamber where Crow Mother was being held. Her friend was an unconscious, half-dangling silhouette against the light of an ornate, crystalline window there. Even in sleep she looked in pain. However, more crows had received the message that the Grand One had arrived. They flocked in behind her and resumed smashing their bodies against the three remaining appendages harnessing Crow Mother in place.

The Grand One noticed her friend's mask laying against the far wall. She collected the thing and quickly placed it over

Crow Mother's naked head. She sang, "Come on Crow Mother, we have so little time."

Crow Mother's breathing gained some normality and the alien even raised her head in greetings, "Grand One. You have come for me."

"Yes. We must hurry. Can you help?" The Grand One tried to pull at one of those bonds and noticed the blood trickling from Crow Mother's open shoulder, "You were injured."

"I was foolish." Crow Mother's song was filled with agony, "There was... a human. He... hated me."

The crows were making slow work of the bonds, but the crystals were cracking. The Grand One wondered about Crow Mother's words, "A human?"

"Our time is up." Crow Mother had noticed the others before the Grand One could. Yes, the spiders had found them. It didn't take long. They were pinned there, in that room. *Surely, this is where we will die...* The Grand One thought, *together in our foolishness. Perhaps I am like a blue flower after all. And blue flowers are not long for this world.*

Fifteen

Toothache figured it out quickly, what the spiders were capable of. He saw the other sloths flooded with the little terrors and knew he had to act to force them from this place before they were completely overrun. Bites from those tiny mouths were pulling cries from his friends and he could see the blood of them coming from the holes the spiders were creating.

Wild eyed, he shouted, "Pull back! Into the canyon! Into the canyon! Retreat!" His words were heeded by all who heard him, and the escape was in full swing.

The megatherium burst forth from the main doorway of the tower, stampeding away from the myriad small spider people who quickly spread along the arcades and courtyards of Bo'No'To and up along the canyon walls.

Vicaltorbissus felt the human body being lifted up by some force, carried down the pathways by the hands of the little bodies their siblings now inhabited. The body of Silent Wolf was crowdsurfing toward the mirror room. It did not wish to wake up. Vicaltorbissus and the human were both active proponents of staying in this false slumber because the alternative was quickly developing into an unacceptable fallacy. If this was life in this verse, Vicaltorbissus did not want it... if this was life on this world, Silent Wolf could no longer live it. They would sleep together in mourning for as long as they were allowed... which was not very long.

The siblings carried them to the wet room. They laid the human body there beside the vacated cavity of Eccioporte which, though very dead, still pumped out baby spiders from its engorged belly. One of those spiders offered them the cruel words, "This is no time for slumber."

Their human eyes opened once again. They sat up, seeing the true army spreading out before them. Together, they hated it. But they could not deny its existence. Vicaltorbissus could not deny that their siblings had defied them and for the first time in their fifteen million years of life, they were afraid.

Crow Mother was awake. Her friend was with her. She had not left her to die alone in that place. Unfortunately, the new threat was staring them both in the face and Crow Mother understood that her death song had only been sung a brief few moments ahead of schedule. The spider people lined the walls and ceiling, leaving no space visible there. The doorway was jam packed with the little things. There could be no escape in that direction.

Yet, for some reason, the horrid creatures had left a small circle in the center of the room empty around her and her companions... showing some kind of cerebral activity — a sort of reverence toward the two masked figures was evident, as if they knew Crow Mother had played a critical role in their birthing. Knowing that to be the case, she was an unhappy wet-nurse. She understood that her little abominations would kill and eat her as they had done to the others on Botto. She wished they would just get it over with already.

"What are they?" Her friend sang softly. She had a gorgeous, husky voice in that moment. Crow Mother was glad to hear that ephemeral beauty before the life could be pulled from her.

"A nightmare of our own making I am afraid." Crow Mother's voice, she thought, did not gift that same beauty to her friend. She was sorry for that.

"What can we do about them?"

The memory of the full grown spiders that had destroyed her home world filled Crow Mother's mind. She had no real answer to offer. She was defeated.

A crack began to spread along the remaining arm harness. The crows had been trying even in the face of the maw. They were breaking through and Crow Mother felt a jolt within her. Her friends had returned to rescue her. She could at the very least help them to die as heroes might die.

"First..." Crow Mother's voice cracked, but the sound got out regardless, "we must jump." She turned her head and eyed the crystal-sealed window behind her. The Grand One followed her gaze. "Then, in death, we can figure out the rest."

Crow Mother did not know if the Grand One understood or agreed with her suicide pact, but their time was clearly up. They had to do something. She pulled her stuck arm harshly and the pillar shattered, sending her whole upper body heaving forward. Her head was pounding, her shoulder wound festering. She accepted the pain gratefully slamming her good arm down against each of the footholds in turn.

"Help me!" She sang out to the Grand One.

The Grand One reached out for her catching her waist in a great bear hug and wrenching her free from the crystals. She was free... even if it was only for a moment, she was free. Her friend held her like a crutch. They limped persistently toward the window. The spiders in their path lingered, but gave space as they walked. *Why do they still not touch us?* She wondered.

Eighteen

This is crazy, the Grand One caught herself thinking. *This is foolish. Is this the only option left to us?* And yet the maw did not consume them. The spiders let them make their move toward the window as if approving of their choice of death. What would it matter to them if they ate her flesh up at the top of the tower or down below?

She heard the many small voices ringing in her head then, not so much accepting of the act, but confused by it.

"What is she doing Sacarrentio?"

"She is changing the timeline."

What do they mean by that? She wondered.

"She cannot change the timeline, we must do it."

"Then do it Dongojio. You know as well as I the need we have of their power."

"Yes, but the time is... incorrect. The cycle has yet to be fulfilled."

"Well then we should stop them."

"Yes Husceratti, we must stop them, but do not eat them until the cycle is fulfilled."

"Yes."

"Yes."

Their general words of agreement were disconcerting to the Grand One. She thought about what they must have meant. What was the cycle? Why did they still need her friend alive? Were they still drawing power from her somehow even without the crystalline appendages holding her? She decided that must be the case. *Then we must end it.* The spiders would not get what they wanted from them. She would pull her friend to the very edge... and they would die before their time. She hoped their sacrifice would be worth it. Her universe deserved to be free of these terrible creatures.

The spiders began to act. They crawled forth covering hers and Crow Mother's bodies, but they were such little things and they did not bite. The Grand One steeled herself against the eerie feelings that came along with so many tiny legs covering her skin. The need she felt was greater than her fear. She had to escape the tower even if it killed her... which it probably would. Heck, she was meant to be dead already. So she did as Crow Mother asked. She broke the crystal window sending some of the spiders flying with the violent motion. She dragged her friend through the pile and looked down to the ground far below. Her breath became constricted with the weight of the moment and she had to force her lungs to take in air.

The Grand One peered back and looked into Crow Mother's vizor. They nodded one to the other, and together, they jumped.

Nineteen

They were falling. Wind rushed up to meet them sending the little terrors into disarray — flurrying things trying to hold to their larger bodies — trying to tug at them — to hold them in the moment. Gravity would not let it be so. Gravity was more certain in this universe than their expectations.

Her crow friends must have rushed out the window of the tower just behind them, because Crow Mother could see their feathers flashing in her peripheral vision. The wind thwop thwop thwopped against the fabric of her shawl smacking it awkwardly against her mask. The ground was getting closer.

Crow Mother felt several talons pulling against the fabric on her backside. *Not quite strong enough my friends,* she thought not noticing that the fall was slowing — becoming more akin to a tumble down a hillside. Still, the fall did not stop altogether. She and the Grand One became two odd piles surrounded by scatterings of crows — ragged balls made up of limbs.

The piles thudded violently against the muddy ground of the canyon courtyard.

Twenty

Through a window in the temple, Vicaltorbissus watched the falling aliens. The forces of this planet had pulled back to the canyon's mouth and left them with a brief pause to recollect themselves. In their mind, they struggled with the concept of fate. That one should die and one should live. That the one that died should have such a greater impact on the trajectory of the universe than the one who lived ever could. They watched the crows try to save the aliens. They wondered if they truly knew the outcome of this war, for the pathways were muted to them, their siblings stunned into silence by the actions of those that now fell.

The moment was long. Too long. And Vicaltorbissus was surprised to find that the human they wore was holding his breath. They asked Silent Wolf a question then, *Is this the result you had hoped for boy?* But the boy did not know how to respond. He winced in pain. His attempt to reuse his own body after the habitation of so many other minds had cleared was like trying to learn to run after one's legs had been broken for several years. Even if Silent Wolf could clear his mind, he would not be the same person he was before the Spider Woman had controlled him.

Vicaltorbissus saw this in the boy. They repossessed the form knowing the pain was not quite surpassable at this time. As they returned their focus to the viewing portals that were the human eyes, they watched the splat of the falling ones.

The sound that accompanied it was wrong. A little too light. A little too peaceful. The two armies had stopped any other activity to witness the two forms falling from the tower; a clandestine sense of foreboding in that moment — for both sides.

Have they died at last? The boy huffed from within that mind, meekly breaking the blockade that held him from himself. Vicaltorbissus could see from where they stood the smacking mess on the ground there — the twitching forms of the crows that had landed on the sides of the piles — the various other stilled forms. *Must we continue on now that they are gone?* Silent Wolf was assuming that nothing could survive such a fall. The spider within him remembered the moment before them and knew that it was wrong. What they saw now was not what the pathway would become.

They reached out for their siblings' minds knowing with spite in their heart that they would not be a general of an army when they reached them, but rather a slave to fate.

Twenty One

The Grand One lay in a heap sandwiched between several of the birds. *We're dead. We're all dead,* she thought morbidly, *myself included.* She felt her breath however — felt her eyes open and close. Slowly the million aches within her body registered to her mind. She sat up and looked around with a sense of shock and uncertainty.

"Crow Mother. Are we still living?" She sang.

Her friend's arm pressed out of the other pile limply, but still moving, "I cannot say for certain." That was Crow Mother's voice for sure, "I fear many of our friends have just perished on our behalf."

The Grand One knew this to be true. She peered around at the flattened crows surrounding them, tears filling the space between her skin and her mask. "Can you move?" She had to fight to sing then — she was responsible for these deaths too. Those birds did not deserve such a fate.

Crow Mother managed to sit up as well. The pain in her body was evident from her slow, trembling movement. "With difficulty," she responded, weakly.

The Grand One was relieved to see her friend sitting up. Then she felt a sort of burning sensation — prickling — all over her body. It occurred to her to look out across the floor of the canyon at the too many eyes watching her from all sides of the warscape: megatherium and glyptodons on one side, spiders upon spiders on the other. "They are all watching us..."

"They need us." Crow Mother sang distantly.

"Every one of them," the Grand One replied, "Both sides." A new foreboding was heavy within her and their conversation only compounded that sense.

Then a barrage of strange little voices emanated again from the spider side of the courtyard.

"They have survived."

"There is still time."

"Take them."

"We must get them to the Nexus."

"Keep them. We may save the timeline yet."

The spiders were moving again, encroaching upon the Grand One's pile. As her eyes swept past the tower, she noticed a human-like form on the doorway in silhouette. She could not make its features out in that light, but the spiders were imminent — scuttling toward them on those miserable little legs.

"What should we do?" She asked her weakened friend.

"I am afraid I am out of answers."

Hopeless. The Grand One reached for her kopa, a constant source of inspiration in her times of need. But it was crushed. The weight of the fall had finished her instrument along with all of the crows. In her frustration, she tossed the crumpled remains of the reed at the oncoming spiders and allowed her tears to gain volume, "Mother Tree, if only you were here to guide me."

It was odd though. In that moment, Mother Tree was with her. She felt her spirit in the air. She felt her hand on her shoulder. A spirit now of the earth — her earth — Orotti. The presence of that specter gave her clarity. She must not stop until her job was done. She must get up and take the next step. She turned her head to smile at the ghost of her former tutor but realized then that it was not Mother Tree's arm at all. It was a crow's wing that touched her. Some of the crows had stopped their twitching... and gotten up. Some of the crows were still alive!

Twenty Two

Toothache saw the movement of the Grand One and Crow Mother... of the birds. They had made it through the fall unscathed. He knew the other sloths saw it as well. Heard the glyptodons' cool baroo against the echoing canyon walls. The Grand One's Army was bustling back into action.

"We can still help them!" He cried, the de facto leader of this sect, "Hurry! The hour is not too late! Charge!"

The Grand One's Army took up his call. They charged toward the tower and toward the spiders. They charged toward the very concept of hope.

Twenty Three

Vicaltorbissus and the boy Silent Wolf stood in the buckled threshold of what had so recently been Eccioporte's temple, occupying the same body between the two of them. They watched the army of this world charging toward the army of the other realm. They spoke to the spiders who had woken them, "What would you have us do?"

Several spiders spoke in unison from the greater maw, "Kill the army. Then collect those two for us. We are incomplete. Their energies are needed to finish us. We need their flesh to make us whole."

They felt a gnawing pang of regret. Looking toward one of the open turrets they flashed through moments they had impressed upon their memory back in the Realm of the Spider. Such moments meant very little to them then in that place, the human hands holding to those controls, the emanating blast, the searing of flesh... the broken mask. Vicaltorbissus shared these things with the human and the human's emotions filled them, a choking, guttural warmth, a desire to be done with these aliens and this reality. Vicaltorbissus and Silent Wolf were in some odd state of agreement to see the destruction through no matter what it meant for each of them personally. They ran through the spiders unencumbered.

Twenty Four

The Grand One climbed to her feet. She reached down and helped Crow Mother up. The vibrating pound of her army galloping toward them gave her new confidence and she turned to see the other force making that sliding, skittering sound as it approached already substantially closer than her own force. The maw reached them and the surviving crows leapt forth pecking and swallowing, clawing at the little things, desperate to keep their aerial advantage, desperate not to be pulled down and consumed themselves. The Grand One swatted the beasts away with what little strength she could muster. But Crow Mother had none left and was already half covered by the terrors. So the Grand One focused on her friend, scraping the creatures from Crow Mother's body with her hands in a reduced shovel motion.

Her army reached the epicenter then. They slammed their bodies against the hoard of spiders, stomped them. This time they better understood their formations and seemed to stand a chance — not a bunch of individual animals fighting for their own survival, rather a super entity — a frenzy capable of going toe to toe with the alien swarm. The glyptodons formed ranks and spiked and crushed the things while the megatherium utilized their superior reach to pluck individual arachnids from their packs on their long fingers — or crush them with their thick herbivore jaws and spit them out again.

Toothache bashed into twenty or thirty spiders who had been primed to bury the Grand One.

"Thank you Toothache!" She sang back to him.

If only that early success were sustainable. The spiders quickly recognized the Orotti creatures' tactics and reformulated their own. They formed up their factions, once again surrounding individual megatherium, individual glyptodons, finding naked patches and filling them.

Crow Mother, in her tedium, had been looking off toward the distance. She noticed one of the turrets moving in its circle and tugged at her defender, "Grand One. Look."

Turning her attention to the place where Crow Mother pointed, the Grand One saw the body of the human in that rig. "It is Silent Wolf. I thought he was dead."

"He is the human that stabbed me through." Crow Mother emphasized the notes for 'human' and 'stabbed', a rage in the former that the Grand One did not like to hear.

"W-why would he...?" The Grand One realized she had no time to ponder. The turret was preparing its charge, it was turned directly toward them. "Oh no! Toothache!" She called for her friend.

Toothache spun away from his personal, losing battle with the arachnids and galloped to the Grand One's aide huffing, "I am here for you Grand One!"

"Can you carry us both?" She meant herself and Crow Mother.

"I can!"

Quickly, the Grand One helped Crow Mother onto Toothache's back. She herself returned to that spot on his upper shoulders.

"Where are we going?!" Toothache asked without hesitation.

"To the turret!" She sang back.

The way was blocked by the main body of the spider army and the canon of the turret was already beginning to exude a pale blue glow. Not a good sign. They were already most likely too late.

"So be it!" Toothache did not care about any of that. This was their fight. He would do what was necessary. He launched into a mad dash across the battle field, crushing as many spiders as he could get his feet on along the way. The Grand One took to swatting at those pests that managed to crawl onto his back. *We can make it!* She thought, *We can make it!*

Twenty Five

Vicaltorbissus was already manning the turret. The foreign heat of the Nexus chopped and chopped at the human skin of Silent Wolf and Vicaltorbissus cringed at the boy's pain — a thing a spider never had to feel in their own realm. They swung the cannon toward the army of this world, but the little spiders were too deeply enmeshed within the other force for them to comfortably fire.

"I cannot find a clear shot," they mindspoke the mutiny of spiders.

"It matters not." One of them replied.

And another pushed further saying, "Fire!" without resignation.

"But the children!" Vicaltorbissus cried back, angry at the sacrificial demotion they bestowed upon the body he was trapped in. The little ones could not yet control such a device as the turret. Silent Wolf had to do it, die for it, kill Vicaltorbissus' own kind alongside the creatures they fought — sacrifice them as well for... for what?

"They are just the first of many. They will resurrect in time." That one was Sacarrentio. Had Sacarrentio become the new leader of their kind? They did not deserve that throne.

Still other spiders spoke up reprising the thought, "Do it!" and "Fire!" and "Now!"

The turret was aimed toward the heart of the skirmish. Vicaltorbissus noticed a megatherium there. It had allowed two riders to mount. They were heading directly for Vicaltorbissus and the turret. The riders were masked but Vicaltorbissus (and Silent Wolf for that matter) recognized them as the singers from that other world. One was that same Being that had tried to strangle them, the other wore that mask that had to be broken in the dream. Their fate had shown itself to them. Now was the time to find completion — for Vicaltorbissus to return to the Realm of the Spider to try Eccioporte for her crimes — for Silent Wolf, they did not know what awaited that one after death.

Focusing the turret on the singers, they fired. The blast leapt from the cannon with the force of a moon separating against its world's Roche limit. Negative energy plastered backward against the human body chopping its flesh into petals, rubbing away to the muscle and tendon of the boy. The pain was unbearable.

Twenty Six

Earth tore away beneath the armies. A boom had ruptured the canyon floor and anything within that space was either launched backwards in all directions or pulverized into dust. Toothache and his riders must have been above the beam. They were thrown high into the air and landed with a hard smack against scorched soil.

On the edge of this huge, newly formed crater, the Grand One struggled to rise. She held her arm where the Jomony had pulled the infection clean. That old pain returned to her. She wondered that perhaps when they had saved her from that earlier death, they must have given her an abnormal agility — it would explain her most recent series of close calls... but it could not explain any of the things she had done before the gully. Still she imagined that there must be a limit to that survival acuity. Now that she felt the pain from the source of infection again, she wondered if that limit had been reached.

It occurred to her then that she was alone. Her friends had not landed nearby. She looked around and spotted Crow Mother and Toothache lying in separate heaps a good distance from her along the crater's rim. The armies were gone. She could not see hide nor hair of either of them at that moment. She felt a terrible throbbing in her head. Her blood was boiling. And she attempted to sing one of her songs of summoning.

Only then did it occur to the Grand One that her Sun Mask had broken. Half of the device remained on her face, charred and crumbling. She was suddenly very upset that none of the Jomony had joined them on their journey to this, the other side of the world. If only Eldest had brought them along and played the drum to keep them running. Eldest had refused.

Morning Singer was with child. The Jomony would not function on their own. Such a terrible restriction for such skillful task doers.

The Grand One limped over the edge of the crater until she reached Toothache. The sloth's eyes were filled with panic. He had been horribly gashed across his torso. He was suffering and she did not know how well she could communicate to ease his fears without her mask's power. She touched him just above the wound as Mother Tree had touched the crushed girl called Red Lips that day she had tripped on a wet stone in the creek Antan. That wound had always stayed with Red Lips but she had survived. The Grand One was not certain Toothache's fissure would heal.

"It is alright my friend." She tried to sing it to make him feel better, but she knew the tune was wrong. She sang on regardless, "This wound need not be fatal."

The sloth shook his head. His panic did not clear from him.

"I know you cannot understand. I am sorry."

The Grand One turned her attention to Crow Mother who, after everything she had been through of late, looked significantly worse off than the sloth. Her mask had also been pulverized. Her breathing was short and pained as it had been when they found her in the tower. She was dying.

"Crow Mother, can you walk?"

Crow Mother wore the same shroud of panic as Toothache, but at least she seemed to comprehend some aspect of the Grand One's song. She even responded with a horribly pained bellow that sent the Grand One back into the dark vacuum of thought. The shuttle — she showed her — the shuttle still rested above the canyon.

Of course! “Yes, I remember.” The Grand One tried to force the song into sense, “Tell Toothache. He cannot understand me without my mask.”

Crow Mother crawled her way over to the downed sloth and sang what the Grand One barely recognized as a song of direction. Toothache’s eyes calmed. He worked to rise and, shaking dust from his bloody fur, presented himself limpingly to the singing alien. The Grand One helped Crow Mother up onto Toothache’s back again. They did not wait for goodbyes. Their wounds were too severe and the trek up the canyon was a frustrating obstacle given the likelihood they would bleed out on the way if they took the path too slowly. They rode off toward the canyon mouth leaving the Grand One to stand alone at the crater line in resolution.

There were survivors of the blast, she thought as she began again assessing her surroundings... but they did not yet stir. The Grand One prayed that she had not led all of these innocents to their deaths as well. They had to be alive somewhere. Walking, she cusped the crater and saw the mounds where glyptodons and megatherium had landed against the hard walls of the canyon. The snickering sound returned across the way and she peered out to find the source of it. Well most of the spiders had survived the explosion. They were riled up and rallying themselves for more battle. *Damn this!* The Grand One knew she was on the losing side of this thing. But she had stayed behind because she thought there might be a chance she could change the trajectory of their fate. She had felt it from the spiders when they spoke to each other around her, had felt the confusion they bore toward her. Something about her had given them pause — it was not simply their need of Crow Mother that had stopped them from eating her at the top of the tower.

Crumpled and seared behind the turret, she could see the body of Silent Wolf — the last dying member of her tribe — whom she had so many times rejected out of some foolish sense of duty. She would not reject him any longer — faded as he had become. *I will go there*, she thought. And she spoke aloud in the dead language of Tetset since she no longer had anyone to sing to, "There is still time. We have to stop this invasion. Somehow." Her legs limped with the ache of far too much activity. Her knees wanted to surrender. She would not let them. She picked up speed as she descended the crater and began to run.

From the center of the great hole in the ground, she felt the strange, empty wind — heard no sound of her earth as if the universe did not exist in that place. Pushing forward, she broke through that vortex, her breath intact. She ran, ignoring the hoards of spiders banking over the side of the crater toward her. The Grand One would reach the turret. The answer was there — the solution was in that nasty force that could create such desolate emptiness.

Megatherium and glyptodons began to stir then. They were in time to witness the Grand One's mad dash, the peril she faced from the maw. Some glyptodons awoke very near other battered spiders they had been struggling against before the blast. They continued to fight, but their eyes kept returning to the inner crater, in awe of the Grand One — her run — her pride — even in the wake of so much death she still gave them reason to hope.

As the Grand One approached the turret side of the crater, it became clear the spiders would reach her before she could get to the top. Her army saw this. They would not wait any longer. Several megatherium led the charge down into the scorched pit. They would defend the Grand One, help her perform whatever final task she had chosen for herself.

"Silent Wolf!" The Grand One found herself shouting the closer she came to the far edge. She pulled her weight up with her one good arm as her army smashed against the maw one final time. She stood above the expunged body of her tribesman, weak and out of breath. "Silent Wolf." She kneeled beside his mangled from.

Shredded as he was, he still managed to turn his head to look upon her, finally seeing the girl he had known in Tetset behind the broken remnant of the alien mask.

"You." He seemed to cough each word out with a thread of smoke, "Blue Flower. I must be dreaming."

Blue Flower. Her old Tetset name. It brought her back to a world that still felt vibrant. A world she was not meant to hold a place in. She stared at the broken form of Silent Wolf lying on the ground. Remembered how proud he had been in his warrior robes beside their chief. She remembered the day he had been given his first hunting assignment. How proud she had been of the boy she had known back then. How quiet she had remained as she watched him grow into someone who could live in that community. How hurt she had been to know her place in that. She had so wished to be seen as someone who could grow old in Tetset. A thing she was never meant to do. But none of that was Silent Wolf's fault.

"No." She said. In Silent Wolf's dying moments, she could at least give him one of the things he had always desired of her — attention — presence. She wrestled the remainder of the mask from her head, "It is me. I am really here."

Twenty Seven

The human had known this other — this unmasked singer — so similar in form to the body they currently wore. Vicaltorbissus remembered the broken mask from the future sight of the pathways — remembered what they thought it had meant — understood now that the message had been saved, not for the spider, but for this dying human body — this moment. They wondered why that would matter. This body would not last much longer. What purpose could such a message serve to them now as their life giving blood loosed from nearly every orifice. But then again, time did have a way of moving differently in this strange universe.

They were distracted by the human's slow death. However, the human Silent Wolf apparently held his pain in lesser regard than Vicaltorbissus. That boy forced himself to the fore-conscious of their mind — remembered the mouth as his own. Vicaltorbissus was impressed when the boy actually managed to form a sentence without their help. He said, "Why do you come to me now..." a cough interfered briefly, there was more blood there, but he found that strength again as soon as it let up, "when our time has already passed."

Something about those words reverberated off the pathway memory in Vicaltorbissus' own mind. They already knew the girl known as Blue Flower's response as if they had been born with the words:

"Because I believe it is not too late to fix this."

Strangely, Vicaltorbissus found themself liking these humans. Their resolve was unlike that of the spider's and they found it peculiar — amazing even — that in the wake of this undisputed failure, these so easily broken creatures could still hold onto any semblance of hope. Then Silent Wolf asked Vicaltorbissus if he could tell the girl about the pathways before they died. In their weakened state, Vicaltorbissus likely would not have been able to stop the boy, but the spider found themself appreciating the gesture of respect. They accepted. "We have welcomed the spiders into this world through the pathway in Eccioporte's womb. It is already done. That other singer made it so."

Vicaltorbissus felt a curiosity then about that other Being, a new respect for it and its kind that they had not felt before. They asked from the boy's mouth, "Is it... is it dead?"

"No." The girl responded sharply — emphatically.

Silent Wolf regained his mouth again, tedium setting in across the overworked body, "Shame," he said, "It killed our people."

"No." Her will was stronger than theirs. She had the objective truth on her side, "That turret..."

They struggled to turn their head so they might spot the big gun from the corner of their eye. It was nearly impossible to move even that small amount. "I was there..." the boy replied, "when they died."

The alien's song reverberated in their head then, the last one it had choked them with in the temple. Darkness. The bodies of Tetset falling from the sky, wearing fear on their faces.

"So was I." The girl responded.

The silhouette of Blue Flower appeared within Silent Wolf's vision. She had been looking out the windshield of the shuttle. She had been lifting them up. She had meant to rescue them. Silent Wolf saw it now and Vicaltorbissus let him see. Ultimately, the truth did matter, even when it worked against you and your kind. "It tried to tell me." Silent Wolf whispered, his mind racing through the moment when the alien had held him by the throat — had shown him the turret and the beam on repeat.

The Grand One was surprised by the statement, "It?"

"That other Being," the boy had only been told what Eccioporte wanted him to know. He did not have a reference to The People as a genuine culture. He had not heard that the singer could have a name.

"Crow Mother," the girl said, "My friend."

Silent Wolf was growing angry. Vicaltorbissus chose to no longer interfere in this. The spiders were wrong — would have been happier remaining in their own realm — just let the truth bleed out with the rest — let the pain end. Still, Silent Wolf felt the need to speak his mind, "It tried to show me the truth," he nearly yelled the words, "but I could not see it. I had so much pain in me... and the Spider Woman..."

"She manipulates," the girl took Silent Wolf's singed hand gently in her own, "and destroys worlds. You were one man against a god. But you are not alone any longer. I am here and I have brought friends. Creatures of our world... and others. Some survived even the turret blast. They fight on. For us and our entire world. Even now."

The maw began to claw their way atop the crater wall then, approaching the two human forms. They had broken through the Orotti army who could only struggle desperately to keep from being buried by the overwhelming sea of spiders. Vicaltorbissus noticed them first, the humans entrenched in their conversation. They retook control of the mouth and howled in a voice no human could make, "Stop!"

The spiders did stop. They remembered their general. Even after the mutiny of Sacarrentio and Husceratti, they remembered Vicaltorbissus. Some fidgeted with confusion. Some fought in the distance, not hearing or rather not wishing to hear their true general's command.

They asked, "Why do you have us stop?"

"Why do you command this?"

"What else would you have us do?

Vicaltorbissus did not answer their questions. Instead, the minds of the boy and the spider general worked together as one. Silent Wolf rose to his feet. The pain was unbearable, but pain would not matter on the path they agreed then to travel. "We will need you and your army to get out of the canyon if you can. Get as far away as you are able."

"We will try," she said.

The spiders wanted to talk to Vicaltorbissus, but they would not listen to those pleas of genocide any longer. Vicaltorbissus and the boy had made up their mind, this was not their world to take. They said to the girl, "Be well on your journey."

"And you. Blood of my blood." She embraced them gently. The only act of love Vicaltorbissus had ever felt in this verse... it hurt like shit! But it was worth the pain. Silent Wolf remembered the image of the lovers in the mirror room — at least he had thought them lovers at the time. His reflection had been entwined with Blue Flower's form in that ancient mural behind the waterfall. The Spider Woman had been a terrible soothsayer now that all was becoming clear. This moment was never about lovers.

"Go." Vicaltorbissus did not wish to waste any more time and the maw was getting antsy, "Before they decide that I am not their general once again."

Twenty Eight

It hurt to be running again, but the Grand One ran none-the-less. She sprinted toward the mouth of the canyon raising her breaking voice to a howl. The animals would not understand anything she tried to sing to them, so she hoped the motion of her body and the cry she exuded would at least get them to follow her. They had done so moments ago, rushed into the crater to help her though she could not command it. They would do so again.

Five megatherium remained, twelve glyptodons, and only a handful of crows. They followed her because they trusted her. She did not know if she was worthy of their trust at that point, but damnit, she would get the survivors of her mess out of the canyon as Silent Wolf requested.

Out the corner of her eye, she watched the last man of Tetset approach the turret and she knew what he intended to do. Then the canyon mouth swallowed her and her army up — the long canyon trail and Kyun'Bon'On becoming all they could see as they hurried desperately to escape the place she recognized for what it truly was, a death trap.

Twenty Nine

Together, Silent Wolf and Vicaltorbissus placed their singed, pulsating hands upon the controls of that same turret that had nearly killed them moments earlier. They toggled the grips not actually feeling the strange metal at all. In their constant state of pain, their sense of touch was fading into numbness. *Oh well. No use for it. Just press the buttons,* they told themselves.

Spiders called out to them, "Vicaltorbissus!"

"You are letting them escape!"

"No!" Vicaltorbissus and Silent Wolf replied, "I have fooled them. I will shoot them as they run." But they did not turn the turret toward the canyon mouth. They turned it on the temple itself. They let the beam charge up. They hoped the one called Blue Flower could get far enough away for this shot would not be like the others.

The spiders had heard their manipulations, had accepted them as truth. They did not seem to mind that they turned the canon in the wrong direction. They were too busy praising the general concept of deception, clumsily unaware that they were the ones who had been deceived. "Yes!" Said the spiders.

And, "This is well!"

"Yes children," Silent Wolf and Vicaltorbissus nearly sagged, their blood was almost gone, "I know." As they said those words, they pulled the triggers. The turret lit up in full and the beam erupted out across the crater. It smashed into the maw of spiders first — burst through them and the ground beneath — killed hundreds — thousands of them on impact. Their little eyes had no time to show any kind of surprise as they burnt up in the strange heat of the gun.

More blisters and boils formed across Silent Wolf's body. Still they maintained control of the canon, not relenting the blast that usually only lasted a single cycle through. The beam held continuously. They pulled the arc of that beam across the surface of the temple and that heat feasted on the then crumbling walls, the interior pillars, the pathways. As it struck the most active of the pathways, Nexus energy bled out creating several new eruptions — a chain reaction occurred, not dissimilar to a nuclear explosion (though more web-like and plasmic in appearance).

Finally, the beam and its accompanying Nexus explosions made their way into the mirror room where the greatest store of spider realm energies had been kept. And that ethereal blue-white overtook everything.

The entire temple erupted outward with that light — lapped over Bo'No'To consuming all the spiders that remained. Silent Wolf and Vicaltorbissus watched the reflective cloud come toward them. They welcomed that death — welcomed their own disintegration. The cloud billowed through them and in an instant they were no longer there.

The Realm of the Spider was full once again.

Thirty

Injured, nearly dead, pained by the too quick run they had been forced to perform, Crow Mother rode Toothache's shoulders along the upper cusp of the canyon, up through the dry land to the scorched tree and the waiting shuttle beyond. Crow Mother removed herself from the sloth's shoulders and opened the bay door allowing a large ramp to protrude. Toothache walked gingerly up that ramp. Crow Mother waited. Her exhausted eyes remained open, limply viewing the explosion below as it worked its way up toward them. Her breath caught on one of the minerals in the Orotti air. If the atmosphere of that world wasn't out to get her, that billowing cloud of anti-Nexus certainly was.

She hurried inside. Closed the bay door. Activated the shuttle's engines. They rose into the air just as the blue-white light came up to meet them.

Thirty One

The Grand One had been welcomed onto the shoulders of a megatherium she had known as Corkeye. She was a sour beast, but like all the others, she had quickly grown fond of the human that played an alien. The Grand One wished she had taken more time to speak with that one before the powers of her mask had been lost. She wished she had better gotten to know all of the creatures that had fought for her. Unfortunately, the time for that had passed.

They ascended the wide canyon path with greater speed than her own legs could accommodate. Yet in the back of her mind, the Grand One knew the megatherium were slowed by the many small wounds the spiders had inflicted upon them. Death by cactus pricks — death by rose thorns. A million little injuries could kill as well as one big one. Still she hoped they could make it to some safe space and recover before they all inevitably bled out.

Looking down then, the Grand One saw the frenzy in Corkeye's face. The other animals showed that same fear. They had heard or felt something the Grand One's limited senses could not yet pick up on. A glyptodon stumbled as it rushed along and she watched it slip from the edge of the path. It could not recover its grip and it fell from the ledge. She knew it would die down there in the lower canyon whether it be a slow death from its injuries or a rapid one from...

...What the creatures had sensed ahead of her. A blue-white light that blared toward them from the canyon mouth they had just escaped. They were too late. The turret had done its work too quickly. She wanted to thank Silent Wolf even so. He had been brave in the end — even if it meant they all had to die because of that bravery. She tried to lean in and whisper a calming sound to Corkeye as they approached the top of the wide path — tried to soothe her knowing what came to meet them.

"We do not die for nothing. We do not die alone." She knew the words could not be understood. She only hoped she had imparted enough kindness in the sounds.

Turning her head, the Grand One could see the blue-white light folding over megatherium, glyptodons, and crows that lagged behind. It showed no signs of slowing. She closed her eyes then. She thought to whoever in the universe might be listening, *My name was Grand One. I fought for Tetset. My people. When that failed, I fought for Orotti. My world. My fear will forever remain that my struggles came at too great a cost.*

The light came for her then. She was enveloped in it. She felt nothing, emptiness, silence.

Thirty Two

Qotle walked with his sister. The remaining members of Hen'Bon'On followed slowly behind. They sought an oasis that existed in their old myths amidst the Dry Land far from the canyon and Bo'No'To. They had tried to follow Kyun'Bon'On to a safe point, but nothing felt far enough away from Eccioporte for Qotle. So he had changed tactics and veered them from the river toward the myth.

It had been hours since they had taken up the hike. They had not yet rested since the nighttime crow attacks on the temple. They were burnt out — wishing to be done — to make camp already — to eat some coneys and pok'yu.

Shi'Yun turned her head to look back the way they had come. She stopped in her tracks and tugged at her brother's arm. Qotle turned to look as well. He could not see the other clansmen. He could not see anything but the blue-white light. He was grateful to hold Shi'Yun's hand in his own.

Thirty Three

From that small pocket of Orotti, that canyon on the face of a continent that might one day have come to be called an America, the anti-Nexus cloud surged out expanding across the globe like a cancer.

The light spread and spread reaching out to the gully on the far side of the world. It spread across Morning Singer and her unborn child. It overtook Eldest, the apes, the Jomony. The entire forest disappeared into a thick cloud of unavoidable fog in an instant.

That world was covered. A cold cloud settled in. Like Venus, the atmosphere became dense and poisonous in a way the planet had not known for sixty-five million years. The cloud hung over it all for a great while, perhaps a day... a day of nothing — an emptiness so full, had anyone been conscious to see it, they would not have attempted to breathe.

Then, the cloud dissipated. For a long time, nothing moved. The world was silent.

PART VII - SILENCE

One

Little remained of Bo'No'To. The once complex, mica colored walls smoldered with mocking shades of grey and black. The spiders were no more — burned up — decimated. Only the huge crater and some few remaining sections of the lower temple structure gave evidence that anything had ever lived there.

Along the base of the lower canyon, where Kyun'Bon'On flowed without volume, carcasses lay intermittently upon the bank or in shambles on the rocks above. Glyptodons, megatherium, crows. Some had fallen, others were simply too slow and too close to the burn up from the blast. Those latter dead retained little of their skin, fur, feather, or muscle.

High above that mess, on the crest of the upper canyon where the Dry Lands began, not far from the Fingers of All, the Grand One and Corkeye had been thrown clear of the burn up. There were other intact specimens there in that place as well. Several glyptodons had been lifted to that higher ground, perhaps two more megatherium, and a minuscule selection of crows. They all lay there peacefully as if dead and primed for a funeral ceremony.

But those specimens were not dead. The Grand One suddenly pulled in a deep, concerted breath... another return from the afterlife a full sun cycle after the explosion had propelled her forth. Opening her eyes, she turned her head to see the few remaining soldiers of her army stirring as she did. She opened her mouth to laugh... a laugh that could not be heard. She said something joyful in the words of Tetset... and it took her a time to realize that no sound came out — though she felt its resonance in her chest and vocal cords.

The animals did not so much as turn their heads at her words. They looked around in pain. Shock filled their eyes. So the Grand One attempted to speak again. She wanted to offer them that calming sound she had given to Toothache. Again, the words did not produce. The Grand One felt a new terror rise up within her. She lifted herself from the sun baked dirt and walked slowly among her animal friends, checking for injuries, tears seeping down her face like blood from a wound that only then had discovered its opening.

She was deaf. So were they all.

Kneeling down, the Grand One hoped to help a bleeding glyptodon. But the creature barely even responded to her touch as she began to press its wounds with both of her hands. Nothing helped. The blood continued to trickle. So she let go and shuffled herself over to look the dying glyptodon in its big eyes. She tried to sing to it knowing her voice would not materialize. She wanted to thank the creature for its sacrifice. She wanted to make it feel at ease... To let it know that a great burden had been removed from the face of their world. To let it know that it had played a critical role in saving life all throughout the universe. But the dying soldier could not understand...

The Grand One stood up brushing her bloodied hands across her muddied clothes. She turned and behind her, to her surprise, Crow Mother's shuttle was landing nearby. The gust hit her then, but the sound of the thrusters did not lead or follow.

Toothache exited first. He approached and nuzzled the Grand One's shoulder with his head and passed on to see after the other animals. He was no longer bleeding and she was grateful to know their mad dash, at least, had saved them. Crow Mother stood in the bay door. Maskless, she was still a bit worse for wear, but she was alive having been able to subsist on the atmosphere of her shuttle. This heartened the Grand One further. But a single crow popped up then and looked to caw at her, again reminding her of her deafness. She slumped her head, waved her hand backwards in gratitude to her army's great sacrifice, and entered the vehicle without attempting to sing to her friend. She wished she could make sense of that fate to herself, but she was at a loss. They had won, hadn't they? Well this did not feel like victory.

Two

Ocean waves passed across the face of the shuttle. The Grand One stood watching for the sight of one of those massive water beasts though none breeched the surface to see them pass. Likely the creatures could not hear the thrusters either and did not realize there were travelers to greet. Water birds flew and landed on the surface of the waves. They were out of sync and bumped into each other awkwardly as if a limb had been removed and they had not yet figured out how to make their bodies work without it.

The Grand One saw it for what it was. An illness had swept across the entirety of Orotti in an instant, and what it meant... and how far it reached... were simple and obvious truths to which all life on her world would have to grow accustomed. Her entire world was now deaf.

They landed in the gully where the Jomony lived but, very much like the fish, no Jomony rose to greet them. Instead, Morning Singer sat beside Eldest. Their heads hung low. Some apes rattled around by the trees uncomfortably. But the Jomony remained unmoving; prone.

Crow Mother strapped a short-term breathing mechanism (just a bag with no noticeable technology that the Grand One could see) to her face and rushed out the bay door. The Grand One watched her go knowing in her heart that Crow Mother's greatest desperation was yet to come. *She will try to fix it,* the Grand One thought after her friend, *She will try.* Crow Mother ran to the drum stump and tried to make a beat, but her mind was wrong. The rhythm was not consistent — it couldn't have been for the Jomony remained still and useless. Crow Mother became irate. Sound was everything to her and her People. And they too had lost that sense. She tore at the ground like a wild animal knocking the strap from her face and quickly dwindling into pre-suffocation. Morning Singer raised her head but did not approach to console her kin.

So it was up to the Grand One. She stepped out the bay door and walked along the field of stilled robots to the place where her friend had collapsed. She lifted the breathing apparatus from the mossy ground and delicately placed it over Crow Mother's shoulder. At first, the alien appeared not to want the thing... content to choke. But the Grand One nudged it against her shoulder a little harder and Crow Mother finally accepted the stupid bag and placed it back over her beak.

Three

Perhaps an hour later, the Grand One and Crow Mother entered the cave beneath the New Mountain together — though they both knew that only one was meant to enter at a time. They lit the wall fire as a team but could not tell if the mountain's drumming heart had begun to beat. Assuming it had, they continued through the lighted hallway. The Grand One saw, with Crow Mother there to show her, that there was indeed a cleaner way to start the burning that did not produce flames in every corner of that hall as she had experienced her first time through that place... but that information no longer served any purpose to her.

Somehow the Golem was moving around within the deeper chamber, so some rhythm had been accomplished with the fire. But something was not quite right there either. The large robot's presence felt uncertain. It did not step easily. It lacked control of its speed. And it wobbled and nearly fell into them as they entered. It occurred to the Grand One then that the anti-Nexus had not simply affected basic auditory functions in living organisms across her world, rather the entire mechanic of sound had been disturbed and altered in their pocket of space. The Golem regained some semblance of control over its equilibrium — though a slight tick still denied it fluid behavior. The robot came to Crow Mother first. Processed. Nodded. Then it touched the Grand One.

She thought she felt an emotion coming from the Golem, like sadness or uncertainty, as it cupped her chin in its massive clay hand, raised a half finished almost mask up into the air and let it fall to the floor. The Golem shook its head. There was nothing more it could do to help them. Then it lurched backward and collapsed into a seated position against the nearest wall. There it has remained these last one hundred thousand years in slumber.

Next day, they attempted to carry several of the smaller Jomony to the cave to see if they could reactivate for longer with the fire's beat. The result was the same, or worse. Some of the clay dolls overexerted themselves building up too much heat in their dash to regain proper function. Those ones burned themselves out or burst from the built-up pressure. It was hopeless. Those little robots might have been able to heal them if they could only get the things running properly but that was clearly a pipe dream.

The Grand One and Crow Mother would not earn new masks on Orotti. They would not heal or regain their sense of sound. And neither would anyone else. Even Morning Singer's and Eldest's masks would only help them to breathe in the mineral heavy atmosphere. They would have to lend their devices to Crow Mother from then on if she were ever to spend more than a few hours on the planet's surface.

Rejoining the group in the gully, they felt the difficulty of their strange defeat. Ape and crow, Morning Singer and Eldest, the Grand One and Crow Mother all sat around in forced silence — meditative. The shells of the Jomony dolls became an abstraction of sorrow in that place that had once been so lively and full of hope. They knew then that for the foreseeable future:

The Crows would not caw.

The Sloths would not yowl.

And The People would not speak.

Five

Crow Mother flew them back to the other continent in silence. She touched the shuttle down near a large water filled crater somewhere south of the canyon. The Grand One, or perhaps she had become Blue Flower once again — no longer the strong, self-fulfilling general who stood tall for her world — rather the little flower that could be trampled under the great foot of fate — exited the bay door with her head hanging low. She walked a few paces and stopped, not so comfortable with the awkward goodbye to come.

The People were going away to find another world they could settle where the atmosphere would not choke their lungs. Blue Flower would not likely survive such a journey with her expected human lifespan. Even without a proper form of communication these facts were clear.

But Blue Flower still had affection within her. An ability to love. She lived yet as did her alien friend. So she turned around and ran back to Crow Mother who waited on the ramp. There they embraced each other and cried and tried to wish each other luck in whatever nonverbal way they could manage.

After a long while, they let go of one another. Blue Flower turned her eyes to the lake within the crater where a small tail of smoke had begun to form beneath the setting sun. That was where she belonged, her own world, not some great cosmic journey to find The People a truly livable new home. She was a human of this planet, one of the few who understood what had happened to everyone and why. And she was responsible for it all. She would have to find a way to help make the deafened place livable once again. She would take responsibility for her actions

— give her service for all those who had sacrificed so much to her cause.

Blue Flower approached that campfire alone, the sunlight quickly dwindling to the west. But Qotle recognized the girl from the teosintl immediately. He stood up too suddenly, accidentally dropping his meal of coney and grain in the process. Shi'Yun and the few other remaining members of Hen'Bon'On looked up from their food. They welcomed her and offered her a bite and she sat with them and not a one attempted to use words. At least, not for a time and never again in the way they had before.

Six

The woman Blue Flower had become lived in a safe, damp cave in a distant but plentiful part of the world — far from Tetset and Bo'No'To — far too from the Great Forest, the New Mountain, and the gully — on another continent entirely. She and Qotle had led their small tribe across a long land mass that had previously lay dormant beneath the sea and once across they had found a new home like nowhere they had been before. A new world practically, devoid of the many tragic memories they all quietly shared with one another.

There were reasons to be joyful in that new place. Blue Flower was with child. She and Qotle had grown rather fond of one another with no words to speak between them. They had grown to trust each other in that silence. Blue Flower, feeling she better understood the man, had learned to separate him from the memory of the spider. Qotle, knowing how very much he owed to her, had made a point of working always harder to bring her joy and fond new memories.

A small fire burned in their little den. Blue Flower dipped her hand in a bowl of muddy clay. She traced swaths of goopy stuff onto the wall. Drew giant ground sloths, people with spears, a great tower, and strange beings dancing in their various masks. Shi'Yun picked up some muddy clay as well and joined Blue Flower in her drawing.

Qotle caught Blue Flower's eye and they shared a smile. Yes. That was joy. That would have to be good enough for them.

The fire was almost out and the three humans lay fast asleep. But in her dreams, Blue Flower fell into blackness. She saw her friend Crow Mother's mask within that pit. And she awoke in a sweat. Blue Flower felt at her belly for those maternal pains, but she was alright, and her baby was fast asleep within her. Still, she felt she had to sit up. My, she was groggy at that time of the night.

Raising her eyes up, Blue Flower peered with difficulty toward the fire. Crow Mother *was* there. She was *actually there...* in the flesh. She was sitting by the wall where Shi'Yun had been drawing her funny little patterns.

Blue Flower stood and approached her old friend with wonder. Crow Mother was distracted when Blue Flower reached her. They only nodded to each other. *How many years has it been?* She wondered as she looked to the place on the wall where Crow Mother had been focusing all of her attention.

Shi'Yun's symbols were not like Blue Flower's at all. Not man or beast or alien in representation. They were kind of place holders instead, like a collection of differently sized spheres — like stars — bouncing up and down in... well in some organized sort of pattern. The fire flickered against the wall forcing Blue Flower to see the inherent motion within the images and she pointed out with her index finger forming an imaginary bounce. Her throat rumbled up in a soft whisper of... music.

Crow Mother turned her head to look upon Blue Flower. She knew she was humming something. And even though neither one of them could hear her, they both knew exactly what it was she was meant to be singing. A tale of the ending of one world and the beginning of another. The death of defeat and the birth of hope. The tale of the cycle of life and death on constant repeat. Crow Mother followed Blue Flower's lead and, in their deafness, the images helped them both to synchronize their voices. They sang on quietly together all that night. And Blue Flower wondered that if she made a point of recording songs in that way, perhaps some future generations might regain their ability to hear and learn from those symbols the true Songs of The People.

The End.

A Note from the Author

First and foremost, thank you for picking up this book. It is readers like you that allow writers like myself a platform to eccentrically present little forms of madness to the world. I hope you've enjoyed the ramblings of my mind as you read through The Ancient Ones as much as I enjoyed the process of putting pen to paper.

With that in mind, I want to take a moment here to explain some incongruities that come into play within this particular novel to anyone who is interested in diving just a little bit deeper. As you are likely aware, at this point in time, the year 2023, it is the common opinion of most scientists that human civilization did not really get going in the Americas until about 10,000 years ago. Obviously, The Ancient Ones takes place 100,000 years ago, so how is it that Tetset and Hen'Bon'On exist? I posit that people did visit the "New World" much earlier than most have been willing to consider. They came, tried to live here during the Wisconsin Glaciation, and left across the land bridge of the Bering Strait before their great great (ad infinitum) grand children eventually about-faced and tried the Americas once again.

Quite recently, remains have been uncovered — homosapien remains — that have tentatively been dated all the way back to this exact period. Whether this dating is accurate or not, the possibility remains, humans might very well have visited the Americas far earlier than previously thought. This being stated, one might feel free then to argue that some form of civilization must have been at play among these early explorers — tribal or clan-like — gatherers and hunters doing their best, socializing in whatever way early human could have. So, Tetset and Hen'Bon'On. Not necessarily the ancestors of any one people, these two communities (and others briefly referenced within this book) might have lived, travelled, become Hun, Anglo Saxon, Czechoslovakian — The swaths of time that linger between The Ancient Ones and the birth of civilization as we have come to know it are so vast that much would have been lost, forgotten, destroyed.

This brings me to the other primary incongruity within my work of fiction. Teosintl is wild crop from South America. It is recognized the world over as the likely ancestor of modern corn. It is short and spreads along the ground wildly over great distances like a weed. Modern Teosintl only has a few kernels per stem. Obviously, the great Megatherium — a Giant Ground Sloth as big as a bear — would not be able to hide within such a short crop (the word crop should not even be used here) — much less the girl, Blue Flower running from the invading Hen'Bon'On — escaping below the Teosintl's "tall" kerneled tops. I fully admit, I have taken great liberties with the term Teosintl. My only intention in using this word is to imply the concept of ancestral corn — and a hundred thousand years ago "ancestral" corn would be extremely ancestral indeed — likely baring almost no similarity at all with corn stalks as we know them today. Perhaps ancient wheat or rye could have served a similar purpose, though this thought is trivial at best. I used the word Teosintl to address the indefinable for as much reason as any other because I thought it sounded cool. I feel little shame in this. Fiction is the author's own playground. However, I do humbly hope this note helps to clarify the intended meaning of my words.

- c.b.strul

Acknowledgments

Thank you Madison for putting up with me all through the Covid lock downs. It was a long, difficult time, but your presence and understanding, your willingness to give me the time and space I needed to finish this and all the other work, and your genuine compassion are the primary reasons I was able to get through that time and come out the other end with something of value rather than a bunch of 100% video game files. I love you so much!

Thanks to my mother who championed the concept of this story the first time she heard about it and has continued to lend a hand all the way through to these final moments of completion. I'm glad we've found this kind of project to bond over.

Thanks to Johanna and Solomon for always answering when I called even if my words didn't quite make sense at the time. Having multiple worlds in your head at once can sometimes muddle the tongue. You two never made me feel like I was crazy in these moments and I really appreciate it.

Thanks Dad for all the long car rides across the country as a kid. They certainly impacted this novel whether on the surface or in subtext alone. Also, those late night shows you used to watch probably gave me more than a few of these ideas over the years.

Thank you so much to my illustrator Aurelia. You did such a fabulous job in helping me to define the images of Crow Mother and Eccioporte. The Eakress (The People) and the Spiders would not be the same without you!

Thank you to Don and Kristal and Tyler and Brenda for putting up with me! You gave me a safe haven to live and write in troubled times.

Thanks Alyssa, my developmental editor. You helped me such a great deal in fleshing out Silent Wolf and filling in the gaps in my story.

Thank you Denise. In the earliest stages of this concept you welcomed my thoughts and gave me clarity on ancient civilizations that helped to keep me from over expounding on a topic I might not have been equipped to discuss. I hope you're well.

Thanks to John for giving me pointers on the publishing side of things and showing me that it really can be done.

Thank you Max for driving me out to Trona Pinnacles all those years ago. Yes! This is that same story!

Thanks for the music Carter!

And thank you so much Erica, Walker, and Frank for understanding my needs perhaps even before I did and giving me the time and space away to be able to make this content.

The body of this book was printed in 12 point Hoefler Text.

The chapter titles appear in Trattatello,
both 12 point bold and regular.

The cover appears in eroded Uncial Antiqua.